Praise for VOICES OF THE DEAD:

"If you haven't read Leonard before – and you must –
this is a great place to start."
– *The Guardian*

"*Voices of the Dead* is Peter Leonard's most ambitious
book to date."
– Bookreporter

"Tautly plotted and gripping on every page…. What a
story – fine, fine writing Peter Leonard!"
– Crystal Book Reviews

"For those who like noir fiction that's infused with a
good dose of testosterone, this should prove an enjoyable
read."
– Jewish Book Council

"A great read…. Highly recommended!"
– CMash Loves to Read

"I read this book in a day and a half because I just couldn't
put it down. From page one, it's nothing but action that
leaves you dying to know what happens next."
– The Top Shelf

"Leonard delivers the goods. It's a complex plot driven
rollercoaster of suspense, tension, and chills and a great
read. Enjoyed it. Definitely recommended."
– Spinetingler Magazine

Voices of the Dead

Peter Leonard

Studio Digital CT, LLC
P.O. Box 4331
Stamford, CT 06907

Copyright © 2011 by Peter Leonard
Cover design by James Tocco

Story Plant paperback ISBN-13: 978-1-61188-032-8
Fiction Studio Books e-book ISBN-13: 978-1-943486-59-5

Visit our website at www.thestoryplant.com

First Story Plant Trade Paperback Printing: January 2012
First Story Plant Mass Market Paperback Printing: January 2022
Printed in The United States of America

Acknowledgments

I want to thank my publishers, Lou Aronica and Peter Miller, my agent, Jeff Posternak at Wylie, New York, and my editors, Angus Cargill and Katherine Armstrong at Faber, UK.

I couldn't have written the book without the help of the librarians at the Holocaust Memorial Center in Farmington Hills, Michigan.

Thanks also to Tony Fiermonte, former Detroit Police Precinct Commander, prosecutor Steven Kaplan, Marvin Yagoda, Jean Acker, Gregg Sutter, Jim Bodary and Debi Siegel.

For Beverly

Introduction by Elmore Leonard

An important difference between Peter's books and mine, he writes his prose on a computer while I put down the words with a ballpoint pen. That's all right. David Mamet said, "I think there are people who are sufficiently driven that even a computer is not going to stop them from writing well."

And Pete is sufficiently driven.

After twenty-five years running a successful advertising agency—all while reading hundreds of popular novels and making judgments about their worth—Peter has attacked the world of fiction with a vengeance, writing five novels in the past five years and his publisher is after him to write another, a sequel to *Voices of the Dead*.

The key to writing successful books is developing the right voice to tell the stories, one that's natural to the writer and flows without strain or too many words and uses the voices of the people in the book, their attitudes, showing rather than telling who they are. Peter read a lot of Ernest Hemingway and John Steinbeck—not so much the popular names on the *Times* list—none of the authors who have a co-writer on the cover along with theirs, though much smaller. It causes you to wonder who actually wrote the book. Peter has read my Ten Rules of Writing and it shows; he always leaves out the parts readers tend to skip.

I remember him giving me the manuscript of his first novel *Quiver* with some hesitation, expecting me to begin marking up the pages to underscore awkward sentences, tired expressions. But right from the start I liked *Quiver* and Peter's dead-on style; no long-winded parts of it over-written, no show-off descriptions that say,

"Hey, look at my writing." I think my only suggestion was to move a key scene to a place where it would get more attention. Reading his work since, I haven't done much more than circle typos.

Four books later *Voices of the Dead* shows a remarkable leap in story content, a terrific plot told with Peter's ability to write quiet scenes packed with suspense.

The story takes place in 1971. Ernst Hess, a diplomat visiting the German Embassy in Washington, is still a dedicated Nazi 25 years after the war, loving the time he was an SS officer in charge of a killing squad; and he's still at it, looking for Jews he might have missed.

In the other corner is Harry Levin, who escaped from a Nazi death camp when he was a boy. Now Harry's a scrap-metal dealer in Detroit who goes one on one with the cunning Nazi.

Read the first chapter and you won't sell this scrap dealer short.

Chapter 1

Detroit, Michigan. 1971.

11:30 in the morning, Harry Levin was on Orleans Street, cutting through Eastern Market on his way back to the scrap yard. He'd just withdrawn fifty thousand dollars from the National Bank of Detroit. Now he was driving past turn-of-the-century brick buildings, seeing signs for Embassy Foods, and F&S Packing, another one for Market Seafood, brick bleeding through faded blue paint. There were delivery trucks parallel parked on the street, and Hi-Los carrying pallets of food, zigzagging through the loading areas of wholesale food emporiums.

The sun had risen over the buildings and he could feel its warmth through the open windows of the Mercedes. It was a perfect blue-sky day, one of about fifteen a year you got living in the Motor City. The Chevy Nova in front of him was slowing down and Harry hit his brakes. Beyond the Nova, a semi with a forty-foot trailer, a heavy, was blocking the road, trying to back down a narrow street to a loading dock, blue cab at a severe angle, looking like it had jackknifed. But it kept moving, the driver angling for position.

Harry sat against the leather seat and waited, sitting there awhile, getting impatient, had a meeting at his office in twenty minutes. He glanced in the rearview mirror and saw a black guy approaching the car from behind, watching his cool economical strut, man wearing white bellbottoms and a maroon shirt with collar points that reached his shoulders.

He looked straight ahead, saw the semi backing down the alley almost out of view when an arm came through the side window to his left, holding a carving knife with a long blade under his jaw, pressing it against his neck.

"Stay where you at, motherfucker," the black guy said.

His eyes were bloodshot. He had a sparse mustache and a scraggly goatee and a high Afro with a putty-colored comb stuck in it at an odd angle. Man was a junkie and Harry knew he'd cut his throat without thinking about it. He heard a door open, glanced in the rearview mirror, saw the guy that was coming up behind him getting in the backseat, closing the door. This one was clean-shaven and more alert than the junkie, with shiny hair that looked like it had motor oil on it, combed back.

"Motherfucker, see where I'm at? See what I got, you don't do what you tole?"

He had a pocketknife with a six-inch blade in his hand, leaned forward, put it against Harry's jugular, pulling him back against the headrest, Harry smelling aftershave and sweat. Afro's hand moved out of the window, and he went around the front of the car and got in next to him.

"What in the case?" guy in back said.

"Transaction reports."

"Yeah? The fuck's that?"

"I buy and sell scrap."

"Know what we do? Take your money." Afro gave him a sleepy-eyed grin. "Like this. Gimme your wallet, motherfucker," he said, pointing the carving knife at Harry.

Guy in back said, "Let see what else in there you got?"

Harry saw him in the rearview mirror, watched him sit back and put the briefcase in his lap, fooling with the clasp, trying to open it with the tip of his knife blade. Tried for a while, gave up and looked at Harry.

"Where the key at?"

"In my pocket," Harry said. He reached behind his back, felt the grip of the Colt Python, pulled his wallet out of the back left pocket of his khakis and threw it on the floor mat in front of Afro. Keep him busy.

Afro bent forward, reaching with his long arms, and now Harry drew the Colt, turned in his seat, back against the door as Afro sat up with the wallet, spread it open, looking at $750, grinning till he saw the gun.

"Easy," Afro said. "Be cool." He handed Harry his wallet back. "See? It all there. No harm done, nobody lose nothin'."

Harry turned, two hands on the revolver, aimed at the guy in back, the guy preoccupied, still fooling with the briefcase. Harry pulled the hammer back and now he looked up. "Drop the knives out the window or I'll blow your head off." He said it calm and measured. They tossed the blades out and Harry heard them hit the street. "Give me your wallets."

Afro took his out and put it on the edge of Harry's seat. Guy in back slid his between the seats on the console.

"Now get the hell out of here."

They did, and Harry left them standing on Orleans Street, wondering what had just happened. He looked straight, the Nova was halfway down the block, put the Mercedes in gear and took off.

In addition to junkies trying to rob him the IRS was trying to take his money in a more legitimate way. First he'd gotten a letter that said:

Dear Recycler:

As part of our review of tax compliance, the Internal Revenue Service has determined records maintained by S&H Recycling Metals may be insufficient to verify the accuracy of purchases of recyclable materials. It is the responsibility of taxpayers to maintain adequate records to substantiate items on their tax returns, including purchases of recyclable materials. Failure to maintain such records could result in the assessment of additional tax due to the disallowance of deductions. We appreciate your cooperation and willingness to work with us on this matter. If you have any questions, please contact the examiner named at the heading of this letter.

Sincerely,
Chief Examination Division

13

Harry was thinking, come on. What is this? Now they were preparing to audit his company. Harry had asked his secretary, Phyllis, to pull all the records, back up that supported his tax returns, everything from 1969 and '70. He had no clue why they were coming after him. He'd maintained accurate, up-to-date records. The examiner named at the top of the letter was William Decker.

He was in the waiting room when Harry arrived, stood up and introduced himself as Bill. Looked like a former athlete, six three, a couple inches taller than Harry, but about his age, early forties, hair going gray, cut to the top of his ears, big hands, firm handshake.

Decker told him the audit was random, not personal, but Harry had trouble believing it. He paid cash for scrap, and a business like his was an easy target. Harry and his scale operator, Jerry Dubuque, loaded a dozen banker boxes in the back of Decker's Fairlane station wagon, three years' worth of shippers, cash slips, weight tickets, metal settlement reports, bids and contracts. The IRS would match it all up with what Harry said on his returns or Decker would give him a call.

Harry owned twelve acres on Mt. Elliot near Luce just east of Hamtramck. He'd bought the business from his uncle, in '62. Worked there since he was seventeen. Harry had six million pounds of scrap, a mountain of auto parts, refrigerators, bed frames, steel beams, railroad tracks and farm equipment that rose up five stories and extended five hundred feet from end to end. To move the mountain he had two hydraulic crawler cranes, one outfitted with a magnet, the other a grapple. He also had three scales, a baling press, alligator shears, guillotine shears and four loaders to haul scrap to the mills.

When Decker left, Harry took the black guys' wallets out and looked at them. Afro was Ray Jones, eyes closed in the license photo, six one, 180, six dollars and a piece of paper with a name on it: Yolanda, and a phone number in the scuffed-up brown wallet with a ninja in black illustration on it. Guy in the backseat was Darnell Terry, five eleven, 170. He was the high roller, had twen-

ty-seven dollars and two credit cards, a Visa and a Mas-
terCard with different names on them.

Harry owned a three-bedroom Tudor on Hendrie, a
tree-lined street in Huntington Woods. He'd lived alone
since his daughter had gone away to college in Washington DC a year earlier. She'd decided to stay there for the
summer after her freshman year, work part-time and take
a couple classes. Harry couldn't blame her, living in DC
sounded exciting, and beat the hell out of Detroit.

Harry had a thing going with a neighbor named Galina, a big-breasted thirty-seven-year-old Latvian Jew
whose breath smelled like sauerkraut, and privates like
wild geese. She lived on the street behind him and over
a couple houses. Her husband worked for Ford and had
taken a job in London. She didn't want to go to a place
where it rained all the time, so they were in the process
of divorce—although there had to be more to it than that.
She'd call once a week, usually in the evening, say she
was horny and available, drive around the block, and
park in his garage so the neighbors wouldn't see what
was going on. They'd go up to his bedroom, take off their
clothes and spend a couple hours in bed. She'd run down
to the kitchen, naked, bring up snacks and drinks to sat-
isfy some appetites and replenish others. This had been
going on for several months until one day she told Harry she'd met someone and thought it was serious. Harry liked her but it didn't go much deeper than that. He
wished her luck.

He'd also had a recent fling with a girl he'd met at
an Allman Brothers concert at Pine Knob. He noticed this
petite good-looking girl, long hair parted down the middle, skinny arms and big jugs hanging free in an Allman
Brothers tee-shirt, sitting next to him, smoking pot. He
looked at her, she handed him the joint. He had never
smoked marijuana, but thought, what the hell. Took a hit
and started coughing and she looked at him and grinned.

"First time?"

Harry nodded.

After the band did "Statesboro Blues," she stood
up and screamed, and it was so loud his eardrums hurt.

When the noise had died down he leaned over and said, "You're the best screamer I've ever heard in my life. You should be in horror films."

She smiled and said, "You haven't heard anything yet."

And she was right. After "Whipping Post" she let one out that was even louder.

Harry said, "What's your name?"

"Janice Jones."

"You a Playboy Playmate?"

"No," she said, "a bartender."

"Janice, you have any other hidden talents?"

"Call me," Janice said, "and find out."

She wrote her number on his palm with a blue ball-point, and he woke up the next morning looking at it. They met for lunch a couple days later at the Stage Deli in Oak Park. He had chicken soup and the *South Pacific* club. She had a *King and I* with extra Russian. Janice was from Bottineau, North Dakota, a town thirteen miles from the Canadian border.

"How do you get there?" Harry'd said.

"Fly to Minot and have someone pick you up."

Her parents were farmers. Janice said she looked at the future and saw an old, broken-down version of herself by the time she was forty—like her mother—and wanted better. She'd run away when she was seventeen. Went to San Francisco, met some people and lived in a house in the Haight. She was in Detroit for a couple of weeks visiting friends.

After lunch they went back to Harry's house. She put her purse on the kitchen table and looked at him. "Want to get high?"

"Sure," Harry said, feeling adventurous. He watched her take a plastic sandwich bag of marijuana out of her purse, sprinkle some into a rolling paper, and roll a joint that looked like a cigarette with one hand. They smoked it and he gave her the grand tour, and when they got to his bedroom she sat on the bed and took off her tee-shirt, sitting there bare-breasted, patting the comforter next to her leg.

16

"Want to fuck?"

She said it casually like she was asking him what time it was.

Harry walked over, seduced by this North Dakota farm girl with perky tits, sat next to her and they started making out. Next thing he knew they were naked between the sheets and he was between her legs, Janice on top, body erect, breasts bouncing, hands on his chest, riding him. After a few minutes her eyes rolled back and she came, and let out a scream. It was summer and the windows were open. Harry couldn't believe it. "What're you doing?"

"Getting off," she said.

"My neighbors are going to call the police."

Harry grinned thinking about it, and made himself a vodka and tonic, went outside and sat on the patio. He read the *Free Press* and cooked a two-inch-thick Delmonico steak on the grill, watched the Tigers beat the Angels 3–0. Joe Coleman struck out ten. Stanley and McAuliffe both homered. He was in bed at eleven.

Chapter 2

Hess found out the woman lived on P Street in George-town, not far from the consulate. He told the ambassador he was having dinner with potential clients, and wanted to drive himself. It was unorthodox, but plausible. He had been issued one of the embassy's Mercedes sedans. He stopped at a bookstore and bought a map of the area, and located P Street. He drove there and saw the Goldman residence, a federal-style brick townhouse.

Hess went to a restaurant and had dinner and a couple drinks. At ten o'clock he drove back, parked around the corner on 32nd Street between two other vehicles so the license plate was not visible to anyone driving by. He walked to the Goldmans', stood next to a tree in front of the three-storey townhouse. There were lights on the first floor. He walked to the front door and rang the buzzer. He could hear footsteps and voices inside. A light over the door went on. Hess stood in the open so whoever it was would see he was well dressed. The door opened, a man standing there, assumed he was Dr. Mitchell Goldman, dark hair, big nose, mid-forties, top of the shirt unbuttoned, exposing a gold chain and a five-pointed star. Hess smiled. "My car is on the fritz. May I use your phone to call a tow truck?"

Dr. Goldman stared at him with concern.

"I am staying just down the street at the consulate," Hess said, smiling. Now the door opened and he stepped into the elegant foyer, chandelier overhead, marble floor.

"Mitch, who is it?" a woman said from a big open room to his right.

Dr. Goldman looked in her direction. "Guy's having car trouble, wants to use the phone."

"It's ten o'clock at night."

"He'll just be a minute," the dentist said.

Hess could see the woman sitting on a couch, watching television.

"The phone's in here." The dentist started to move.

Hess drew the Luger from the pocket of his suit jacket, and aimed it at Goldman.

The dentist put his hands up. "Whoa. Easy."

"Who is in the house?"

"Just the two of us."

"Are you expecting anyone?"

He shook his head.

"Tell her to come in here," Hess said.

"What do you want? You want money?" He took his wallet out and handed it to him. "There's eight hundred dollars in there."

"Call her," Hess said.

"Hon, come here, will you?"

"I'm watching *All in the Family*. Can you wait till the commercial?"

Hess could hear people laughing on the television.

"Just for a minute," the dentist said.

Hess saw her stand up and step around a low table in front of the couch, moving across the room, still looking back at the television. She turned her head as she entered the foyer and saw him holding the gun. Her hair looked darker in the dim light but he had only seen her briefly that day.

"Oh-my-god," she said, hands going up to her face.

"We're reasonable people," the dentist said. "Tell us what you want."

"The pleasure of your company," Hess said. "Where is the cellar?"

Coco thought he looked familiar, would've sworn she'd seen him in the club before. She usually worked days, was sure he'd been in for lunch. Was a foreigner like a lot of them. This one kinda cute with a goatee and funny accent sound like that Colonel Klink on *Hogan's Heroes*. He was stocky, broad shoulders, dressed nice, suit and tie, big roll he took out, flashed around. She thought of him as Fritz.

Other side of the booth, Extasy, skinny blonde with little biddy tits, was giving Fritz a personal dance, going through the motions, strain on her face like whatever she was on had worn off and she needed more. Coco had just come out the dressing room, smelled like hairspray and periods, slid in next to Fritz, wearing gauntlets, a G-string and stiletto heels. "Ex gotta go on stage, mind I join you, sugar?" Doubted he could hear with the music pounding. But he looked at her and grinned.

Music stop, he reached in his pocket pulled out the roll, peeled off a twenty handed it to Ex, she slid out the booth and disappeared.

Coco touched his arm. "Where you from, baby?"

"Bavaria."

"Where Bavaria at?" And took a guess. "Like in Germany?"

Fritz smiled. "Very good."

"Let me make you more comfortable." She loosened his tie, pulled the knot down a few inches and unbuttoned his top button.

"There," she smiled. "That better?"

Man finished his drink, look like whisky in a lowball glass, throwing it down. Put his arm around her, pulled her closer.

"Need another one, sugar?" She saw Donna, one of the waitresses. "Yo, D, bring Fritz one, and a 7&7." She glanced at him, smiled. "You don't mind, do you, baby?" Slipped a pack of matches in his jacket pocket. Fritz wasn't listening. He nibbled her ear and she flinched. Traced a line around her bare titty with his index finger, and brought his hand down her flat smooth stomach to the band of her G-string, trying to see how far he could go before she stopped him, and he was right there. She grabbed his hand and held it.

"Can't be doing that, honey. No touchin'. They goin' to kick you out. Want privacy? Got to go up to the VIP room." Placed her hand on his thigh, rubbing it. "Got some big, strong legs," Coco said. "Bet you got something else that's big, huh?"

He kissed her neck and she pushed him away, trying to smile, flashing her perfect teeth. "Don't want to ruin the mood, got to talk business. See, got to tell what you can do and what you can't. What you get for how much and such. We take out little Fritz with his German helmet, cost you hundred dollars, plus tip. Tell me what you want, I tell you what it cost, see we can give you a quantity discount."

She ran her hand down all the way to his knee, pretending she was interested in him, attracted to him. Felt something wet on his pants. Rubbed it between her thumb and index finger, brought her hand up, looked like blood. "Baby, you all right? Looks like you cut yourself."

Donna put their cocktails on the table. Fritz took the roll out, slid two twenties off, handed them to her. Coco grabbed her 7&7 and took a sip, looking over the edge of the glass at her Bavarian prize. But something was wrong. Fritz's mood had changed. Man was edgy now. Wasn't interested in her no more. Picked up his whisky, drank it, slid out the booth.

"Yo, baby, what's up?" Coco said.

But he was moving, walked out the club and never looked back.

Sara cashed out her last table, tipped Kenny the bartender, and the busers, and walked outside. It was just past midnight, still hot and muggy. It felt good after being in an air-conditioned restaurant for six hours. It had been a great night. She had made $180 in tips alone. Life was good. She'd been lucky enough to get the job at Bistro 675, a trendy new restaurant on 15th Street, not far from the White House. But it had been a lucky year. She was on the Dean's List at George Washington, and a month before the semester ended, her English professor, Dr. Lund, had asked if she'd be interested in house-sitting for the summer. Two months, anyway. He'd rented a country home in the south of France, three kilometers from Aix-en-Provence, and needed someone to water the plants and bring in the mail.

A chance to stay in Washington for the summer, she'd said to herself. Are you kidding? How cool was that? She'd called her father and told him the good news.

He said, "That's great. I want your life. Things always seem to fall into place."

She hadn't told him about Richard yet, this cute boy in her psych class. They had been hanging out for a few months and Sara liked him a lot, maybe even loved him. Next time her dad came to DC she was going to introduce them.

She found her car in the lot, a baby blue '68 Ford Falcon her father had bought for her, cruising north on 15th, windows down, listening to Joni Mitchell do *Blue*. Passed the statue of Alexander Hamilton and the Treasury building and New York Avenue, approaching Pennsylvania, green light, heading into the intersection, singing with Joni, really belting it out:

Hey blue, here is a song for you...

Hess had no idea where he was. He had been driving west on Pennsylvania Avenue, and now was somehow on K Street. He regretted stopping at the gentlemen's club but he'd needed several drinks to calm him down, he had been so charged up, so high on adrenalin.

To the right was a sign for Lafayette Park, and he realized he was traveling in the wrong direction. The White House was somewhere south through the trees. He tapped a cigarette out of his pack and lighted it with a match, steering the big Mercedes-Benz with his knees. He was drunk, the white line dividing the road, blurring into two. He closed one eye to correct his vision.

Hess brought the cigarette to his mouth, but it slipped through his fingers. He fumbled, tried to catch it with dulled reflexes, cigarette dropping in his lap, falling to the floor. He glanced down, saw it and reached to pick it up, but it rolled toward the accelerator pedal. He looked up now, approaching an intersection, red traffic light sending an alarm to his brain, foot going for the brake pedal, but too late.

He slammed into an automobile, hitting it broadside with serious impact, crushing it, pushing it through the intersection. Hess was conscious of his head striking the steering wheel, the Mercedes spinning, crashing into a storefront. He heard voices and the high-pitched whine of a radiator under pressure, the sound of a siren some distance away, and saw faces staring at him through the windows.

Harry was in his office at the scrap yard, writing a check to the IRS, he couldn't see the amount, but it was enough to put him out of business. He was signing his name when he heard the phone ring, sounding like it was far away. He woke up, opened his eyes, the phone on the table next to his bed, ringing. Slid over, glanced at the clock. 3:17 a.m. Answered it, barely awake. "Hello."

"Mr. Levin, this is the Huntington Woods Police Department."

"Yeah? You know what time it is?" Harry said.

"Sir, your daughter has been in an automobile accident. There is a police officer at your house. Will you please answer the door?"

No way it was Sara. "My daughter's in Washington DC. What's going on?" He heard the doorbell.

"The officer will tell you."

He hung up the phone. It had to be a misunderstanding. Heard the doorbell ring again as he was putting on his robe. He went downstairs, opened the front door. A Huntington Woods cop in a blue uniform was standing on the porch.

"Mr. Levin, may I come in?"

Harry swung the door open further. The cop stepped into the foyer and took off his hat. He looked young, thirty maybe. Blond hair parted on the side, creased where the hat rested, ruddy complexion. Seemed nervous.

"Mr. Levin, your daughter, Sara, was killed in a car accident this morning in Washington DC."

Harry felt like he'd been punched in the chest. Stepped back and tried to take a breath. It couldn't be. He'd talked to her just before she went to work.

But the cop assured him it wasn't a mistake. His department had been contacted by the DC police. Sara was at Washington Hospital. He gave Harry the name

and number of a Washington DC detective named Taggart and a woman named Judy Katz at the hospital. The
cop told him how sorry he was, and let himself out and
closed the door.

Harry went back upstairs, sat on the bed, holding it
in, and called Eastern Airlines, booked a seat on the 6:31
a.m. flight to National Airport.

24

Chapter 3

Harry took a cab from the airport to Washington Hospital Center, a big white building complex on Irving Street. He arrived at 8:37, went to the reception desk and asked where his daughter, Sara Levin, was. A black woman with a well-trimmed Afro, reminded him of Angela Davis, told Harry to have a seat, pointing at couches and chairs arranged in front of a picture window with a view of a courtyard, someone would be out to talk to him.

There was no one else in the waiting area. Harry scanned the magazine rack, picked up TIME. The headline said: "The Occult Revival," with an illustration of a guy wearing a black hood, and in smaller type: "Satan Returns."

Harry sat and flipped through the magazine, but he couldn't concentrate. He was in a daze, nerves on edge, sick to his stomach.

A few minutes later a woman with frizzy shoulder-length dark-hair came across the lobby and stood in front of him. She was cute, early thirties, wearing a sleeveless paisley dress and running shoes, a hippie dressed up for work.

"Mr. Levin, I'm Judy Katz."

She sat next to Harry, body angled toward him.

"Sara was brought to the ER this morning at 1:34 a.m. She had been in a terrible car accident. She was dead. There was nothing we could do. I'm very sorry."

Judy Katz put her hand on his and squeezed it. Harry let out a breath as if he had been subconsciously holding it in. He sat there for a couple seconds, trying to process what he'd just heard. "You're sure it's Sara?"

"We have her driver's license and school ID."

He rubbed his eyes.

"How'd she die?" He rolled the magazine up and squeezed it.

"Internal injuries, Mr. Levin." Judy Katz said. "Sara died instantly. She wasn't in any pain."

"Who else was involved?"

"A man was driving the other car. I don't know anything about him or his condition. He was taken to Georgetown. Another hospital."

"Where is she?" Harry said. "I want to see her."

Judy Katz escorted him downstairs to the morgue. They walked along the spotless hallway that smelled like cleaning fluid, sterile, antiseptic, neither one talking, Harry aware of the sound of their shoes on the tile floor. Hers squeaking, his clicking.

Judy stopped and said, "Sara's in here. This is a viewing room."

There was a body on a stainless steel table, covered by a white sheet. Her feet were sticking out the bottom, Sara's pretty feet with pink manicured toenails, toe tag hanging from her right foot, name and Social Security number and Huntington Woods address in black marker.

Judy pulled the sheet back and Harry saw the lifeless face of someone, a girl with dark brown hair, but unrecognizable, the left side crushed.

"Is this your daughter, Mr. Levin?"

Harry nodded, picturing her the last time he'd seen her, the day she moved into the teacher's townhouse. "You've got the best luck of anyone I know," he'd said.

"The world's my oyster, Pops."

Harry took a cab to the Washington DC Police Department on Shepherd Street, met with Detective Taggart in a room with a long table, two ashtrays on it, pink walls and a clock. Taggart looked about forty, dark curly hair, sideburns, light green dress shirt, brown tie pulled down, slightly askew, revolver in a black shoulder holster under his left arm.

"Mr. Levin, I'm sorry about your daughter," he said, southern accent. "Can I get you coffee, a soft drink, cigarette?"

26

Taggart took a pack of Lucky Strikes out of his shirt pocket, tapped one out and tilted it toward him.

Harry shook his head. "Tell me what happened."

"Your daughter was traveling north on 15th Street. According to the restaurant manager she had just gotten off work. It was around twelve twenty. The car that hit her was traveling east on K Street, ran the red light at 15th, slammed into your daughter's car broadside in the intersection."

"Who was driving the other car?" Harry said.

Taggart glanced away and back at Harry. "I'm not at liberty to give you that information." He looked uncomfortable, squirmed a little in his seat.

"What're you talking about?"

"I don't blame you," Taggart said. "But there's nothing I can do. He's a foreign diplomat."

"I thought I was at the police station."

"It's out of our hands," Taggart said.

"You didn't arrest him?" Harry said, shaking his head. "What the hell's going on?"

"I shouldn't be telling you this—" He paused. "We held him till this morning, and I heard he was still drunk when we let him go."

"You mean he's out on bail?"

"There was no bail. Guy from the Chief of Protocol's Office and a lawyer from the Office of the Legal Adviser got here at six thirty this morning and we had no choice but to let him go. This guy's connected, somebody important."

Taggart slid a business card across the table to him. Harry picked it up and looked at it: James Vander Schaaf, State Department of the United States, Office of the Chief of Protocol.

"You want to know what's going on? Talk to him. But I doubt you'll get a straight answer. This is Washington."

Harry took a cab to 320 21st Street, got out in front of the sand-colored Department of State building. Vander Schaaf had a nice office with a view of the Potomac. He wore a seersucker suit and a bowtie. He was tall and thin and personable. Harry sat facing him behind a mahogany desk the size of a Volkswagen, framed photos on it and a coffee mug that said "World's Best Dad" in a big cartoon typeface, and wall-to-wall bookshelves behind him.

"Mr. Levin, on behalf of everyone here at the State Department, I want to offer you our sincere condolences for your loss. Unfortunate, tragic, you have our deepest sympathy," he said.

It sounded like practiced sincerity. Bereavement 101.

"I can definitely relate. I have children of my own."

"I don't want your sympathy," Harry said. "I want to know what you're going to do about it."

Vander Schaaf put his palms together like he was praying, gave Harry a solemn nod. "Mr. Levin, I just want you to know that I'm here for you. We all are."

Whatever that meant.

"But what we have here is a very difficult situation. Are you familiar with diplomatic immunity?"

Harry had an idea, but let him keep going.

"It's a tradition that dates back to the ancient Greeks: Sophocles, Aristotle." He picked up a pen like he was going to start writing, using it as a prop, giving him something to do with his hands. "They believed foreign emissaries traveled under the protection of Zeus." He paused. "Today it's designed to protect diplomats who travel abroad. Mr. Levin, we can't in good conscience send our ambassadors to places where an unfriendly government might try to bring false charges against them. Sir, it's a safeguard. It was all codified at the Vienna Convention in 1961. A complete framework was established for diplomatic relations on the basis of consent between independent sovereign states. It set out special rules, privileges and immunities—which allow diplomatic missions to act without fear of coercion or harassment of local laws. Is any of this making sense, Mr. Levin? If not I can have John Brennan, an attorney from 'L,' what we call the State Department's Office of the Legal Adviser, come by and explain it further."

He put the pen on the desktop, picked up the coffee mug and took a sip.

"A foreign diplomat kills an American citizen and there's nothing you can do about it. Is that what you're telling me?"

"Unfortunately, yes," Vander Schaaf said. He picked up a piece of paper and started reading. "Article 29 provides inviolability for diplomats, and Article 31 established their immunity from civil and criminal jurisdictions."

"Don't read anything else, okay?"

"Mr. Levin, I understand how you feel."

"You don't have a clue," Harry said. "Where is he?"

"Who, sir?"

"The guy that killed my daughter."

"I have no idea."

Vander Schaaf looked worried.

"Who's your boss?" Harry said.

"The Chief of Protocol, Mr. Emil Mosbacher Jr."

"Get him on the phone, tell him I want to talk to him."

"Mr. Levin, that's impossible."

"I thought you were all here for me."

"Mr. Mosbacher is with the president."

"Then call the White House, let's get Nixon himself involved."

Vander Schaaf was flustered, didn't know what to do. Harry got up and started for the door.

"By way of reparation, Mr. Levin, I have a letter of apology from the diplomat himself."

Harry moved across the room.

"He's very concerned about the matter," Vander Schaaf said, on his feet now, coming around the desk. "And has offered to pay funeral expenses."

Harry was at the door, he turned and said, "Funeral expenses? You think that's why I'm here?"

"Mr. Levin," Vander Schaaf said, crossing the room, trying to catch him, but Harry had already gone.

He phoned Detective Taggart from a payphone in the lobby, got him on the line and asked where Sara's car had been taken.

"What are you going to do with it?"

"Look at it," Harry said.

"It's in a lot on North Pearl Street. Got a pen?"

Taggart gave him the address and Harry wrote it on the back of Vander Schaaf's business card.

"I'll call and tell them you're coming. Get anywhere with the State Department?"

"They should call it the Anti-state Department."

"I tried to find out who the diplomat is," Taggart said, "but they've covered this thing up, buried it deep. All I know, the guy's a German. Good luck."

Taggart was a standup guy. Harry thanked him and hung up. He went outside and hailed a cab and took it to the DC police impound lot, rows of cars behind chainlink fence topped with razor wire. There was a single-storey cinderblock building just inside the fence. Harry went in the office and showed his driver's license to a clerk behind the wood and Formica counter. He wore a police uniform shirt but looked like a mechanic, long greasy hair combed straight back over his collar, a few days of reddish-brown stubble on his face.

Harry told him about the accident and said he wanted to see the car, a 1968 Ford Falcon registered in his name with Michigan plates. The clerk flipped through a stack of papers that had a staple through the top left corner.

"Here 'tis, '68 Falcon." He looked up now. "In fact, they're both out there side by each. Your car, what's left of it, next to the one that hit it. 1972 Mercedes-Benz 450 SEL, costs more 'n I make in a year, probably two. Tow trucks brought them in within a few minutes of each other, explaining their close proximity. Row A, spaces seventeen and eighteen. Walk out that door, take a right, can't miss it."

Harry approached the Falcon from behind, and even from this angle he could see the damage. He walked up to it, stood next to it, looking inside the car. Everything on the left side from the front fender to the trunk was crushed, pushed halfway through the interior. Roof peeled back like a sardine can. Steering wheel bent out of position. Driver's seat angled sideways against the front passenger seat. There were spots of dried blood on the seats and dash and passenger-side window.

Now he glanced at the black Mercedes parked next to it, twice the size of the Falcon, had to be two tons. Stepped over and looked at the front end crushed all the way to the dash, left wheel and tire trapped in the wreckage.

He opened the driver's door. Except for blood on the sill and the bottom of the window the interior was untouched, intact. Harry could understand now how the diplomat had walked away. He looked on the floor and saw a cigarette next to the accelerator pedal. He reached and picked it up, a Marlboro burned about halfway. Ran his hand under the driver's seat, felt a pack of matches. It had a black background with the red silhouette of a naked girl. He opened the cover and saw 'Archibald's Entertainment for Gentlemen' with an address on Q Street. Under it, a note in blue ink said: "You want it, baby, I got it, Coco XOXO" and a phone number.

Harry walked around to the other side of the Mercedes, opened the front passenger door, sat on the black leather seat, and scanned the interior. Reached over and checked behind the visor on the driver's side. Nothing. Checked behind the visor in front of him. There was a vanity mirror. Stared at the close-up of his face. He looked tired and needed a shave. There was a console between the seats and a compartment under the center armrest. He opened it and looked in. Empty. Checked the back seat. Spotless. Checked the glove box, took out a black leather folder, opened it. Car was registered to the Embassy of the Federal Republic of Germany, 4645 Reservoir Road NW, Washington DC, 20007.

Harry took a cab to Archibald's, walked into the dark room, loud pulsing music, beams of light crisscrossing the interior like air-raid strobes. There was a naked girl on stage, spinning upside down on a silver pole. Other girls in various stages of undress were dancing tableside. Harry asked the bouncer if Coco was working and he pointed to a petite, light-skinned black girl giving a lap dance to a customer at a corner table.

The hostess, a fortyish brunette with fading looks, escorted him to a booth.

"I'll have a vodka tonic, and will you send Coco over when she's free?"

"Sure, hon," she smiled. "No problem."

His drink came, and when the song ended so did Coco.

"How you today, baby?" she said, sliding in the booth in a G-string, full of energy and personality. Afro accentuating high cheekbones and caramel skin, petite body making her seem younger than she was, girlish.

"My German friend told me to ask for you."

"What German friend you talkin' about?"

"He was in last night."

She gave him a big friendly smile. "My man, Fritz." Gave his arm a light squeeze. "What I call him. What's his real name?"

"I can't tell you," Harry said. "It's sensitive due to his—" He led her and she picked right up.

"Don't have to say no more." Coco touched his arm again. "Fritz okay?"

Harry said, "Yeah, I think so." No idea what she was talking about.

"Thought he was hurt."

"Why's that?"

"Had blood all down his pants."

"You saw it?"

"Felt it. Was all wet."

"What happened?"

"Dint say. But when he leave I went to the ladies, washed my hands. Was red blood come off in the sink."

Chapter 4

Harry took a cab to the Four Seasons, checked in and called his office. It was 3:38 in the afternoon.

"Harry, where are you? People have been calling for you all day, including some detective from the Washington DC police," Phyllis said. "Is everything all right?"

"I'll tell you later," Harry said. He didn't want to get into it right now. "How about the guy from the IRS?"

"Haven't heard a thing. Harry, you coming in today?"

"I'm not feeling well." Which was not far from the truth.

"Can I do anything for you? Pick up some medicine?"

"I'll be okay," Harry said and hung up. Phyllis Wampler had worked for him for ten years. She was forty-two, never been married, lived in Ferndale with her dog, a little shorthaired, two-toned thing named Lily. Harry had stopped over one time to drop something off. He rang the bell, Phyllis opened the door with the dog in her arms.

"Lily, this is Harry, the man I work for," she'd said in a baby-talk voice. "Look at her, Harry, she just had a baffer. That's a pretty girl. She's a good girl getting her baffer, all pretty girl now. Aren't you?" The dog barked and she grinned. "Yes her is."

Phyllis had dates periodically, but if the guy didn't like Lily it was all over. Some people liked dogs more than people and Phyllis was one of them.

He took Detective Taggart's card out of his shirt pocket and dialed the number, heard him identify himself.

"It's Harry Levin."

"I've got something for you. But I'd rather not say it over the phone."

"I've got something for you, too."

They agreed to meet in the Four Seasons bar in thirty minutes.

"I was investigating a double murder in George-town," Taggart said. "Didn't get to the station till seven. By then, as I told you, the diplomat had been released."

He drank Budweiser from the bottle, fingers wrapped around the neck, looking out of place in the swank mahogany-paneled room in his light green shirt, brown tie at half mast, brown plaid sport coat, and brown hat on the seat next to him. Just the two of them sitting at the empty bar, bartender working, mixing drinks and serving customers at tables.

"What I didn't know, he'd been read his rights. Printed and photographed before anyone knew about his diplomatic status. He'd caused an accident and he was drunk. Looking at involuntary manslaughter at the very least."

Harry picked up his vodka tonic and took a sip. The glass was sweating, so he wrapped a cocktail napkin around the bottom. Taggart reached in his jacket pocket, took out a folded piece of paper, and handed it to him. Harry opened it, studied the face in the photo. Drunk eyes staring at him, mustache and goatee, dark hair flecked with gray, early fifties. Something familiar about him.

"Name's Ernst Hess," Taggart said.

"Who is he?"

"German diplomat. That's all I know."

"Was he hurt?"

"I don't think so. Why?"

"There was blood in the car and blood on his pants."

"How do you know that?"

"I've got my sources." Harry sipped his drink.

"What do you mean you've got your sources?"

Harry told him about Coco.

"You investigating this on your own now?"

"I'm trying to find out what happened."

34

Taggart looked offended, like Harry was stepping on his toes.

"Look, I appreciate everything you're doing," Harry said. "I'm not trying to get in your way. But I've got to find out who he is and where he is."

"My guess, on a plane back to Germany. Get out of town, avoid any further embarrassment. What do you think?"

"I don't know," Harry said. Taggart's conclusion made sense but he wasn't so sure. Taggart picked up the beer bottle and drained it.

"Another one?" Harry said.

Taggart shook his head. "Got to get back to the office. What about you?"

"I have to go to the hospital get the medical examiner's report, official cause of death, and have Sara's body shipped home."

"Take care of yourself." Taggart slid off the bar stool and they shook hands.

Harry went back up to his room. Found a phonebook in the drawer of the bedside table. He looked up the German Embassy, got the phone number and made a call.

"German Embassy, how may I direct your call?" a woman said, Berlin accent.

"Will you connect me with Herr Ernst Hess, please?" Harry said in German.

"I am sorry, Herr Hess is out of the building. May I take a message?"

"I'll call him back," Harry said.

Harry dialed the front desk and asked where the nearest car rental place was, and found out there was an Avis office right down the street. He rented a black Mustang with tan interior. He studied a map of DC that came with the car, and found Reservoir Road. It ran east and west just north of Georgetown University.

He stopped at a sporting goods in West Village and bought binoculars. Then he drove to the embassy and parked across the street in a metered space in front of a redbrick colonial. The embassy was nothing like he expected. It was a modern six-storey steel and glass building inside a gated complex. There was a guard shack with a security gate, and a wide sweeping driveway that extended from the street to the building. Harry watched visitors drive in, have their ID checked by a security guard, then drive up to the entrance and park.

He unfolded the Xerox shot of Hess that Taggart had given him and waited.

At 6:15, a black Mercedes-Benz, twin of the one that had hit Sara, drove in the gate and pulled up to the front door. Harry zoomed in with the binoculars, turned the dial, adjusting the distance, and saw a man in a dark suit, white shirt and tie get out the left rear door and walk around the car, talking to a silver-haired guy getting out on the opposite side. Harry had gotten a good look at him, comparing what he saw to the mug shot of Hess, and was sure it was him. The Mercedes pulled away. Hess and the other guy went in the embassy.

At 7:55, the black Mercedes returned, stopped at the guard shack and pulled up in front of the building. He looked through the binoculars, saw Hess and two other men come out and get in the car.

Harry followed the Mercedes down Pennsylvania Avenue to Wisconsin, took a right and then a left on M Street, and a right on Pennsylvania Avenue past George Washington University to 17th Street, catching glimpses of the White House, Richard Nixon probably in there somewhere, shaving. He'd read an article that said, on occasion, Nixon had to shave five times a day.

On his right was the Washington Monument, and in the distance the arched dome of the Capitol. The Mercedes pulled over in front of a restaurant, Les Halles. Harry knew it, had taken Sara there at the start of the school year. The three men got out of the car and went inside. Harry waited till the Mercedes pulled away and valet parked.

The restaurant was one big room, bar in front, with maybe a dozen stools, the dining room behind it, crowded, bustling. Harry found an empty stool, sat on the side of the bar and ordered a Canadian Club and soda. He could see the Germans twenty feet away, three men at a table for four, speaking German, their voices rising above the din like smoke from their cigarettes. Harry unfolded the Xerox mug shot, positioned it next to his drink, studying the face of Hess in the photograph.

The same man was sitting at the table, no mistake about it, same mustache-goatee, same sturdy jaw. Harry sipped his drink and watched Hess. Hess telling a story maybe, or a joke, having a good time. Harry reached for his wallet, took out a ten and put it on the bar top. Folded the Xerox page and put it in his shirt pocket.

Harry picked up his drink, slid off the bar stool, walked to the table where the Germans were sitting. "Gentlemen, good evening, I heard your Bavarian accent," he said in German, looking at Hess, "and for a moment I thought I was back in Munich. May I join you?"

The silver-haired guy was about to object until Hess raised an arm to stop him.

"It is all right. He is one of us."

Hess nodded at Harry, and he sat in the empty seat. "So you are from Munich?" Hess said.

"I was born there," Harry said. "In 1927. I remember Hitler driving around the neighborhood in his open car, giving speeches." He threw that out and had their attention now. The third man was big and solid, built like a linebacker, looked about fifty, quiet, didn't say a word.

"That was an unprecedented time in our history. Unparalleled," Hess said. Looking like he wanted to relive the past, pumped all of a sudden, grinning, recalling the good old days. "What part of Munich are you from?"

"We lived on Sendlinger Strasse," Harry said.

"Altstadt," Hess said, smiling. "I know this street." He paused. "And where do you live now?"

"Detroit."

"You must work in the automobile industry?" Hess sipped his drink.

"I sell scrap metal," Harry said, still in German.

Hess said, "What brings you to Washington?"

"I came to see my daughter," Harry said, holding him in his gaze. "I had to identify her body."

Hess looked nervous now, face turning serious.

"You killed her last night, and you're out having a good time," he said.

"It was an accident," Hess said. "I am truly sorry for your loss."

"Yeah? Doesn't look like you're sorry. Doesn't look like you care one way or the other."

Hess was flustered, got up and started moving across the dining room. Harry went after him, reached out, grabbed the collar of his suit jacket, aware of diners at other tables looking over now. Hess stopped and turned but the big man was on Harry, holding him from behind. He could feel his strength. He went along without resistance for a few steps and then turned his body quickly, slipping out his grasp. The big man came at him again and Harry threw him over his hip on top of a long table, and watched him slide across taking plates and glasses with him onto the floor.

Harry kept moving, heading for the door, but two DC cops in uniform intercepted him before he got there. They cuffed him, took him outside and put him in the back of a squad car.

7:30 in the morning, Detective Taggart woke Harry up, escorted him out of jail and took him back to the station. They went into a big open room, a bullpen with rows of desks lined up, detectives at work, phones ringing, cops moving around. Taggart's desk had piles of papers and folders on it and a couple white Styrofoam cups with coffee stains on them. There was no place for Harry to sit, so Taggart went down the row to an empty desk and wheeled a chair back. Harry noticed crime-scene photos amid the clutter, eight-by-ten black-and-white shots of a man and a woman naked on their stomachs, blood pooled around their heads. Taggart picked them up and turned them over.

"Shouldn't be looking at those."

"I already did," Harry said. "What happened?"

"Shooter took them down the basement, bam, bam, one each in the back of the head."

"Looks like they were executed." The photographs reminded Harry of something he'd seen a long time ago. "Why are they naked?"

38

"Good question."

"Who are they?" Harry said.

"Dentist and his fiancée. Maybe it's a pissed-off patient, guy got a bad root canal," Taggart said. "This is why I missed the diplomat yesterday morning."

"Who found them?"

"Somebody called it in."

"The killer?"

"Crossed my mind. Anxious for us to find them. Maybe that's part of the buzz." Taggart sat in the chair behind his desk. "Harry, I appreciate your interest but I think you should be concerned about your own situation."

Harry sat, blew on his coffee and took a sip.

"I guess I had you all wrong," Taggart said. "You don't strike me as the vigilante type."

Harry pictured Sara's battered face and felt himself getting angry. "Guy killed my daughter, you think I'm going to let that go?"

"I don't know but you're being charged with assault. The bodyguard needed four stitches to close a cut on his face." Taggart sipped his coffee. "How'd you do that?"

"Judo."

"Judo, huh? You don't look Oriental. Where'd you learn that?"

"I took lessons," Harry said.

"You a black belt?"

"Brown."

Taggart drank his coffee. "They also got you on destruction of property." He took out a piece of paper. "Restaurant says you owe them for six Bordeaux glasses, four Limoges plates." He pronounced the "s." "Total of two hundred and eighty dollars."

Harry sipped his coffee.

"German consulate says they'll drop the assault charges if you go home, promise to get counseling."

"Counseling?" Harry could feel his bile rise. "They've got a lot of nerve."

Chapter 5

He watched the SS guard shout angry words in German, spit flying, the mouth working hard, opening and closing in cadence with the harsh guttural command. He saw the scene in hazy gray monochrome. Harry was standing on the muddy yard at Dachau with a group of prisoners, barracks on both sides of them. Guards were beating them with whips and clubs, herding them into the back of a truck that was covered by a tarpaulin. They had been told they were being transferred to a sub-camp, so there was hope because anything was better than where they were.

"*Komm, komm,*" the guard said. "You look like you don't want to work any more. Get on the truck. *Schnell.*"

Harry and his father were the last two on, prisoners packed in front of them. The tarp was pulled closed but not all the way. Harry could see through the opening. The truck drove out of the camp, turning right, engine laboring in low gear until it reached the main road, heading toward Munich.

A few minutes later, Harry saw a stone marker on the other side of the road. *Dachau 4 km.* They drove a little further and the truck turned right onto a two-track path that wound through the trees, and now there was a feeling of panic among the prisoners. They weren't being transferred to a sub-camp. Harry tried to convince himself it was a work detail but knew they had been selected.

Harry looked at the raggedy figures pressed around him, shifting to the sway of the truck. Glanced the other way through an opening in the tarp at the guards following them in two *kubelwagens*, four men in each. As they wound their way through the trees the guards would disappear from view. Harry's father told him to jump off the truck.

"You have to do it," his father said.

"I want to stay with you."

"In a few minutes there will be nothing left of me, or any of us. Save yourself."

Harry hugged his father, waited for the right opportunity, slipped through the tarp and over the rear gate, dropped to the ground and rolled into the trees. He heard the motorcade drive by, got up and ran, following the sounds of the truck engine.

SS guards with machine guns herded the prisoners through the woods to a clearing. He could see dirt piled up on the other side of a pit that looked long and deep.

Harry was so afraid he was sick to his stomach, body shaking, could hardly breathe. The prisoners stood side by side at the edge of the pit, twelve to fifteen at a time. When a whistle sounded SS guards walked up behind the Jews and shot them point blank, blowing their heads apart. Harry would jump when he heard a volley of gunfire. Some of the SS guards laughed, making fun of each other for getting blood and brains on their uniforms.

His father was in the second group. This time a young SS officer in a black uniform walked behind the prisoners and sprayed them with machine-gun fire, the velocity of the rounds blowing them into the pit. The SS man was grinning, enjoying himself.

"That's how you kill Jews," he said.

A third group was brought into position. He could hear moans and screams coming from a few who were still alive. A rabbi wrapped in a prayer shawl said, "'Comfort ye, comfort ye, my people.'" A guard knocked him unconscious with the butt of his rifle, and dragged him to the mass grave.

Trucks dropped off groups of Jews and went back for more—fifty people at a time. They were led to the pit and shot. Harry had seen the Nazis do terrible things, beating and humiliating Jews on the streets of Munich, and even murdering them at the camp but nothing like this.

41

The young SS officer started passing out bottles of schnapps while the killing continued. When the last transport arrived many of the Nazis were drunk. His mother was with a group from the women's camp, led to the pit and shot like the others. Harry was numb, couldn't watch. Closed his eyes and heard the shots. When it was over, the SS guards, twenty killers, stood around talking and laughing, drinking schnapps, smoking. Someone was playing an accordion. Others were taking photographs. It was festive now, lighthearted, a party after murdering almost six hundred innocent people.

He saw two guards walk past him into the woods, and decided to get out of there as fast as he could. He was moving, crouching behind a tree when a rifle shot blew off a chunk of bark next to his head. Felt it sting his face and stopped. One of the guards had seen him and was coming toward him with his rifle.

"Look what I found," the Nazi said, bringing Harry to the pit. "A hiding Jew."

The SS officer who'd shot his father whipped Harry across the face with his riding crop. "What should we do with the little kike?"

"Let him go," a guard holding a bottle of schnapps said.

"Are you drunk?" another guard said.

"If not, I soon will be." He brought the bottle to his mouth and took a big drink.

The men standing around the pit laughed. The SS officer placed the barrel of his pistol against Harry's temple. Harry closed his eyes, expecting the blast. But it didn't come.

"Sir, you'll get Jew blood on your uniform," a guard said.

"You have a better idea?"

The guard standing next to the SS officer stepped over and drove the butt of his rifle into the side of the Harry's face. Harry staggered and the guard pushed him into the pit. He landed on top of bodies, burrowing between a dead woman and an old man, hearing gunshots above him before he passed out.

Harry opened his eyes. It was completely dark. He was having trouble breathing. Something was in his nose and throat choking him. It was in his eyes too and all over him, and he now realized he was in the pit, covered with dirt, the weight of it and the corpses, heavy, pressing down on him. He could hear moans and cries from people who were still alive. Pushed his way through bodies, clawed his way through the layer of earth, feeling the cool night air, spitting dirt out of his mouth, wiping it out of his eyes, taking deep breaths.

Harry climbed out and saw the bodies of others lying on the ground where they'd fallen and died. The scene so surreal, was it a dream? He scanned the woods and saw a girl running, disappearing into the trees. So at least two of them had survived.

The sky was overcast. No stars or moon. Harry followed tire tracks through the woods to the road. One way went to Dachau and the other to Munich. He walked along the side of the road for a couple kilometers until he heard dogs barking in the distance, and followed the sounds to a farm, fields of crops that had been harvested. Beyond the fields he could see lights on in a house, and next to it the dark shape of a barn.

Harry waited till the lights went out before crawling three hundred meters across the fields, resting now, leaning against the back wall of the house. He could see windows open on the second-floor rooms above him. The dogs were on the other side of the house, barking occasionally, but they hadn't seen him or caught his scent. He moved around the house, looked in the kitchen window, saw a loaf of bread on the counter.

He came to a door, turned the handle, opened it and heard the hinges squeak, slipped into a hallway. He stopped and listened, didn't hear anything, moved into the kitchen, picked up the bread, tore off a piece and ate it.

Behind him he heard the twin hammers of a double-barrel shotgun being cocked. "You know what this is?" a man's voice said in German.

"I'm starving," Harry said. "I just need something to eat."

"Turn around."

He did, and saw a big man holding the gun at his waist, barrel pointed at Harry's chest.

"Uli, put down the gun. He is a boy," a woman said, coming in the room. She was short and wide, blond hair pulled back in a braid.

The man cradled the barrel over his left arm like a bird hunter. "He is a thief."

She turned on the light, looking at Harry in his striped, dirt-caked, bloodstained uniform, shaking her head.

"Look at him," the woman said to her husband. "He is from the camp. My God, what did they do to you?"

Harry was wondering where to begin.

"How old are you?"

"Fourteen." He was big for his age, already five foot nine, but skinny after meager rations for six months.

"Where are your parents?"

"Dead."

She came across the room, eyes fixed on him, put her arms around him, pulled his skinny frame against her heavy bosom, holding him. Harry looking over her shoulder at the husband, wondering what he was thinking.

The woman released him and opened a drawer, took out a towel, wet it under the faucet and touched his face. It was cool and felt good on his swollen cheek. She washed his face, rinsed the towel and washed it again. She took him to the table and sat him in a chair. Served him chicken and dumplings, bread and milk. The husband telling her in hushed tones that helping a Jew could get them killed. The woman, whose name was Margot Schmidt, telling him to go to bed, she was going to look after the boy. She sat with him while he ate. Told him to slow down, there was no hurry, he could have as much as he wanted.

"Of course we knew what was happening at the camp. We heard the trains arriving. Saw the work details, prisoners in striped uniforms like the one you are wearing. Heard the rumors of medical experiments and firing squads killing political prisoners and Jews. We are farmers. We have nothing against you."

When he finished eating she took him to the bathroom, filled the tub and closed the door behind her. Harry dipped his toe in, getting used to the heat, and then lay down in water up to his chin, the water turning brown.

When he was finished she gave him clothes and shoes that she told him had been her son's. The son had enlisted and was killed in action during the French invasion. She was angry, bitter, didn't understand why Germany had gone to war in the first place.

She took his blood-stained camp uniform downstairs, burned it in the fireplace. Harry slept in a bed for the first time in six months, nervous, getting up every few minutes, looking out the window, expecting to see Nazis.

He was dreaming of food, seeing a plate of bratwurst and sauerkraut and potatoes, when he felt someone shaking him and thought he was back in the barracks, block 21. He opened his eyes and saw the woman. She put her hand over his mouth. Told him there were Nazis outside, looking for prisoners that had escaped. They were searching the barn. He could hear the dogs barking.

The farmer stood in the doorway and said, "If they find him they will kill us too."

Harry got out of bed, ducked down and went to the window. He looked out and saw two open military vehicles parked in the yard. Four SS soldiers were walking toward the barn and four more coming toward the house. He recognized the young SS officer from the massacre in the woods.

"Get away from there. If they see you—" Her words trailed off.

She took him down to the kitchen, opened a trap door that led to the cellar. He climbed down a ladder into the musty darkness and waited.

Soon he heard the heavy sound of footsteps above him and voices. Then the trap door was pulled open. Light from the kitchen shone down illuminating the ladder and a section of cellar floor. Harry moved back and bumped sausages hanging on ropes from the ceiling, sent

45

them swinging. Moved back farther and felt glass containers of fruits and vegetables stored on shelves. Harry worried the husband had told them where he was.

He saw black boots coming down the ladder, and the gray jodhpurs of an SS soldier. Harry moved to the far corner of the cellar, going to his knees behind bins of apples and squash, he touched them, onions and garlic, he smelled them. Harry going down on his chest as the SS soldier's feet landed on the dirt floor. The soldier moved to the right, training the flashlight over the contents of the cellar, the light lingering and holding on objects and then sweeping across the back wall, coming toward him, light reflecting off the glass containers on the shelves, then tracing a line where the walls met, going from dirt floor to beamed ceiling. Then moving across the sidewall, and over the bins, Harry holding his breath, curling up, making himself smaller.

He heard a click and the beam disappeared and the soldier was on the ladder climbing back up.

"Nothing," the soldier said.

The trap door was put back into position and it was dark again. He heard the soldiers leave the house. Heard the vehicles start up and drive out of the yard and let out a breath.

Margot Schmidt, against her better judgment and the protests of her husband, drove Harry to the outskirts of Munich in a rickety old truck that backfired and burned oil. She told him he was crazy. He should stay with them at the farmhouse. They would hide him until the insanity was over, until it was safe. Harry knew the husband didn't want him. That was obvious, and sooner or later someone would find out he was there and tell the SS.

She pulled off the road and gave him bread and sausage wrapped in butcher paper tied with string. He put it in the pocket of the coat that had been her son's. She leaned across the bench seat and hugged him. Harry thanked her and got out of the truck. He pulled the brim of the cap down over his eyes and headed for the towers of Altstadt.

Twenty minutes later he was across the street from the building his father owned at Sendlinger Strasse 43. The bottom floor had been rented to a pharmacist who appeared to still be in business. Harry and his parents lived in the top two floors. He crossed the street and tried the door. It was locked. He remembered his father kept a spare key on the stone ledge over the rear entrance. Was it still there? Even so, if someone were living in the house they would have changed the locks, wouldn't they?

Harry walked around the block behind the building. Stood in front of the door. He jumped up and felt the key and knocked it off the ledge, heard it hit the cobble-stone entranceway. He picked it up, slid it in the lock and opened the door.

Chapter 6

Detroit, Michigan. 1971.

Harry glanced at the row of black Cadillacs parked on the street, a group of friends and relatives around him at Sara's casket, waiting for it to be lowered into the ground next to her mother. Rabbi Rosenbaum delivering the Mourner's Kaddish.

"May His great Name grow exalted and sanctified."

"Amen" from the mourners.

"May He give reign to His kingship in your lifetimes and in your days, and in the lifetimes of the entire family of Israel, swiftly and soon. Now say: Amen. May His great name be blessed forever and ever. Blessed, praised, glorified, exalted, extolled, mighty, upraised, and lauded be the Name of the Holy One."

And now everyone said, "Blessed is He."

Harry felt like he had slipped out of his body, watching himself in a black suit, white shirt, black tie and black yarmulke, hands clasped together, holding them over his groin, solemn expression, mind flashing snapshots of Sara like frames in a slide show.

An hour later Harry was sitting in his crowded living room, Aunt Netta, an Orthodox Jew, holding his face in her hands.

"Harry, did you shave? You are not supposed to shave or get a haircut. Harry, don't you know this?"

"It's okay," Harry said.

"It's not okay. You should be sitting in a low chair."

"I don't have a low chair," Harry said.

She glanced at his shoes, black ankle-high Bally boots with a zipper on the side. "And no leather. You should know better, Harry. It's rabbinically mandated."

Telling him what a mourner should do during shi-va. Netta was short and wide like his mother, about five two. She pinned a piece of ribbon, a keriah, on his shirt pocket.

After the Nazis murdered his parents, Harry doubted the existence of God, and stopped practicing the rituals and traditions of the faith.

"Harry, I arranged a minyan for tonight's service," Netta said. Which meant ten men from Temple would arrive about 7:00 p.m. to recite Kaddish.

Most of Harry's family had emigrated from Germany in the late thirties. His father's side of the family was tall, thin and good-looking. His mother's side was short and stocky. The men had round faces and thinning hair and wore glasses, black horn rims with lenses so thick you got dizzy if you looked through them.

Harry's uncle and former business partner, his dad's younger brother, sat next to him and grinned. Sam was seventy-one and always had a gleam in his eye.

"A Polish terrorist was sent to blow up a car," Sam said. "He burned his mouth on the exhaust pipe."

Harry grinned.

"Two Jews, Saul and Sheldon, were walking past a church. They saw a sign that said: *Become Catholic. We pay $100.* Sheldon says, "I'm going to do it." "No," says Saul. "Yes, I am," says Sheldon. "You can't. Your family, your friends, they're all Jewish. You go to shul for the High Holidays." "I'm doing it," says Sheldon walking into the church. Saul paces back and forth until Sheldon walks out with a big smile on his face. "No," says Saul. "You didn't." "Yes, I did," says Sheldon. "I'm baptized. I've become Catholic." Saul says, "Tell me, did you get the hundred dollars?" Sheldon looks at him and says, "Why is it always the money with you people?" Sam laughed, patted Harry's cheek. "So how you doing?"

"Holding up," Harry said.

"What choice do you have?"

"I miss her," Harry said, feeling a heavy sadness like he might break down, took a deep breath and it calmed him.

Peter Leonard

Sam put his arm around Harry's shoulder. "We all do. That kid was something special."

Harry saw Phyllis and Jerry, dressed up, standing in the foyer. "Excuse me, will you?" he said to Sam, got up and went over to them. They'd never been in his house and looked nervous. "Thanks for coming," Harry said.

"Harry, why didn't you tell me?" Phyllis said. "I'm so sorry." She hugged him and handed him a glass canning jar. "I made this for you. Salsa, extra spicy, the way you like it."

He took it and put it on a table and helped Phyllis off with her coat. "Come in, have something to eat."

Jerry shook his hand. "Harry, I don't know what to say."

"You don't have to say anything."

"I can't stay long," Phyllis said, out of her comfort zone, ready to leave right then if she could've.

"There're no rules," Harry said. "Go whenever you want." He escorted them into the dining room, people moving around the table, filling their plates. "But first have something to eat." A tall dark-haired kid with a beard and glasses with silver rims appeared next to him.

"Mr. Levin, I'm Richard Gold, friend of Sara's."

"She mentioned you," Harry said.

The boyfriend. Clearly uncomfortable, palms clamped together, but it was an uncomfortable situation.

"We were going out, seeing each other," Richard Gold said. "I was in love with her. Sara was going to introduce us the next time you came to visit."

Richard was choked up, and Harry was too. He could hear Sam behind him firing off more jokes.

"Doctor, my leg hurts. What can I do? The doctor says: Limp!" People were laughing.

He patted Richard on the back. "I appreciate you being here. Excuse me." He walked past him into the kitchen and there was Galina. She had just come in the door, carrying a family-size bowl of borscht and a platter of gefilte fish covered in cellophane. She put the food down on the kitchen table.

"Come here," she said, moving toward him, hugging Harry, pulling him to her, whispering, "I can come back later, give you back rub."

Her euphemism for going to bed with him. He hoped Aunt Netta wasn't listening. She would have said, "Harry, no sexual relations during shiva."

Harry said, "What happened to your boyfriend?"

"Is over," Galina said. "The man is a schmuck."

The idea of sex with Galina, being smothered by her massive earth-momma breasts, appealed to him. It would take the edge off, take his mind out of the funk he was in.

At 9:30, after everyone had gone, Harry went in the kitchen and made himself a vodka tonic with a slice of lime. All the leftover food had been put in the refrigerator. All the dishes and glasses and silver had been washed and put away. He realized he hadn't eaten anything all day but wasn't hungry.

Harry took his drink and went upstairs, walked in his daughter's room, turned on the light and looked around, the room telling a lot about eighteen-year-old Sara Levin, revealing a curious blend of girl-woman. Harry sat on the bed, knowing he was never going to see her again, felt tears come down his face, staring at the posters on the walls: the Beatles in black and white, shot on a TV sound stage, could've been *The Ed Sullivan Show,* a color close-up of Jimi Hendrix playing guitar at Woodstock, Bob Dylan wearing a hat in a dark moody shot. He got up, wiped his eyes with his shirt sleeves, looking at tennis trophies on top of the bookshelves, and under the trophies books lined up: the *Nancy Drew* mystery series, *The Sun Also Rises, Of Mice and Men, The Catcher in the Rye,* and *The Bell Jar.* On the desk was a framed photo of Harry and Sara posing in their white judo outfits. He walked out of the room and turned off the light.

Harry was brushing his teeth when he heard the doorbell. He went downstairs, opened the front door. Galina was standing on the front porch in a raincoat on a warm August night. She came in, brushed his cheek with her palm. "Expecting rain?" Harry said, closing the door.

She started unbuttoning the coat as she walked to the stairs, took it off, draped it over the banister and walked up naked, wearing high heels.

Halfway up she turned, glanced at him and said, "You coming, Harry?"

Chapter 7

Munich, Germany. 1942.

The key worked. Harry slid it in and unlocked the door, but someone might be living there. He rang the buzzer and waited, thinking about what he would say if the occupant came down and asked what he wanted. He moved back into the alley and looked up at the second-floor windows, the afternoon sun reflecting off the glass making it look dark.

Harry heard a truck, turned and saw a military vehicle coming toward him, stepped back to the door, turned the handle and went inside. He moved up the stairs and stood looking at the door to the house he had not seen in more than six months.

He went in and listened. Heard the faint sounds of traffic on Sendlinger Strasse. Closed the door and went into the kitchen. He opened a drawer and grabbed a paring knife with a four-inch blade. Opened cupboards and saw his parents' glasses and dishes.

Harry went into the living room. It was their furniture, the chrome-and-leather Marcel Breuer chairs and couch, chrome-and-glass Bauhaus end tables and von Nessen lamps. Harry's father, the BMW designer, telling him about the quality and craftsmanship of the pieces. Not that Harry had cared about such things when he was younger, but he'd listened and learned.

The Bechstein grand was across the room. His mother had played professionally until Hitler outlawed Jews from participating in the arts. His father wanted to destroy the piano after he read that Edwin Bechstein, an ardent Nazi, had given Hitler a Mercedes-Benz as a gift.

His mother had said, "Julius, pianos are not political."

"Today," his father had said, "everything is."

On the wall behind him, above the mantle, was a black swastika reversed out of a circle of white on a square of red cloth, the flag of the Third Reich. Below it was his mother's prize Doxia clock, with its silver deco numerals and hands, and frosted silver dial.

On the opposite wall was a framed photograph of Adolf Hitler, little mustache perched like a bug on his upper lip. Harry had seen him driving through Munich on numerous occasions. His parents thought Hitler was crazy and couldn't understand why the German people had elected him. It was a nightly discussion at the dinner table until his mother would say: "Can we talk about something else?"

There was an eight-by-ten photograph in a sterling silver frame on the end table next to the couch. Harry picked it up and studied it, an SS officer posing with his wife and twin sons, the boys about Harry's age, wearing lederhosen. They had taken over the house and everything in it.

He went to the window and watched the traffic below, cars and military vehicles passing by. He went to the third level where the bedrooms were. His parents had the big room with the bath. Harry's room was at the opposite end of the hall, guest room in between. His room looked the same, the single bed, the six-drawer dresser, desk and bookshelves. He looked in the closet. His clothes had been replaced by light brown shirts and dark shorts of the Hitler youth, by lederhosen and other clothes he didn't recognize.

He walked down the hall to his parents' room. It too looked the same. The art deco armoire, the light brown furniture with black lacquered trim, the nine-drawer dresser and oval nightstands. The same deco furniture grouping in front of the fireplace where his parents sat in the winter and read. The same double bed and white chenille bedspread.

The closet was divided between men's and women's clothes. On the left were military uniforms lined up on hangers. Three black jackets with black-white-red swastika armbands and matching jodhpurs. Next to the black jackets were three pale-gray uniforms cut the same way, with an eagle on the sleeve in place of the swastika. On a shelf above the uniforms were three peaked caps with the same eagle above the skull and crossbones.

Below the uniforms were two pairs of well-shined black jackboots. He got on his knees and moved the boots aside and crawled to the back corner of the closet, dug the tip of the knife blade into the seam between the floorboards and pulled back. The plank came up and Harry reached in the opening and took out a thick wad of marks, a photograph of Harry and his parents in front of the house, three sets of identification, and his uncle's address and phone number in Detroit, Michigan, USA.

His dad had said, "If something happens to your mother and me, I have left something for you."

It confused Harry at the time. He had said, "Papa, what's going to happen?"

"I hope nothing. I hope the Allied forces defeat Hitler. But we have to be prepared."

Harry placed the floorboard back in position, went back into the room and stood by the window. He looked at the ID cards, one each for him, his mother and father. Their photographs, but different names, aliases, and nothing that said they were Jewish. If his father had these documents, why didn't they leave the country? He put his parents' papers back in the floor. They weren't going to need them now. He was counting the money, already up to five thousand marks when he heard voices downstairs.

Harry stuffed everything into his trouser pockets. He moved into the hall and looked over the banister. The twins were coming up the stairs, wrestling. One had the other in a headlock, crashing into the wall. He heard a woman's voice telling them to stop or they would be punished. It didn't seem to do any good and now the mother came up the stairs and separated them.

"Boys, go to your rooms," she said.

Harry went back in his parents' bedroom, crossed to a door with glass panes that led to a balcony on the alley side of the building. He opened the door and went out. There were two chairs and a table. He looked through the glass and saw the woman enter the room. She stopped and turned, yelled something down the hall and moved toward the closet unbuttoning her dress. Harry crouched and froze.

She came back from the closet wearing a robe, the curves of her body visible under the thin fabric. She had short brown hair and pale skin and heavy red lipstick. She picked up a magazine from the nightstand and sat on the edge of the bed with her back to him.

Harry went over the balcony railing and climbed under it, wrapping his arms and legs around a support beam, looking down at the cobblestone alley ten meters below. A couple minutes later, he heard the door open and felt the wood creak above him. He saw her in the openings between the boards, barefoot, sitting in a chair. Saw her get up and move to the railing, looking at something. He heard voices. She turned as the twins came out, Harry catching glimpses of them pushing each other, one grabbing the other's arms behind his back.

The mother said, "Stop this now or I will tell your father."

They stood at attention, clicked their heels together.

"No mamma, please. We will be good."

They acted like little kids, Harry thought.

"Any more of this your father is going to hear about it."

One of the boys leaned over the railing. Harry could see his head upside down, hair hanging, until his mother pulled him up.

"Go to your rooms," the mother said. "I will let you know when you can come out."

The boys went in the house and she followed them and closed the door.

Harry held on with his left hand and arm and reached over half a meter, grabbed the downspout with his right hand. He took a breath, pushed off with his legs, lunged and grabbed the downspout with both hands, clung with his knees, got his feet in position, pushing up to secure himself. He shimmied down a few inches at a time, and when he was a meter from the ground he jumped.

He took a left on Westenriederstrasse. Passed the butcher shop, Joseph Bamberger, where his father used to buy meat—boarded up now. Harry and his father would stand in front of the glass display case, talking to friends until it was their turn. A few doors down was the poultry shop, still in business, but the Jewish proprietor had been deported. There were only a couple Jewish-run businesses still in operation. Thinking about it, Harry wondered why his father had been so stubborn.

Harry cut over to Frauenstrasse, where his parents' good friends the Fabers lived in an apartment down the street. He found the building, checked the directory, but Faber was not among the names listed.

Frauenstrasse turned into Blumenstrasse. He took it to Lindwurmstrasse and went left, walked to 125, and went to the rear of the building, to the makeshift synagogue where his family had worshiped since their synagogue on Reichenbachstrasse was destroyed by the Nazis on Kristallnacht in November 1938. The door was locked. There was no one around. Harry didn't know if people still came here. He didn't know if there were any Jews left in Munich. It was late afternoon. He took out the bread and sausage Frau Schmidt had given him and ate, leaning against the wall of the building, wondering what he was going to do. He had to get out of Munich, but how?

When it was dark the door opened and an old man came out of the building and saw him.

"What are you doing here?"

"I used to come here with my parents," Harry said.

"What's your name?"

"Harry Levin."

"You're a Jew, why aren't you wearing your star? They'll execute you on the spot."

"They're going to kill us all anyway," Harry said. "Why advertise it?"

57

"Are you a partisan?"

"Whatever I have to do," Harry said. "How many of us are left?"

"I don't know," the old man said. "The Nazis have taken most of the Jews to the settlement in Milbertshofen, Knorrstrasse 148, and the housing area in Berg am Laim before deporting them to Palestine."

"They're not going to Palestine, they're going to concentration camps: Dachau, Theresienstadt and Auschwitz." He had this on good faith from prisoners he had met and worked with. Harry could see the bewildered look on the old man's face. "We have to get out of Germany."

"Come with me," the old man said, taking him to the cellar where services were conducted. He gave Harry a name, Recha Sternbuch, and an address on a piece of paper. "If you can get to Montreux, Switzerland, this woman will help you. Do you have money?"

Harry nodded.

"You can take the train. But you will have to bribe the Swiss police. A boy your age traveling alone raises a red flag. I will pray for you."

Harry slept on a bunk in the cellar of the warehouse synagogue and left the next morning. It was strange walking through the city not wearing the yellow star on his coat, seeing Nazis everywhere. He was nervous at first, and then got used to being disguised as a normal German, no one taunting him, giving him a hard time, no one even noticing him.

He walked two miles to the train station, stood in the terminal, studying the board that listed departures, and bought a ticket to Montreux. He went to track 23. He would be out of Germany, free in a few hours.

The train was there, so he got on and took a seat in the middle of the car next to the window. He watched people come down the aisle and fit their luggage on the overhead rack. He heard the soldiers before he saw them, six SS officers in gray-green uniforms, peaked caps, jodhpurs and black jackboots. They sounded drunk, laughing and talking loudly.

Harry sank down in his seat and looked out the window. A train had just pulled in on the next track and people were getting out. He glanced over at the soldiers, accidentally made eye contact with one of them, and looked away. He saw the man out of the corner of his eye, saw him get up and start down the aisle.

Harry could feel his heart banging in his chest.

"You are traveling alone?"

Harry looked up at him and nodded.

"Where are you going?" He had a pistol in a black holster on his hip.

"Montreux," Harry said. "To visit my grandmother."

The Nazi glanced at the empty luggage rack. "What is your name?"

"Volker Spengler." That was the name on his ID, the name his father had chosen for some reason. Probably because it sounded so German.

The Nazi said, "How old are you, Volker Spengler?"

"Fourteen," Harry said, trying to stay calm.

The Nazi sat down next to him, and Harry felt his pulse take off. He leaned back against the window, trying to move away from the man, give himself a little room.

"Are you all right? You seem nervous."

"I'm fine," Harry said, heart pounding.

The Nazi said, "What do you have to be nervous about?"

"Nothing." He could feel his palms sweat and rubbed them on his pant legs.

The Nazi was staring at the sleeves of his coat covering half of his hands.

"This is yours? It looks too big for you."

"My cousin grew out of it and gave it to me."

"Let me see your papers."

Harry took the ID out of his shirt pocket and handed it to him. The Nazi opened it, looked at the photograph and back at Harry.

"Where are your parents?"

"My father was in the Heer, killed in action. The battle of Kutno." Harry remembered his father talking about

Peter Leonard

it at dinner one night. "My mother works at Dachau, secretary to the commandant."

"What is his name?"

"Herr Weiss."

The Nazi nodded and got up, keeping his eyes on Harry. Handed him his ID and went down the aisle.

Chapter 8

Detroit, Michigan. 1971.

"He's a voting member of the Christian Social Union of Bavaria," Bob Stark said. "The CSU operates in alliance with the Social Democratic Party. Each maintains its own structure, but they form a common caucus in the Bundestag, the German parliament."

"What the hell're you talking about?" Harry said.

"Ernst Hess is politically well connected. I'm not saying he's going to, but some day he could run for chancellor of Germany."

They were in Stark's office on the fortieth floor of the Penobscot Building. Stark was a friend, an international attorney, tenacious, self-made, put himself through law school working a fulltime job. Spoke fluent French and Italian, and passable German. The smoke from his cigarette drifted up toward the ceiling. Stark picked a piece of paper up from his desktop and started reading.

"The German government has a democratic constitution that emphasizes the protection of individual liberty, and division of powers in a federal structure."

Stark looked over the top of the page, met his gaze.

"Protection of individual liberty, huh?" Harry said. "That's not how I remember it."

"They've changed," Stark said with a grin.

"Seven hundred and fifty years of anti-Semitism and now they're tolerant. What do you think was the big influence?"

"Got their ass kicked in World War Two." Stark puffed on his cigarette.

"What was Hess doing in Washington?"

61

"Meeting with construction companies, selling the capabilities of his airships. Hess builds Zeppelins." Stark put his cigarette out in the ashtray. "Claims he's a distant relative of Count Ferdinand von Zeppelin, who invented the first one in 1900."

"How do you know that?"

"I looked it up," Stark said. "Remember the Hindenburg? Crashed and burst into flames over New Jersey in 1937. It was the largest flying machine of its kind ever built. Eight hundred and eight feet long. Almost three football fields." He paused, straightening the knot of his red paisley tie. "Hess is trying to revive the concept. He's developed an experimental line of airships that are smaller, lighter, faster and more practical. We're not talking about the Goodyear blimp. Hess' airships have an internal skeleton, built to carry more weight. Perfect for transporting heavy equipment and supplies to inaccessible areas: ski resorts, coastal developments."

"Doesn't this strike you as a little odd, a German politician with diplomatic status coming here for personal gain?"

"What's good for Ernst Hess is good for Germany," Stark said. "I've looked into it. You want to sue him? Say the word, I'll file charges."

"What's that going to do?"

"Bring attention to what happened to Sara, public outrage.

"I don't want to start a crusade," Harry said. "This is personal."

"It might get you a settlement."

"I don't want money."

"What do you want?"

Harry said, "Where's he live?"

"I don't know," Stark said. "Somewhere in Bavaria would be my guess. What do you have in mind?"

Harry looked at him but didn't say anything.

"You want to find out more about Hess, I can call Fedor Berman. Private investigator, lives in Munich. He's a survivor like you."

Harry went to the gun range on Grand River. Took the .357 Mag out of his pocket and pushed in his earplugs. He held the revolver with two hands. Fired six rounds at a paper target from thirty feet, putting all of the shots, perfect cylindrical holes, where he wanted them, mid-chest on the black outline of a man. Reloaded and did it again.

After, he went to his office where he hadn't been for almost two weeks, sat at his desk, shuffled through the mail, opened a letter from the IRS. According to their audit findings, S&H Recycling Metals underpaid on its 1970 Federal Tax return and owed $17,500, payment due by September 15, 1971. Harry paid all the bills and signed a dozen blank checks. Picked up the phone and told Phyllis to come in.

She knocked on his door and opened it. "Need something, Harry?"

"Sit down," Harry said.

She sat in a chair across from his desk.

"I'm going to take some time off."

"Harry, you just got back."

"I'll be gone for a while, couple weeks, a month."

"If you don't mind my asking," Phyllis said, "where're you going?"

"I'll call you when I get there," Harry said. He handed her the checks he'd just signed. "Keep these in the safe till you need them. There's also plenty of cash, sixty grand. Don't take it and run off to South America."

Phyllis gave him a dirty look. "Harry, I wouldn't do that."

"I'm kidding."

Harry called Pan Am and booked a flight to Munich with a stopover in London. He called the Free Press and told them not to deliver the paper till further notice. Called his niece, Franny, and asked her to bring in the mail and water the plants while he was away. He'd left two hundred dollars and a key to the house for her in an envelope in the garage.

Upstairs, Harry put his American Tourister suitcase on the bed, the one that had been tested by a four-hundred-pound gorilla in a TV ad. He folded clothes and fit them in. Grabbed his shaving kit from the bathroom. When he was finished he went to the desk, opened a drawer and took out a dog-eared, sepia-tone photograph of him posing with his parents in front of their house on Sendlinger Strasse. Harry in a wool cap, standing between his parents in stylish hats and overcoats. He'd turned thirteen a few weeks before, on October 7, 1941.

He slipped the photo in his passport and put it in the inside pocket of his sport coat. He closed the suitcase and took it downstairs. Turned on a light in the foyer, walked into the den and stood at the window. An airport shuttle pulled up in front and drove him to Metro.

He picked up his boarding pass at the gate in the international terminal. Flew first class to London on a 747, had a couple drinks upstairs in the bar, and a filet and baked potato at his seat. He slept for a couple hours, arriving at Heathrow at 8:36 in the morning. He had a two-hour layover, and took a Lufthansa flight from London to Munich, arriving at 12:17.

Harry took a taxi from the airport to the Bayerischer Hof hotel on Promenadeplatz, seeing Munich for the first time in thirty years, the snow-capped peaks of the Bavarian Alps on the horizon, perfect blue-sky fall day. Stomach knotted up, feeling strange, a lot of memories. Half expected to see Nazis on the streets. The city looked different, bigger and more modern on the outskirts but when he got to Altstadt it was much the same as he remembered it.

He checked in and went to his room and stood at the window, looking out at the twin onion-domed spires of the Frauenkirche cathedral and the Neues Rathaus in Marienplatz, and he felt like he was home.

At 1:45 Harry walked out of the hotel toward the Frauenkirche, crossed Frauenplatz to Kaufingerstrasse, saw the Renaissance tower of Peterkirche and the red tile roof of the Alter Hof, and there gliding over the rooftops was a silver Zeppelin that said HESS AG in black letters on the side. It was as if Hess knew he'd arrived and was following him, watching him.

Harry went left to Marienplatz and stood in front of the Glockenspiel, looking up at the mechanical figures, thinking about coming here on weekends with his father, standing in the same place, watching the figures doing the Coopers' Dance.

He stopped at a cafe and had bratwurst and a beer. Then he walked down Sendlinger Strasse, past the Asamkirche to his old neighborhood, the silver Zeppelin hovering over him, moving southwest.

He found his house and took out the photo. By rights Harry now owned the building, not that he was going to try to get it back. The ground-floor space that had been a pharmacy thirty years ago was now an antique shop. He thought about the last time he'd been here, getting his fake ID, and leaving his parents under the floor in the bedroom closet, assumed they were still there.

Harry had contacted Wilhelm Martz, a good friend of his parents and uncle. He had gotten his address and arranged to stop by. Martz lived on Kreuzstrasse, a couple blocks away. He found the house, a Bavarian Tudor, and rang the bell. The door opened, and a good-looking woman with dark curly hair and glasses eyed him with caution.

"I'm Harry Levin."

Now she smiled. "Harry, how are you? I'm Lisa. Do you remember me?"

Remember her? She was the cutest girl in the class, in the whole Jewish school. He'd had a crush on her, felt like a bumbling fool in her presence. He used to sit in class and look at her, thinking she was perfect except for her nose. It had a sexy hook, one little imperfection that made her all the more attractive. "I think so," Harry said.

"You think so? Harry, I have to tell you I was crazy about you."

"Really?" He grinned and walked in and she closed the door.

"Really."

"Why didn't you say something?"

"Girls weren't supposed to make the first move, Harry."

She escorted him into a room with dark wood trim and plaster walls, old-world craftsmanship. It was stuffy like the windows hadn't been opened in years. Martz was sitting in a heavy overstuffed chair, an alert old guy with a permanent grin. He stood up, fixed his rheumy gaze on Harry. He was tall and stoop-shouldered, with long silver hair combed back and dark eyebrows.

Lisa said, "Nice seeing you, Harry," and walked out of the room.

"You look just like your father," Martz said staring at him.

Everyone told him that.

"Your parents used to have parties. You would come down the stairs and ask us to turn down the music."

"I remember everyone dancing, having a good time."

Martz directed him to a green velvet couch that was next to the chair he'd been sitting in. "I think about your parents every day," Martz said. "Your father was well liked by everyone. Jews in the neighborhood would come to him for advice instead of the rabbi. I used to call him Sol, short for Solomon." He paused, taking his time. "It is amazing how much you are like him, same voice, same mannerisms. Your father used to pick his fingernails like that."

Harry looked at his hands, not even aware he was doing it, and stopped.

Martz pushed his hair back with his right hand. "Your mother was a great beauty. She had her pick of the men. But when she met your father that was it."

Harry took the photo out of his shirt pocket and showed it to him.

"Both of your parents had exquisite taste. Always well dressed." Martz glanced across the room. "It is too bad."

"I remember seeing Hitler in the neighborhood," Harry said.

"He lived not far from us. He would drive around with his Nazis, honking the horn at people on the street, saluting. In the early years he was a curiosity. We made fun of him. Didn't think he would last. How could he?

That was in 1928. Five years later he became chancellor," Martz said. "Do you remember the food rationing and the curfew for Jews?"

Harry nodded.

"By 1940 we couldn't buy shoes or clothes. Then we couldn't have cameras. Then we couldn't buy coffee, chicken, fish, or vegetables. We couldn't buy coal to heat the house. In September '41 all Jews over the age of six had to wear a yellow star."

"I remember," Harry said.

"I was taken to Dachau about six months before you. I was in the yard the day the SS put you and your father on the truck. There was no logic to the selection. The important thing, Harry, you survived."

The silver Zeppelin was gone when Harry came out of Martz' house an hour later and walked back to his hotel. He crossed the lobby, stopped at the front desk and asked the clerk if there were any messages for Harry Levin.

"Herr Berman is in the lounge waiting for you."

Harry saw him sitting at a table, a stocky, ruddy-faced man wearing a tweed sport coat, reading the newspaper. Stark said Fedor Berman had spent three years at Auschwitz. He was the only person in the bar, and looked up as Harry approached. "Herr Berman, Harry Levin."

The man stood up and they shook hands. He pulled a chair out for Harry. "*Bitte.*"

They sat at opposite sides of the table. "Will you join me in a drink?"

Harry ordered a beer. "Bob Stark tells me you're a skier."

"I spend the morning hiking, walking up the hills I will be skiing down in a couple months. Must get the legs ready."

Berman poured schnapps in his coffee and sipped it. Opened a briefcase on the chair next to him, took out a manila envelope and handed it to Harry. He opened the envelope and slid out the contents, a dozen photographs of a country estate shot from different angles, and several pictures of Hess' airship factory. "Where does he live?"

Peter Leonard

"Schleissheim," Berman said. "His main residence. Thirteen kilometers north of here. He has a sophisticated security system and a security team watching the estate."

"Who's the big guy that's always with Hess?"

"Arno Rausch. His bodyguard. He's worked for him since the end of the war." Berman paused. "Hess also has an apartment in the city."

Berman handed him a photograph of the building, the address written at the bottom in the margin. He drank his coffee and schnapps.

"Have you been to Munich before, Herr Levin?"

"A long time ago," Harry said.

"Enjoy your stay. If I can be of further assistance—"

"There is one more thing," Harry said. "I need a gun."

68

Chapter 9

Montreux, Switzerland. 1942.

The four Nazis got off the train at Konstanz, the blond SS Sturmbannführer eyeing him as he walked by. The train stopped again at the border. The rabbi had told him Swiss authorities were cracking down on refugees trying to enter the country. Jews who were caught were deported or handed over to the Nazis.

Swiss police boarded, checking papers. A heavyset officer, hat pulled low over his eyes, looked Harry up and down the way the Nazi had, as if he was guilty of something. Studied his identification, glanced from the photo to his face.

"Volker Spengler," he said. "A German boy traveling alone in a time of war. Where is your visa?"

"I don't have one," Harry said.

"How do you expect to enter this country without a visa?"

"I'm going to stay with my grandmother."

"Where does she live?"

"Montreux," Harry said. "She is the only relative I have left. My father was killed in France during the invasion, my mother in Hamburg by an Allied bomb."

"We have a strict policy concerning refugees."

Harry had five hundred marks folded in his pocket, hoping it was enough. The rest of the money was hidden in the linings of his shoes. He handed the bribe to the policeman. "My grandmother asked me to give you this. To thank you, to show her gratitude for helping me."

69

The policeman looked at the folded pile of bills, tucked it in the front pocket of his uniform shirt. "Welcome to Switzerland, Herr Spengler."

He was finally free but didn't trust the feeling. After all that had happened he couldn't let himself relax. Thought about his parents, took the photograph out of his pocket, Harry posing with his mother and father in front of their house. He slid the picture in his pocket and looked out the window at the lush countryside, mountains in the distance, reminding him of Bavaria.

The train went on to Montreux, arriving in the late afternoon. He got off, walked into the station and found a city map in a rack next to the ticket booth. He went outside, studying the street grid of Montreux. He had no idea where he was going and asked a policeman for directions. It took twenty minutes to walk to the Sternbuch residence. He found the address and knocked on the door. It opened and a bearded man in a fedora said, "What can I do for you?"

He looked about forty, wore round tortoiseshell glasses and a shirt and tie.

"I'm looking for Frau Sternbuch."

"And you are?"

"Harry Levin."

"I'm Yitzchok, her husband."

They talked for a couple minutes, Yitzchok asking where he was from, and where were his parents, and how he had escaped?

There were tables set up in the main room, people sitting around them drinking coffee and talking. It looked like a party. Yitzchok led him through the house to the dining room. A woman wearing what looked like a turban was sitting at the middle of the table, speaking to a group of bearded men wearing hats like the husband's. She saw them enter the room and stopped talking. The men at the table turned to look at him.

"Recha, I want to introduce you to Harry Levin, a Dachau survivor from Munich."

The woman stood and came around the table, her face telling him she understood what he'd been through.

She put her arms around him, held him the way his mother did.

"Harry, there is nothing to worry about. You are safe," she said, wiping tears from her eyes. "It is a blessing you have joined us for Shabbos."

Now the men got up, came over and shook his hand. It was a bit overwhelming these strangers welcoming him like this.

They lit candles and had Shabbos dinner, Recha Sternbuch, her family and forty displaced French, Czech and German Jews, a rabbi saying prayers, people passing platters of food. After dinner the tables were taken out of the rooms downstairs and replaced by mattresses where the refugees slept. It was an open house for anyone who didn't have a place to stay.

Recha put Harry in a room upstairs with her son, Avrohom, who was thirteen, nice quiet kid who had a book in his hands, reading by lamplight.

"What is that?" Harry said.

"Talmudic scripture. Historical writings of the ancient rabbis. It is the legal code that forms the basis of religious law."

"This is what you read for pleasure?"

Avrohom looked like he didn't understand.

"What does it say? Read something."

"Here is a passage: Babia Mezia 114b. 'The Jews are called human beings, but the non-Jews are not humans. They are beasts.'"

"It should be changed to 'the Nazis are beasts.'"

"You were in Dachau, my mother said. What was it like?"

Harry told him the whole story, the kid listening without expression.

"God was sitting up in the sky watching over you," Avrohom said.

Harry didn't see it that way, but didn't say anything. The Sternbuchs were deeply religious Orthodox Jews. He didn't want to offend them.

Recha cabled his uncle in Detroit the following week.

71

Harry Levin is alive and well, living with us in Montreux, Switzerland. Will arrange for passage to the United States when possible. Please send visa.

Yours sincerely, Recha Sternbuch.

Harry stayed with them in Montreux till the end of the war. Recha and Yitzchok were gone most of the time on their crusade to rescue Jewish children, the orphans of Europe. She was the toughest woman he'd ever seen, standing up to the police in Switzerland, and the authorities in other European countries, protecting refugees, saving thousands of kids.

When the war ended, Harry and a group of five hundred Jews sponsored by Recha took a train to Lisbon and boarded a ship on August 20, 1945, arriving in the port of New York two weeks later.

With the American visa Harry had gotten from his uncle, he went right through customs and immigration, no one giving him a hard time, no one to bribe. He had money and a place to live and nothing to declare. He exchanged his Swiss francs for American dollars at a bank on Fifth Avenue. Harry walked the streets, looking up at the tall buildings, amazed by the size of New York, almost overwhelming. He had seen shots of it in movies, but nothing like the impact of being there.

He stopped at a bookstore and bought an English–German dictionary and a map of the city. He walked to Grand Central Station at 42nd Street and Lexington Avenue. Bought a one-way fare to Detroit, a fourteen-hour trip with all the stops, arriving on September 4, 1945 at 8:17 in the morning.

Harry took a taxi to his uncle's house on Elmhurst, between Dexter and Linwood, the directions said, riding in morning traffic on Woodward Avenue, four lanes of automobiles in both directions, seeing Detroit for the first time, the city waking up, alive. It was small compared to New York, but still larger and more modern than the European cities he'd been to.

It was a nice-looking house, two-storey brick with a big porch in front and a green lawn, in a pretty neighborhood with a lot of trees. Harry was excited. He hadn't

seen his aunt and uncle since they left Munich in 1940.
He rang the buzzer, waited, the door opened, his aunt
looked at him and yelled.

"Sam..."

Harry stepped into the foyer, Esther hugging him,
hearing Sam's voice in another room. "What is it?" And
then Sam appearing, coming down the hall toward them.

"My God, am I seeing who I think I'm seeing? Harry, why didn't you tell us?"

"I wanted to surprise you."

"Surprise us? I almost had a heart attack. Where are
your things?"

"This is it."

"Esther will take you to Hudson's; it's a department
store. You've never seen anything like it."

"I've never seen anything like any of this."

"You like baseball, Harry? That's right, you don't
know from baseball. I'm going to take you to see Hank
Greenberg, greatest ballplayer in the world."

"Harry, you're going to like it here," Esther said.
"We can buy fruit and vegetables even in winter."

"How about apples?" Harry said.

"As many as you want."

"You hungry, Harry? Of course you are. Esther, get
him something to eat."

It didn't take any time, Harry fell in love with American girls and baseball, playing in the street and going
with his uncle to see the Tigers. He fell in love with the
pickles from Grunt's market on Dexter, and television,
watching Roy Rogers and Gene Autry and *The Milton
Berle Show*. He loved going to movies at the Avalon Theater and going to Boesky's and Darby's for lunch and
dinner. But mostly he liked the fact that in America you
could do or be anything you wanted.

Chapter 10

Munich, Germany. 1971.

9:15 the next morning, Harry was having breakfast, studying the grainy photographs of Ernst Hess' estate taken with a long lens. The house was big, a classic Tudor with dark exposed timbers, with stucco walls, steep roof lines and half a dozen tall chimneys. The windows were rectangular, with one- and two-storey bays and decorative leaded glass panes.

It was more mansion than house, ten photos showing the front, sides and rear, and the gardens, pool and tennis court behind it. There were several shots of Hess taken at different times. Hess in business attire, coming out the front, getting into a black Mercedes, Rausch, the linebacker he'd thrown over the table at Les Halles in Washington DC, standing in the frame. Hess in bathing trunks, climbing out of the pool, gut hanging out. Hess in the garden with a tall, slim dark-haired girl, identified as his daughter, Katya, age seventeen. There were also photos of Hess AG, the Zeppelin factory, two airplane hangars and a three-storey building built on an alpine meadow outside the city, the snow-capped Bavarian Alps in the background. And a final shot of Hess' apartment building in downtown Munich.

The phone rang, Berman saying he had the merchandise Harry ordered. Harry took the elevator down and met him in the lobby. Berman handed him a rectangular package wrapped in brown paper that weighed about four pounds. Harry handed Berman a hotel envelope that had five hundred-dollar bills in it, thanked him and went back to his room.

Harry sat on the bed and pulled the tape off, unwrapped the paper and took out the gun, an untraceable blue-black Colt .38 Special, and ten rounds. He picked up the gun, pushed the latch forward and the cylinder popped open. The chambers were empty. He anchored the butt of the revolver against his belt, muzzle pointing at the floor. Held the cylinder with his right hand and fed rounds into the chambers, leaving one empty so he wouldn't shoot himself by accident. He swung the cylinder closed with his left hand and heard it click. Harry thought about what he was going to do. Knew what Sara, the anti-war activist, would have said. She'd driven to Kent State on May 5, 1970 to join the protest after National Guardsmen fired sixty-seven rounds into a crowd of students in thirteen seconds, killing four, wounding nine. He took out her picture he carried in his wallet, a snapshot from a summer party, staring at his daughter's innocent face, getting angry, thinking what he was going to do was justified. He flipped the wallet closed and put it back in his pocket.

Harry rented a BMW 2002 a block away from the hotel on Prannerstrasse. Drove north out of the city and arrived at the Hess estate thirty minutes later. The house was set behind a brick wall on ten wooded acres. Hess' neighbors' homes were on similar-sized lots spread throughout the rolling hills. He parked the BMW, the car hidden by trees unless you were driving by slowly looking for it. He got out, closed the door, and walked across the road, moving along the six-foot-high wall bordering Hess' estate, following it as it curved into the woods.

He reached up and grabbed an oak limb and hoisted himself up on top of the wall, dropped to the ground on the other side. He picked his way through heavy timber and thick brush, and came out in front of the massive Tudor that had to be ten thousand square feet. There was a circular drive and two black Mercedes sedans parked near the front door.

Harry moved through the trees on the west side of the house, catching glimpses of the wide sweeping lawn and gardens, the swimming pool and pool house on the opposite side of the property, tennis court just ahead.

He could hear voices and see movement behind the fence. Harry crept up close to the court, crouching at the edge of the trees. He watched Hess, in tennis whites, blast a forehand at the girl from one of the photographs, a tall thin teenager whose moves seemed awkward, but she had a two-handed backhand, returned the ball with pace for a winner. Harry stared at the girl, innocent beauty reminding him of Sara, picturing her face in the morgue. He took the .38 out of his pocket, stepped to the fence and put the barrel through an opening, aiming at Hess across the court about fifty feet away.

The girl moved to the baseline. She was serving, and maybe sensing his presence, glanced to her right, saw him and froze. Harry and the girl were looking at each other. He heard Hess ask her what she was doing. She glanced at her father, saw him running toward the net. Then the alarm sounded and Harry was moving back away from the fence, running through the woods.

What was he thinking? Was he really going to kill the man in front of his daughter? Harry ran to the wall, jumped up, got his fingers on the limestone cap and hoisted himself up and over, the sound of the alarm stressing him, getting his adrenalin pumping. He ran to the BMW, got in as a black Mercedes went by, bodyguard behind the wheel. The car slowed and stopped, letting out two armed men who moved along the wall into the woods.

Hess had seen him out of the corner of his eye, someone standing at the fence, wondering what his security man was doing there. But he was not wearing a dark-blue jacket. Katya was turned looking at him, and now Hess saw the gun and realized he was not one of his security men. He was there to kill him.

Hess had dropped his racquet and run toward the net, pushed the button on the net post and the alarm sounded: re-er, re-er, re-er, re-er. The intruder was moving back away from the fence, disappearing into the woods. Hess ran to Katya, put his arm around her shoulders and pulled her with him toward the house as two members of his security team came toward him, pistols drawn.

Harry backed out, swung the car around and cruised through the high-rent neighborhood, thinking he might get out of this yet, the sound of the alarm finally fading. But a black Mercedes was speeding toward him. It went by and skidded to a stop. Harry floored it, watched the Benz spin around and come after him.

The road curved right, left, right. He lost the Mercedes through the turns and then saw it roaring toward him, closing in on the straightaway. Up ahead was the two-lane highway to Munich, running perpendicular, traffic steady, heavy. Harry knew he didn't have another choice, he braked hard and went right onto the shoulder, backend sliding, horns honking as he cut into traffic. It was risky but it worked: the Mercedes was stopped behind him, waiting for an opening.

He got off at the next road, went right into the village of Schleissheim, pulled over on Haupstrasse and waited. Sat parked, watching people walk by and cars pass him in both directions but didn't see a black Mercedes, and after fifteen minutes put the BMW in gear and drove thirteen kilometers back to Munich, parked at the hotel and went up to his room.

Hess was trying to make sense of what had happened. He had finally managed to calm his daughter. Thank God Elfriede was out of town. He'd never hear the end of it.

"Papa, who was that man?" Katya had said. "What is this about?"

Hess had asked himself the same questions and there were no clear answers. He had lied and said, "The man is a lunatic from the factory. The police have arrested him. Don't worry. You will never see him again." Hess smiled to reassure her.

"Papa, if anything happened to you I don't know what I would do." She hugged him and went upstairs.

An hour later, Hess was sipping a glass of single malt, his third, trying to relax. He tossed a pile of surveillance photos onto the desktop. Rausch picked them up, looking at half a dozen shots of the intruder, different angles showing him going over the wall, moving through the trees, standing behind the fence next to the tennis court. But none clearly showed his face. He was about six feet tall, dark hair, medium build. "Do you recognize him?" He stared at Rausch's blank face, waiting for an answer.

"I don't think so," Rausch said.

"Are you sure?" Hess was looking at the scar on his cheek, the red line of tissue where the stitches had been.

Rausch shook his head.

"You should after what he did to you."

"The one in the restaurant?"

"The crazy Jew from Detroit," Hess said. He could not understand the man's behavior, coming to his home with a gun for what had been an accident. It didn't make sense.

"What do you want me to do?" Rausch said.

"Find him."

Chapter 11

Cordell Sims walked out of the brig at the United States Army Garrison in Heidelberg, Germany at 10:00 a.m. on Wednesday, September 10, 1971. He'd been in five days—going out of his mind—for punching out his sergeant. Cordell decided he'd had enough of this man's army.

He'd gone before his commanding officer, Colonel Stubbs, a Korean War vet, career officer, the colonel behind his neat, spotless desk. Cordell in a chair in front of him, looking at this pale-skinned dude white as Cordell was black.

"Private Sims, when you enlisted in the United States military you swore to defend the Constitution against all enemies, foreign and domestic, and bear true faith and allegiance to the same. You swore to obey the orders of the president of the United States, and the orders of the officers appointed over you, according to regulations and the Uniform Code of Military Justice. With that you made a promise to the United States military," Colonel said, giving him a howitzer round of army-speak, eyes on him like lasers. Man paused. "Military discipline and effectiveness is built on the foundation of obedience to orders, private."

Colonel, all worked up now, had white stuff in the corners of his mouth looked like mayonnaise, made him kind of sick at his stomach. "This ain't about defending the Constitution or questioning orders," Cordell said. "It about racism. I think maybe I better talk to a lawyer."

"If your situation had become acrimonious, you should have gone through proper channels and filed a complaint. Was there antilocution?"

Cordell said, "Anti-what?"

"Badmouthing."

"He call me shitskin and nigger," Cordell said. "That qualify?"

Colonel Stubbs opened his desk drawer, took out a folder, opened it and started to read.

"According to Article 90 of the Uniform Code of Military Justice, any enlisted person who strikes his superior commissioned officer or draws or lifts up any weapon or offers violence against him while he is in the execution of his duty; or willingly disobeys a lawful command of his superior commissioned officer; shall be punished. If the offense is committed in time of war, by death or such other punishment as a court martial may direct." He closed the folder and glanced at Cordell. "Private Sims, I'm trying to impress upon you the consequences of your actions."

Cordell said, "You going to put me to death 'cause Sergeant don't like black people?"

Colonel wiped the white stuff off his mouth with his thumb and index finger, looked at it and brought his hand under the desk, probably wiped it on his pants.

"After completing an inquiry I understand there are extenuating circumstances."

"Yes sir," Cordell said. "Like Sergeant Nobis stepping on my spit-shined boots could see your reflection in. Sergeant says, 'Boy, them boots is all scuffed up,'" doing his best Sergeant Nobis impression. "'Better shine 'em real good,'" grinning like a redneck. "Or he check out my bed during inspection, sheet and blanket so tight could bounce a dinner plate off it. Sergeant Nobis picks up the mattress dumped it on the floor, says, 'Private Sims, looks like you had better square up your bunk.'"

Cordell had been there a month, arriving right after he finished boot camp, and this treatment had gone on every day. Cordell took it till Sergeant Nobis called him shitskin. And to his credit, he didn't just swing away. He brought his arms up, fists clenched, gave the redneck a chance. "'Sarge, get ready. Going to knock your cracker head off.' He says, 'Keep talking darkie, I'm going to write you up for insubordination.'"

"You should have come to me," Colonel Stubbs said. "Punching out your superior isn't good for discipline or morale. I might've been able to handle this under Article 15, you didn't knock him out in front of the whole platoon." He stopped like he was thinkin'. "Way I see it there are two ways you can go here, Private. I can dismiss the charges and reassign you, or I can try to arrange a special court martial with a military judge and have you dishonorably discharged from the United States Army."

"I take the discharge," Cordell said. He had had enough of the uniform, the bad food, taking orders.

"Consider your decision very carefully," Colonel said. "A dishonorable discharge is on your record. It could come back to haunt you."

If it got him out the army he didn't care.

The DD was his second break.

First one happened after getting busted for selling heroin to an undercover cop, dude giving an Academy Award performance. Cordell shocked when the man pulled his badge and gun. Looked, smelled, talked like a junkie. Should a handed in his badge gone to Hollywood.

At the time he was trying to make money to support himself, momma had took to the streets, disappeared for weeks at a time. Show up for a few days, disappear again.

Case was going to trial. Cordell's court-appointed lawyer, Mr. Paul Monicatti, told him he could get five years or more, first offense, depending on the judge. But Counselor Monicatti had an idea.

He went to the man said, "Your honor, Mr. Sims is only nineteen years old. He has his whole life ahead of him. In lieu of incarceration, he would like to join the United States Army and make something of himself."

"I'll bet he would," the judge said. "And I agree. Mr. Sims is on probation until he enlists, at which time I will discharge his probation with improvement. The court will have no further involvement. Let the army have Mr. Sims. A tour in Vietnam might do him good."

Maybe his honor had got laid that morning. Whatever the reason for his leniency, a week later Cordell was sitting in a barber chair, Fort Benning, Georgia, getting his Afro shaved.

After boot camp Cordell had looked at his options. No way he wanted to go to Nam, fight some Orientals ain't done nothing to him. So where? Brother from Nashville was shipping out to join the 7th Army at the garrison in Heidelberg, Germany. Looked good. Picturesque town with castles like in a Disney movie. He could see himself all over it. Check out the German food and the German ladies, get himself some German poon. Base was there to keep an eye on the Commies and the Berlin Wall.

Now he was free, a civilian again, wearing a chocolate-brown leisure suit, riding a train, duffel in the overhead, heading for Munich. Had been there once on leave. City with nightlife. He looked out the window, saw Heidelberg back there in the distance and said, "*Auf Wiedersehen*, motherfuckers."

"Gentlemen, the frame has been greatly simplified from the airships of old. There you see." They were in Hangar 1. A team of workers was welding the skeletal frame of a Zeppelin, a long triangle of aluminum girders running from end to end. Hess had flown the heads of three American construction companies over to demonstrate the capabilities of his airships. A shiny new Zeppelin skinned in silver canvas hovered above concrete anchors, moored by heavy rope. "Let's go outside. I have told you what the Hess AG Zeppelin can do. Now I will show you." He extended his arm in a theatrical gesture. "Gentlemen, if you please."

There was an airship hovering over the landing area. "The Hess Zeppelin is smaller, faster and more maneuverable than previous airships. It is designed to transport large and heavy loads to remote locations that would otherwise be inaccessible. It generates lift from a combination of aerodynamics, propellers and gas buoyancy. This airship has the ability to offload payload without taking on board ballast other than the air around it. By compressing and decompressing the stored gas, the Hess Zeppelin becomes lighter for take-off and heavier for flight."

Now the ship started to lift off. "You see, the propellers swivel down for take-offs and landings, and they can be used as a steering system of their own, or coordinated with the rudders via the on-board computer."

Mr. Owen Duvall from San Antonio, Texas said, "How do I know this balloon ain't going to pop when it gets to my site?" He was wearing a white shirt with pearl buttons and a string tie under his fancy Western gentleman's sport jacket.

"You are thinking of the Hindenburg, are you not?" They all did. Seeing 7,062,100 cubic feet of hydrogen explode, destroying the eight-hundred-foot ship in less than one minute, thirty-six people killed. But Hess did not mention this to his prospective customers. "The Hess Zeppelin is filled with lighter-than-air helium." The irony was the Hindenburg was also designed and built for helium, but the United States, the world's main supplier, had imposed a military embargo and, in 1937, would not sell the gas to Germany.

"Why don't I just get me some helicopters?" Mr. Duvall said.

"Is a helicopter able to lift thirty tons?" A rhetorical question.

"No, I guess not," Duvall said, pulling the ends of his tie.

"The Hess Zeppelin can rise vertically like a helicopter. It can turn three hundred and sixty degrees while hovering from a fixed position, and then lower the cargo with astonishing precision."

"OK, Herr Hess, I'm convinced," Mr. Duvall said. "Sign me up for one."

Harry had bought a pair of Leitz ten-by-sixty central-focus binoculars at a hunting outfitter near Bahnhofplatz. Then drove south almost to Forstenrieder Park. Hess Aviation was set back two hundred yards from the highway on a flat piece of land behind a high fence topped with barbed wire, the snow-capped Bavarian Alps in the background. There was a modern three-storey steel and glass building that reminded Harry of the German Embassy in Washington DC, same spare style. Next to it were two hangars and between them a concrete apron and a landing strip.

Harry had followed Berman's directions, pulled off the road and parked. Got out, closed the door and steadied his hands balancing the binoculars on the roof. There was something going on in the yard between the hangars. A short compact Zeppelin moored to a rope was floating above the concrete landing area. He saw Hess talking to a group of men, pointing at the airship and then at heavy construction equipment positioned next to it: steel girders, a dozer, backhoe, air compressor, generator, pile-driving equipment.

He watched as two steel girders were attached by a chain to the underside of the Zeppelin below the gondola, and the airship took off vertically, rising straight up, the steel beams dangling below it. Now the Zeppelin turned in a complete circle, hovering and placing the first girder on the low flat trailer of a semi parked in the background. He saw something out of the corner of his eye, looked up, it was another silver Zeppelin drifting through the clouds high overhead. He hadn't noticed it before, probably because it was so overcast. At first he thought the Zeppelin was moving, gliding through the heavy clouds. He aimed the binoculars at it, and now he could see it was hovering above the airship factory, like it was keeping an eye on things.

Harry looked back at the airship demonstration and saw a car coming down the long entranceway toward him, a silver Volkswagen with HESS AG on the side in black, same logotype that was on the airships. It was time to go. He got in the BMW and got back on the highway, heading toward Munich.

He was looking out at the countryside, green meadow extending to the mountains, the towers and rooflines of a medieval village visible in the distance. The view reminding him of trips he used to take with his parents, car trips to Inzell and Königsee, with its pure green water, and Berchtesgaden, a picturesque village surrounded by nine alpine peaks, the most beautiful place Harry had ever seen, in spite of the fact that Hitler had had his retreat there.

A sign said Munich was ten kilometers away. Harry slowed down behind a semi. He glanced in the rearview mirror and saw a black Audi coming up fast behind him. Thought it was going to hit him, came so close he couldn't see its grill. The windows were blacked out. Harry sped up, put a couple car lengths between them, but couldn't go any faster because of the semi.

Cars were coming the other way on the two-lane road. He couldn't pass. He watched the Audi close in again, and this time it banged into him. He felt the jolt and accelerated. The Audi caught him again and rammed him. He hit the brakes, feeling the impact and weight of the Audi, brake pads squealing, his adrenalin pumping.

Harry waited for an opening in traffic and cut left around the semi, flooring it, passed three cars, saw a Porsche speeding toward him and cut right back into his lane. He could see the Audi four cars back, waiting for a break in traffic. He had empty highway ahead and nailed it, needle climbing, one hundred, one ten, one fifteen. He could see the Audi make a move, swing out into the oncoming lane, passing the slower cars.

Up ahead Harry saw sheep in a tight group on the side of the road. He sped up and had enough room to swerve around two sheep in his lane starting to cross. But the Audi didn't and he saw it hit the flock, sending three airborne, windshield shattered, the Audi losing control, spinning off the road.

Chapter 12

Harry parked in front of the hotel, got out and moved to the back of the car. The bumper and trunk lid were dented. He gave his keys to the valet, glanced toward the Frauenkirche, saw the Zeppelin high in the clouds, glimpses of it appearing and then vanishing. Was it following him?

He went to the bar, ordered Dewar's and soda, and thought about his situation. He was now 0 for 2. Struck out at Hess' house, struck out again at his place of business. What the hell was he doing here? Maybe getting rammed by the Audi had woken him up, brought him to his senses. Was he really going to kill Hess? The idea now seemed absurd. He considered packing his things, going back to Detroit. Then he thought about Sara and knew he wasn't going anywhere.

Harry went to his room and took a shower. He walked back in the bedroom with a towel wrapped around his waist, hair still wet. He was tired, pulled down the spread, sat on the bed, leaned back on pillows propped against the headboard and fell asleep.

It was dark out when he woke up. Harry glanced at the digital clock on the bedside table. 8:17. He dressed and went downstairs and asked the concierge for a restaurant suggestion, a place that served good Bavarian food. The guy recommended a ratskeller a couple kilometers from the hotel. Harry got his car and drove there. Knew the street, and as it turned out, knew the place, his father used to take him there.

He walked through the crowded dining room and sat at the bar, ordered a beer, drank it and watched the bartender, a nice-looking woman with a braided blonde ponytail, fill mugs from a dozen taps. She was fast and efficient, making conversation with the men sitting there, but getting the job done. Harry could have used her at the scrap yard. She asked in German if he was going to eat. He said yes, and she put a menu on the bar top in front of him.

There were two drunk Germans to his right, talking, having an intense conversation, drinking beer, lighting cigarettes, and blowing out smoke that hung in the air over the bar. Their faces reminded him of the faces of Nazi soldiers he'd seen on the streets of Munich in the late thirties, and he wanted to get away from them. He was thinking about picking up his beer, going to a table.

Next to him, on his left, a voice said, "Yo, sprechen Sie English?" in tourist German.

He turned and saw a black guy with a GI haircut in a spiffed-up burgundy outfit, tan shirt and gold chains around his neck.

"Where you from?" Harry said.

"Dee-troit."

"I lived on Elmhurst and then Clairmont near 12th."

"Was an abandoned synagogue near there, brothers turned into a blind pig."

"I recall." He picked up his mug, drank some beer.

"You worship there or party?" He stirred his drink, something dark in a tall glass.

"I'd moved to the suburbs by then," Harry said.

"That before the riot?"

"Yeah. I bought my house in 1963. You remember the riot, huh? How old were you?"

"Sixteen. I was there when it started. Three in the morning, police raided a blind pig was above Economy Printing. Seventy-three people arrested. But they had to wait for buses to take them to the station. Crowd formed out front, brothers throwin' bottles at the police, getting all worked up. From there they moved down 12th, lightin' buildings on fire, breakin' windows, stealin' TVs, anything they could carry."

"Never knew how it started." Harry glanced at his drink. "What is that?"

"Courvoisier and Coke. Also drink it with orange pop."

Harry made a face.

"Gets you where you want to be." The black guy grinned. "Don't knock it till you try it."

"What brings you to Munich?"

"Traveling before I go back. Was in the army. Protecting democracy from the Red scourge," he said, grinning, showing big white teeth.

"What about Vietnam?"

"No, thank the lord. Was stationed at Heidelberg, had an altercation with my sergeant." He sipped his drink. "Got a DD."

"Drunk and disorderly?"

"Dishonorable discharge. You weren't in the service, huh?"

"Missed the draft," Harry said. "I was too old."

"You lucky." He picked up his drink and paused. "Know what the best thing is about being out?" He finished his drink, looked at Harry and said, "Don't have to wear green no more."

Harry looked at the cut of his jacket, a burgundy leisure suit with white contrasting stitching and gold buttons. The shirt had a pattern on it, light-brown illustrations of animals rampant on an African savannah. "You sure don't."

"Got it at Louis the Hatter on Livernois, Avenue of Fashion, if you recall? Know what color it is? Call it claret. Not burgundy, man, claret. Pronounce the 'T.'"

"It's a beauty," Harry said. "Leisure suit, right?"

"Lei-sure rhymes with plea-sure."

He showed his teeth again, couldn't help himself, relaxed, having a good time, couple of guys from Detroit meeting by coincidence.

"I'm Harry Levin." He offered his hand, and they shook.

"Cordell Sims."

"What'd you do before the army?"

"This 'n' that, how 'bout you?"

"I own a scrap yard on Mt. Elliot near Luce, you know where that is."

"Other side of Hamtramck."

"S&H Recycling Metals."

"That's catchy," Cordell said. "What were the names didn't make it?"

Harry picked up his mug, took a swig. "Levin & Levin Ferrous and Non-Ferrous Scrap Metal Recycling Incorporated."

Cordell grinned.

"I'm kidding."

"No shit." Cordell grinned again.

The two loudmouth Germans to his right paid their bill, got up and moved through the dining room, which had thinned out. He looked down the bar, saw a man hunched over his beer at the end, all the seats between them empty. He looked at his watch. It was quarter to ten. The good-looking bartender came out of the kitchen, walked down the bar and asked them if they wanted another one.

Harry turned to the black guy. "Cordell, you ready?"

"Don't mind if I do."

"I'm going to order something to eat, bratwurst. Interested?"

"Their 'wurst is their best," Cordell said, grinning. "Yeah, I'll have some."

Harry ordered a couple of bratwurst plates with fried potatoes, another beer for him and a drink for Cordell. The bartender put their refills on the bar and took their empties.

Harry said, "You enlist, drafted or what?"

"Drafted," Cordell said, "sort of."

"What number were you?"

"I don't know," Cordell said. "But I knew a dude was three."

"What'd he do?"

"You mean when he found out? Got fucked up. What you think?"

The bartender served their food and started cleaning up. He liked looking at her, liked watching her draw pints and serve drinks. Would probably like watching her do laundry, iron a shirt.

He cut off a piece of bratwurst, put it in his mouth. The brat was authentic, better than the one he'd had yesterday, tasted just like he remembered it, grilled meat with a hint of herbs and spices. He glanced to his left. "What do you think?"

Cordell, a napkin tucked in the neck of his shirt, nodded and fanned his mouth, sipped his drink to put out the heat. Harry glanced over for another eyeful of the bartender. She was wiping the bar top, but stopped, her attention fixed on something in the dining room. She dropped the cloth, walked quickly down to the end of the bar, and disappeared in the kitchen.

Harry looked behind him and saw two skinheads in black outfits with red armbands in the back of the room just standing there. The few remaining diners noticed them too, got up and moved out of the restaurant. What the hell was going on?

He turned to Cordell. "We've got company." Looked over his shoulder again, and now there were six of them, reminding Harry of blackbirds on a power line. Look up, see one, then there are twenty. They were coming toward the bar, carrying lengths of wood that looked like ax handles.

They came at them fast, moving through the tables, gripping the wood like baseball bats. Harry slid off his bar stool, squeezed the handle of his beer mug, moving along the front of the bar. Cordell was on his feet, holding the heavy china dinner plate at his waist with two hands.

The first Blackshirt came at Harry, swinging for the fence. He timed his move, faked right, went left as the ax handle swished past his head and hit the bar top like a gunshot. Harry swung the two-pound beveled glass mug on top of his shaved neo-Nazi head, watched him crash into a barstool and take it with him to the floor.

To his right, he saw Cordell launch the dinner plate like a Frisbee into the face of an advancing Blackshirt, splitting open his forehead. Then another Blackshirt was on him, Cordell ducking, bobbing, weaving, throwing punches and connecting.

Harry, moving, grabbed the top of a barstool and flipped it behind him into a charging Blackshirt, trying to slow him down. He ran into the dining room, pulled a chair out from a table, picked it up and held it in front of him, blocking a blow from an ax handle. Harry gripped the back of the chair and swung into the man's upper body. The Blackshirt went down on the floor, looking dazed.

Harry saw a flash of movement to his left and felt his ribs explode as an ax handle thudded into his side. He went down on his knees, wind knocked out, trying to draw a breath. Saw the Blackshirt raise his weapon again, ducked under a table and came out on the other side. Cordell finished the Blackshirt off with a straight right–left hook combination and helped Harry to his feet. They ran out of the ratskeller, down the street lined with cars to the BMW, sidewalk congested with people out for the night. Harry looked back, saw the Blackshirts running toward them, fumbled with the keys.

Cordell, on the other side of the car, said, "Yo, Harry, you see 'em? The fuck you doing?"

Harry got in and unlocked the passenger door. Cordell jumped in next to him. He started the BMW and the Blackshirts were on them, circling the car, waving their ax handles.

"Put the motherfucker in gear," Cordell said.

Harry slid the shifter in reverse, turned the steering wheel trying to maneuver out of the space. He heard a siren in the distance. Saw an ax handle hit his side window. The glass shattered and buckled. Two ax handles smashed the windshield. It cracked and cobwebbed. The window next to Cordell exploded, glass flying. Harry could feel his heart pounding. He shifted into first, cut the steering wheel hard left, floored it and pulled out, hit a Blackshirt, man bouncing over the hood and off. The rest of them were running next to the BMW, ax handles banging into sheet metal. He saw flashing lights approaching, heard the siren getting louder, a police car pulled up in front of him, and the Blackshirts took off.

They were taken to the Kriminalpolizei station, escorted to a conference room, just the two of them. Door closed. Sitting across a long table from each other, waiting for someone to take their statements. They had given their passports to a cop in uniform when they arrived.

Harry looked around the room at the light-green walls and nondescript decor, fixed his attention on Cordell. "Thanks for helping me."

"Didn't have much choice. It was us or them."

The adrenalin had worn off and Harry felt the pain in his side getting sharper, more intense. It was hard to breathe.

"Yo, Harry, you all right?"

"I think so."

"Maybe you better have someone look at that. Might've busted something."

"I'm OK."

"What was that all about back there?"

The door opened and a detective came in. He was pale, mid-forties, thin dark hair combed back, shirt and tie, small semiautomatic in a holster on his hip. He introduced himself as Huber. Sat at the end of the table between them. He had a pocketsize notebook in his hand, opened it to a blank page, put it on the table. Took their passports out of his shirt pocket, opened the first one, looked at the photo and handed it to Cordell. He put Harry's in front of him.

"What is your purpose for coming to Munich?" Heavy Bavarian accent. Sounded like he was interrogating them.

"Visiting," Harry said.

Huber looked at Cordell.

"Same here. Seein' the sights."

Huber turned back to Harry. "What happened tonight?"

He took a pen out of his pocket, pulled off the cap and fit it on the bottom.

"We were attacked by six skinheads carrying ax handles."

Huber glanced at Cordell. "Do you have anything to add?"

Cordell said, "Wore black shirts, had swastikas on them."

"Did you provoke them?"

"Did we provoke them?" Harry said to Cordell.

"Not hardly."

"They came in swinging," Harry said.

"Why do you think they attacked you?" Huber said to Harry.

"Maybe they don't like Americans."

"Or maybe it was me. Black men scare these master-race dudes."

Huber wrote something on the pad. "You are able to identify them?"

"They looked a lot alike," Harry said. "Six skinheads in black shirts. Not much more to tell you. It was dark, it happened fast. Talk to the bartender at the ratskeller. She might be able to give you a description. She got a good look at a couple of them."

"I was you I'd check the hospitals. One of them is going to need a whole lot of stitches in his forehead."

Harry said. "You know who they are, Detective?"

"The Blackshirts," Huber said in the same flat monotone.

"Sound like a heavy metal group," Cordell said. "Teach 'em to play music, spit blood, make a fortune."

Huber ignored him. "They are the new Nazis, terrorizing in the name of nationalism. You are fortunate. You might have been injured or killed. If you see them again, call the police immediately."

"That's it? You're not going to do anything?"

"They have thousands of members. Without accurate descriptions, what can we do?"

Cordell was happy to get out of there. Police stations made him nervous. They stood out front, waiting for a taxi. "These Germans are a lot of fun, huh? Like, could the man be any less helpful? Goin' through the motions, like he don't want to waste his time helpin' a couple Americans."

"He did seem to want to get rid of us," Harry said, "didn't he?"

"I don't trust cops," Cordell said. "Period, in a sentence."

Cordell took out his sterling silver cigarette case, opened it. "Want one? That's a Davidoff, world's finest tobacco."

"No thanks," Harry said.

A police sedan pulled up in front of the building, two cops in uniform got out and escorted a handcuffed prisoner past them inside. They walked out to the street, saw a taxi pull over.

Harry said, "Want a ride?"

"My hotel's just over there," Cordell said, recognizing the museum, pointing. "By the Hofgarten."

"Where you staying?"

"Pension Jedermann," Cordell said. "Man, it's no Ritz. Not even a Ho-Joe's, but it beats the hell out of the barracks at Heidelberg."

"You want to have a drink sometime, I'm at the Bayerischer Hof, on Promenadeplatz." Harry took a business card out of his wallet, wrote on the back and handed it him. "Or call me when you get back to Detroit."

"Be cool," Cordell said. "Keep an eye out for Blackshirt motherfuckers and such."

Harry got in and closed the door, and the taxi cruised down the street. Cordell took a step, something shiny caught his eye, glinting under the streetlight. It was a watch. He bent down and picked it up. Patek Philippe. Black gator band. Turned it over said:

To Harry. Yours forever, Anna.

Slipped it in his pocket.

Chapter 13

Cordell walked to his pension, nice warm September night, nobody on the street, hot wearing the jacket, took it off, draped it over his arm. Stood in front of the pension, was about to go in, still thinking about the watch. Reached in his pocket, brought it out, looked at the time: 11:37. Watch was expensive and he needed money. Cordell thinking, wait, didn't he deserve it for saving the dude's life? Could sell it, travel for a while. But Harry was cool and the watch had to mean something to him.

He took out the man's card: *S&H Recycling Metals*, turned it over, saw Bayerischer Hof, room 573. Where'd he say it was at? Yeah, Promenadeplatz. He walked down the street saw a taxi coming toward him, put up his arm. It stopped, he got in.

Cordell went in the hotel lobby, place quiet, practically deserted at close to midnight. Picked up a house phone, dialed 573. Busy. Waited a couple minutes, tried again. Still busy. Maybe Harry was calling home, talking to Anna, telling her he lost the watch she gave him. He tried the number a third time. Still busy. He decided to go up, surprise him.

He got in an elevator, rode up with three Orientals, watching the lights flash as they passed floors, got off at five, checked room numbers till he found 573. Door was closed but not all the way. He knocked. "Yo, Harry." Pushed it open a crack, saw the phone on the bed, off the hook, two skinheads ripping the place up. Didn't see Harry.

He went in. A skinhead with an ax handle came at him. Cordell went left, ducked, felt it swoosh by his head,

95

and bust a hole in the wall. Cordell hit him and he went down.

Now the second one came at him. Cordell somer-saulted over the bed, landed on his feet, surprised the guy. Moved in, hit him with a combination, left hook, straight right. Skin dropped the wood, ran for the door, first one just ahead of him. Cordell picked up the ax handle, chased them in the hall, watched them run for the stairs, open the door and disappear. Heard someone behind him, turned in a batter's stance, arms cocked, hands gripping the skinny end of the handle, saw Harry.

"You taking batting practice, 12:30 in the morning?"

"You had visitors, Harry. Was just showing them out." He lowered the ax handle. "Man, you are a popular guy."

Harry walked into his room, Cordell right behind him. It smelled like paint and he saw why. There was a crude-looking black swastika sprayed on one of the white walls. Dresser drawers had been pulled out, clothes dumped on the floor. He went over to the bed, picked up the phone, put the receiver back and placed it on the end table. He'd left the photographs from Berman on the desk. They were gone.

"Two of 'em," Cordell said. "Skinheads. Looked like the dudes come to the ratskeller. Same tribe. Missed 'em by a minute." He paused. "What's goin on?"

Harry looked at the swastika again. "I think they're trying to scare me, convince me to leave town."

"They doing a good job," Cordell said. "Maybe you should listen." His eyes scanned the room. "Who are they? Why they after you?"

"I don't know." Were they working for Hess? That was the logical explanation, but he didn't want to get into it right now. Needed time to think.

"Come on, Harry."

"What're you doing here?" Harry said.

Cordell reached in his pocket, took out the watch. "Found it in the street outside the police station. Thought you probably want it."

Cordell handed it to him. Harry, thinking he'd lost it, fit the band on his wrist and fastened it.

Cordell sat on the bed. "Who's Anna? Will you tell me that?"

"My wife," Harry said.

"How long you married?"

"Three years," Harry said, turning the desk chair around to face him, sitting in it. "'50 to '53. She died giving birth."

"What happened?"

Harry said. "Her immune system was screwed up." He paused. "She was a survivor. We both were. I was at Dachau. Anna was at Helmbrechts, a small concentration camp for women, southwest of Hof in Upper Franconia."

Cordell gave him a blank look.

"It's in East Germany near the Czech border."

Cordell got up, took off his jacket and laid it out on the bed.

"In April 1945, the war was ending. The Germans were finished. It was just a matter of time before the Americans and Russians closed in on them. The Nazis shut down the camp and marched these starving women 195 miles to a Czech town called Prachatice. The prisoners were so hungry they ate grass; they ate decaying animal carcasses. The last day, Anna was one of seventeen prisoners marched into the woods. It was an uphill climb for thirty minutes. Anyone who couldn't do it was shot. Fourteen of seventeen didn't make it. The three who did were given their freedom. The American army came through the next day. Anna was taken to a hospital. Emaciated, dehydrated. She was five six, weighed seventy-eight pounds. Two of her toes had frostbite from walking barefoot in the snow, had to be amputated. An army doctor told her she wouldn't have lived another day."

"Where'd you meet?" Cordell said.

"We both ended up in Detroit. I was living with my uncle and she went to stay with a cousin. We were fixed up and hit it off. It was 1949. I was twenty-one, she was twenty. We dated and got married a year later."

"What about you?"

"I was sent to Dachau with my parents. They were killed. I escaped."

"I thought my past history had some crazy shit in it," Cordell said. "Man, you got like a black cloud over you." He fingered the chains around his neck. "How old were you?"

"Thirteen when I went in."

"What'd you think?"

"The world had gone crazy," Harry said. "You trick yourself. You say it's not going to last, it's going to end. But you know it isn't."

"I was thirteen my mom took to the needle, started turnin' tricks, bringin' home these raggedy-ass brothers."

"What'd you think?"

"Same as you."

"What'd you do?"

"Quit school, started working for a dude name Chilly Willy, sold heroin at the projects: Gardens and Brewster. Chill say cop arrest you, what's he going to do? You's a kid. He going to slap your wrist, send you home."

"Who'd you sell it to?"

"Anyone needed a fix," Cordell said. "I made a hundred dollars a day when I started, two hundred when I got busted five years later. Could either do time or join the army. Like there was a choice. Sign me up for the armed services, I said. Judge thought I'd be going to Nam. I did too. Got nothin' against the Viet Cong, but fightin' them was preferable to incarceration."

"I can understand. Listen, I better get the manager up here. I don't want them to think I joined the Nazis," Harry said, looking at the swastika on the wall.

"Call, they come back," Cordell said. "Pension Jedermann. Check on you tomorrow."

He walked out, closed the door.

Harry called the front desk at 1:15, said there'd been a break-in. A man from hotel security knocked on the door a couple minutes later. He wore a blue blazer and carried a walkie-talkie and was the size of a defensive tackle. He came in, looked around and asked Harry a few questions.

Did he know who did it?

No.

Was he in the room at the time?

Dumb question.

Was anything missing?

Just his photos of Hess. Of course, he said no.

Did he want to speak to the police?

Harry shook his head.

The security man told him they were going to move him to a suite for the inconvenience. No charge.

Harry said, OK. Where else was he going to go at 1:30 in the morning?

Chapter 14

Rausch sat in the driver's seat of the Volkswagen, side window cracked six inches. He smoked, flicking ashes and blowing smoke through the opening. He glanced at the clock on the dash. It was 1:42 a.m. Hess had been in the house for almost two hours, and Rausch wondered what was taking him, although Hess had told him he enjoyed walking around before he woke them. Looking at their photographs, their furniture, and their belongings. For Hess it was better to know something about them, to feel a connection, make it personal.

Rausch was parked on Baaderstrasse, in a quiet residential neighborhood. He saw a figure coming toward him on the sidewalk, Ernst Hess in silhouette, the faint glow of a streetlight behind him. He walked to the car and got in. Rausch felt crowded now, two big men sitting almost shoulder to shoulder in the narrow interior. He could see the rush of power, Hess still charged with adrenalin.

"You were in there for a long time," Rausch said. He started the car, slid the shifter into gear and accelerated.

"We were talking. I enjoy conversing with civilized, intelligent people."

"I thought something had gone wrong."

"What could go wrong?"

"Maybe the man had a weapon and surprised you." He saw Hess glance at him.

"How long would you have waited?"

"Until you were finished."

"What if I did not come out?"

"But you did."

"I am asking you this hypothetically."

100

"I would have waited until it was no longer safe," Rausch said, not exactly sure what he was saying, but Hess seemed to approve. He smiled. "Very good."

"What did you talk about?"

"He owned an automobile dealership, sells Volkswagens. Can you believe that?"

Rausch went left on Rumfordstrasse.

"I told him I thought that was ironic, a Jew selling a car developed by the Führer."

Rausch glanced at Hess. "What did he say?"

"Hitler had nothing to do with it. Ferdinand Porsche designed and built the Volkswagen."

"Is that true?"

"I don't know."

"What was the woman's occupation?"

"Retired. She had been a teacher at the Jewish Training Workshop on Biederstein in the late thirties."

"What were the Jews training to be?"

"Swindlers," Hess said, grinning. "What do you think?"

The streets were dark, deserted as they crossed Frauenstrasse, driving into Altstadt. He could see the tower of the Neues Rathaus.

"The Lachmanns were originally from Munich. They had emigrated to New York in 1939." Hess looked at him. "Had I been a Jew that's what I would have done. After Kristallnacht, anyone who did not know what was happening was either naïve or not paying attention."

"Why did they come back?"

"Lachmann said because they are Germans. I told him they should have stayed in New York."

"Did they resist, put up a fight?"

"Do they ever?"

That was what was so surprising. Jews went to their death like lambs to slaughter. If an intruder were trying to kill him Rausch would defend himself. "Were they afraid?"

"Someone woke you up and put a gun in your face, wouldn't you be?"

Peter Leonard

"This isn't happening," Mrs. Lachmann had said. Hess grinned.

Rausch swung around to Kaufingerstrasse and pulled up behind Hess' Mercedes parked on the street. He would leave the stolen VW in a parking garage.

Hess turned in the seat, ears still ringing from the gunshots. He pictured the Lachmanns kneeling naked on the cold hard concrete floor, Hess sitting in a chair behind them. They were always embarrassed taking their clothes off in front of a stranger. It made them feel vulnerable.

He had taken Herr Lachmann's glasses and his wife's engagement ring to add to his collection. He would re-live the encounter later. Now he was more interested in hearing about Harry Levin. The Jew surprising him, first coming to the restaurant in Washington DC, sitting at the table with them, speaking German with his Bavarian accent, fooling all of them. Hess thought that one incident would be the end of it. The man would go home and he would never think about him again. At the urging of the ambassador, he had even agreed to pay for the daughter's funeral expenses, trying to put a positive spin on what had happened. The Washington Post acknowledged his sympathetic gesture in a brief article, and quoted him saying: "My heartfelt apology goes out to Mr. Levin and his family." The carefully worded press release had been written by a publicist at the embassy. It mentioned Hess' involvement but never admitted culpability or guilt.

Two weeks later the crazy kike sneaks onto his estate. Hess couldn't believe it, looking across the tennis court, seeing a man standing on the other side of the fence with a gun, thinking he was going to shoot him, this lunatic from Detroit who sold scrap metal. And although the surveillance photographs were inconclusive Hess was positive it was Levin. Who else? Levin was seen again outside the fence at the airship factory, and Hess knew he had to do something. This Jew wasn't going away.

Rausch had followed Levin to the ratskeller, despatching six men to take care of him, put him in the hospital, but not kill him. With Munich hosting the Olympic Games in eleven months, Hess didn't want the negative

102

publicity of a murdered American tourist, an incident that might imply Munich was not safe.

Harry Levin had escaped again and no one had been able to give him a reasonable explanation as to why. "Tell me how he got away," Hess said to Rausch.

"He was lucky."

"Lucky," Hess said. "There were six of them."

"A Negro was helping him," Rausch said. "He was skilled."

"A Negro? They were together?" Hess said. This was getting interesting. "Who is he?"

"An American soldier. They were sitting next to each other at the bar. My men chased them down the street," Rausch said. "They were about to pull them out the car when the police arrived."

More excuses.

Hess got behind the wheel of the Mercedes and drove to the apartment.

Earlier that morning Rausch had stood tall and erect in front of his desk, military bearing still evident three decades after Germany had lost its army and Rausch his rank. He was a born soldier. Needed to be told what to do, and needed to be complimented after completing a job. They had been together since '43, assigned to Einsatzgruppen B.

As big and strong as Rausch was, he had been bothered by killing Jews. Rausch would feel sick, couldn't eat or sleep. Hess had joked about it. "What is your problem? My appetite has never been better. I sleep like a baby."

They were in Poland in 1945 when the Russians were coming from the east and the Americans from the west and it was a foregone conclusion Germany had lost the war. Hess and Rausch walked away from their battalion one night, stole a military vehicle and drove to Lodz.

Hess had money, diamonds and gold he had taken from the Jews, acquiring a small fortune. He had purchased clothing and an automobile so they could make their way back to Germany. After the war Hess started a construction company to repair Germany's war-torn cities, and had become rich. He had traveled extensively between Munich, Frankfurt and Dresden, often carrying large sums of money, and decided he needed a gun for protection.

Rausch had said, "Do you remember the first one?"

"Do you mean after the war?"

"Yes. I was trying to think of the year."

"1947," Hess said. "I was still following orders."

"Come on. I watched you. You enjoyed it."

"Is it wrong to enjoy your work?" Hess said.

"I don't think it had anything to do with work or taking orders," Rausch said. "The Reich was over. You did this on your own. For yourself. Maybe you couldn't stop."

It was true, of course, although he had never admitted it to anyone, surprised Rausch had been so observant. "We were rebuilding parts of Dresden, do you remember? The city had virtually been destroyed. We used to eat at a certain cafe, and I couldn't help but notice Jews were returning to the city. There was one couple we saw regularly."

"The Jewess you couldn't take your eyes off of," Rausch said.

"You do remember. One day she dined alone and left her gloves on the table. I picked them up and followed her home. She lived in a flat in an old building that had been hit by Allied bombs. Parts of it had been destroyed."

"Were you thinking about killing her?"

"No, I was thinking about returning the gloves," Hess said. "My good deed for the day."

"Is this the truth?"

"Do you want me to tell you?"

Rausch sat back.

"Her flat was on the first floor."

"Was she married?"

"I am getting to that." Hess gave him a hard look. "I rang the bell and heard a dog barking. The woman, her name was Gail Kaplan, opened it a crack and I held up her gloves. She swung it open and a little dog, a dachshund, tried to get out. She said, 'No, Karl.' The dog barked, I squatted and pet it. 'What a beautiful dog,' I said. 'I, too, have a dachshund.'"

"You never had a dachshund," Rausch said. "Did you?"

Hess glanced at him, raised his eyebrows. "The dog snapped at me. 'What is your dog's name?' the woman said. 'Alfonso. We call him Fonzie.'"

"Now I understand," Rausch said.

He was a little slow at times.

"'Oh, how adorable,' the woman said.

"I said to her, 'Before I forget, here are your gloves.'

"'I can't thank you enough,' Frau Kaplan said. She bent down and picked up the dog and held it against her chest.

"'I wonder if I might trouble you for a glass of water,' I said. She said, 'Yes, of course, it's the least I can do. You saw me at the cafe, yes? I know I have seen you before, reading your newspaper.'"

"And then you knew?" Rausch said.

"I thought it might happen. The urge was there. I had the Luger in the pocket of my sport jacket. The woman walked out of the room, carrying the dog. I looked around. There was a grand piano on the other side of the salon. I took off my overcoat and walked to the piano and started to play Mozart's piano concerto number 27 in B flat major. The woman came back in smiling, carrying a glass of water, Karl the dachshund walking next to her like they were a couple. I stopped playing and said, 'Forgive me. I see a piano I cannot resist.'

"'Please continue,' she said. 'I insist. I love Mozart, so does my husband.'

"She handed me the glass of water. I took a drink and put it on a table next to the piano, and played for ten more minutes.

"The woman said, 'Bravo.'

"I stood, picked up my overcoat, draped it over my arm and moved toward the couch. I could feel the weight of the Luger in my pocket. 'Is your husband home?' I said. 'I was hoping to meet him.'

"'No,' she said, 'he is at work. He is an architect.'

"'Another time,' I said. I picked up this small green pillow off the couch. She gave me a quizzical look. I drew the Luger and said, 'Let's go in the other room.' Now the dachshund came toward me, barking. I glanced at the dog and back at the woman and she was gone. I went into the bedroom and there she was sitting on the bed with the phone in her hand.

"'Please,' she said. 'I am pregnant.'

"I moved toward her and said, 'It will be all right.' I held the pillow in front of her face, trying to muffle the gunshot, and pulled the trigger. The pillow caught on fire and the dog went crazy."

"What happened to the dog?" Rausch said.

"It was still barking when I walked out."

"How many others have there been?"

106

Chapter 15

9:15 in the morning, Harry got a phone call from a woman named Colette Rizik, saying she was a journalist.

"I am writing an article for a magazine called *Der Spiegel* about the rise of the neo-Nazis in Germany." She spoke with a British accent. "I understand you were attacked last night."

"Who told you that?"

"I have a contact with the police."

Harry agreed to meet her in the hotel restaurant in an hour. He took aspirin and iced his bruised rib. It felt better today. Showered, dressed and went down to the lobby. He was sitting at a table having coffee when a good-looking woman walked in. Every head in the room—men and women—turned and looked at her. Harry, assuming it was Colette, stood up, waved and she came over. He introduced himself, invited her to sit and she took the chair to his right.

Colette Rizik was blonde, five eight, stunning. She showed him her *Der Spiegel* ID card. It looked official, not that Harry would've known if it were fake. The waitress stopped by with coffee, poured Colette a cup and refilled his. Heads were still turning, looking at her. She reached in her purse and took out a pad and a pen. She had nice hands, long thin fingers with red nails.

"Thank you for seeing me, Herr Levin. As I mentioned I am writing an article for *Der Spiegel*, a magazine like your Time and Newsweek.

Colette turned and took a newspaper out of her bag, unfolded it and showed Harry a short, one column article with a headline that said:

Tourists Attacked at Munich Gaststätte

Harry said, "What do you want to know?"

"It is very unusual for Blackshirts to attack tourists," Colette said.

Harry listened, studying her. She wore a simple white blouse, collar folded over the lapels of a black blazer. He could see the swell of her breasts, the outline of her bra under the thin fabric.

"They have an agenda, you see. People they target to terrorize and harass. Did you provoke them in any way?"

"That's what Detective Huber asked," Harry said. "You think I picked a fight with six guys carrying ax handles?"

"I didn't mean that." She took the top off her pen, and wrote something on the pad. "Did you say anything to them?"

"Not a word," Harry said. "They came in swinging."

"What about your friend?"

"What friend?"

"I was told there were two of you."

He watched Colette sip her coffee, red lipstick leaving a faint stain on the off-white china. She put her cup back on the saucer.

"He was just there," Harry said. "Sitting at the bar. We started talking, found out we were both from Detroit."

"We're undergoing an internal crisis in Germany today. The Blackshirts are one of the subversive groups that have emerged. Most of their members are criminals, thugs and drunks without jobs or money. It reminds many Germans of a time we are still trying to forget." She paused. "But please, Herr Levin, do not judge all Bavarians by the behavior of these fanatics. If you have time I would like to show you the good people of Munich. Are you free this evening?"

"This is what I wanted to show you," Martz said.

Harry stared at the swastikas in black spray-paint on the wall of the synagogue.

"The neo-Nazis who attacked you also did this. They are the new SS, the new stormtroopers," Lisa said. "I feel like it's starting all over again."

They had come from the cemetery where Harry's grandfather was buried. Myron was a funny easy-going guy, always telling jokes like Harry's uncle Sam. His grandfather's gravestone had been spared, probably because it wasn't particularly big or ostentatious, but random markers around it had been desecrated with black swastikas and the words *Sieg Heil*. Some of the headstones had been turned over or broken.

"They won't even let the dead rest in peace," Martz said.

Lisa drove them to her office in an old building on Brennerstrasse not far from Königsplatz. They walked up two flights of stairs, the old man breathing heavy when they got there. She opened the door and they went in.

"Welcome to the ZOB," Lisa said. "It's named after a Polish resistance group during World War Two, the Żydowska Organizacja Bojowa. ZOB. It's a tribute to the parents of my partners killed by Nazis in the Warsaw Ghetto uprising. The English translation is Jewish Combat Organization, which seems appropriate since we're still fighting the Nazis."

There was a row of beige file cabinets lined up across the wall and bookcases filled with binders, and dozens of black-and-white photos of Nazis on a bulletin board. There was a woman on the phone at her desk. She had blonde shoulder-length hair, late thirties, plain but attractive, more so when she smiled and waved. Put her hand over the phone and mouthed something to Lisa.

"Irena, this is Harry, the boy I had a crush on when I was twelve. Harry, meet Irena Pronicheva."

Irena nodded and went back to her phone call.

"What do you do here?" Harry said.

"Keep track of neo-Nazi activities, and try to locate war criminals. Harry, there are still Nazi murderers among us, living normal lives."

They walked past Irena's desk into another room.

"This is my office," Lisa said.

There was a desk and a couch and two chairs. Harry went to the window and glanced down at the street below.

Lisa turned on a lamp and sat behind her desk, opened a drawer and took out a stack of photographs.

"Harry, I want you to see these."

Harry and Martz sat across from her, Lisa showing them shots of neo-Nazis, different angles, walking down a Munich street, carrying ax handles, broken store windows in the background.

"Jewish shops on Maximilianstrasse," Lisa said. "Looks familiar, doesn't it?"

"These could've been taken thirty years ago," Harry said.

"I know. That's what's so scary. And it's going on all over the country."

She picked up a piece of paper and read. "A bomb attack wounded ten people leaving a synagogue in Stuttgart. A Jewish family was terrorized in Dresden. A prosperous Jewish couple, the Lachmanns, were murdered execution-style a few blocks from here last night."

She put the paper down, looked at Harry. "And you were attacked. Another average day in Deutschland."

Harry said, "How do you find war criminals?"

"We have a list of Nazi Party members, those who weren't condemned to death, or are still serving time. What's astonishing, many SS kept their real names after the war and became lawyers, judges, teachers, policemen, and politicians. It's unbelievable when you think about it. A lot of the Nazis that were prosecuted had their sentences commuted." Lisa paused. "A few weeks ago, a Dachau survivor saw a former SS officer coming out of a restaurant on Leopoldstrasse. Her name is Joyce Cantor. She was visiting Munich for the first time in thirty years and ran into a Nazi who tried to kill her."

"Who was he?"

"The SS officer in charge of a killing squad one day in the woods outside Dachau. Harry, didn't the same thing happen to you?"

"I remember him, but not his name or anything about him."

"Joyce called the Anti-Defamation League in New York, and they gave her our number. I spoke to her. She was supposed to come in and look at our archival photographs the next day. But when she went back to her hotel room there was a swastika painted on the wall. Sound familiar? She was scared to death and flew out that evening."

"Did she tell you what happened?"

"I have our taped conversation right here." Lisa pointed to the recorder on her desk. "She had been driven to the woods outside Dachau with a group from the women's camp. It was late in the afternoon. A pit had been dug, and by the time she arrived it was full of Jews, dead and dying. She was told to jump in the pit, the guards shooting at her. But by then they were drunk, and missed her. When it was dark she crawled out and escaped."

Harry could picture the scene, remembered seeing someone running into the woods.

Lisa took out a stack of eight-by-ten black-and-white prints, placed them on the desk in front of Harry.

"These are the photographs I was going to show her. Look at them. You will probably see some familiar faces."

The first one was a brown sepia tone shot of an SS officer, head and shoulders, the man wearing a peaked cap, eagle above the skull and crossbones, pale-gray uniform with a high collar and epaulets, arrogance evident in his thin-lipped grin.

"Martin Weiss," Martz said. "Arrived the 3rd of January 1942. Took over for Alex Piorkowski who was eventually kicked out of the Nazi Party."

"I remember Weiss," Harry said. "He shot a man in the yard after roll call because his shirt wasn't buttoned all the way."

"We don't have to worry about him any more," Martz said. "He was sentenced at Nuremberg and hanged."

"The question is, who did Joyce Cantor recognize?" Lisa said. "Forty-one other men at Dachau were tried with Weiss after the war. That seemed like a logical place to begin. All were found guilty of war crimes. Thirty-five were sentenced to death, the remaining six to various terms of imprisonment. Max Lengfelder, Sebastian Schmidt and Peter Betz—do you remember any of them?—received life sentences."

Harry glanced at their photographs, but no one looked familiar.

"The final three, Hugo Lausterer, Albin Gretsch and Johann Schoepp, were given ten-year sentences. So any one of them could have been on Leopoldstrasse, coming out of the restaurant that day."

He looked at their photos. "Familiar faces," Harry said. "But not the one we're looking for."

Martz handed him another photograph. "You remember Egon Zill?"

"I do," Harry said. "He'd have guards tie a prisoner's hands and feet together and make them crawl, squealing like a pig. Food was thrown into the pigsty and the Jew would have to fight the pigs for it."

"This is Himmler," Martz said. "Remember the day he came, April 11, 1941."

"We weren't taken there till November," Harry said.

"The SS were nervous, making the prisoners clean up the yard, the barracks, burning bodies in the morgue or burying them. Word was Reichsführer Himmler had a weak stomach." Martz took a breath. "We were in the yard, standing at attention after roll call. Himmler came out to inspect us. I remember his eyes, dark and small, close together. He looked like some kind of rodent."

"Here are a few more," Lisa said, sliding the pile over the desktop to him.

Harry shuffled through the pictures and shook his head. "I don't see him. Now what?"

Chapter 16

The beer garden was crowded when Harry got there at 6:15. He had walked through the Augustinerkeller, and it was like going back in time, the beer hall much the same as he remembered it: dark wood, heavy pine tables, timber-frame ceiling, and animal heads on the walls.

He went out back and saw Colette sitting at a long table under the linden trees. She was with a group of locals decked out in Tracht clothing, home-sewn Tyrolean outfits that made them look like friendly mountain people, smiling ruddy-faced men and women who drank goat milk and lived humble honest lives.

They were talking, drinking beer, listening to the oompah band, its members wearing lederhosen, having fun. It was a scene from his past when everything was good, before all the craziness.

Harry watched Colette for a couple minutes, Colette the quintessential fräulein singing, hoisting her mug, enjoying herself. She looked over, saw him and waved. He walked to the table, sat next to her and met the people she was with. This was the custom, you found a space at a table and mixed with whoever was there. The waitress, a sturdy blonde with huge bazooms, came by and he ordered a beer. The band started up again and the Bavarians were singing and swaying in their seats, really getting into it.

"Ein prosit, ein prosit der Gemütlichkeit," Colette sang, smiling at him. "Come on, Harry, try it."

"I only sing in the shower," Harry said.

"Here, everyone sings."

"I better not."

"Then you have to dance with me."

113

Before Harry could object, Colette stood up next to him, took hold of his hands, pulled him up and hooked an arm around his, moving for the dance floor. He held her right hand and she put her left on his shoulder. He put his other hand on her hip and brought it up and felt the firm tautness of her waist. He twirled her a couple times, Colette really into it, laughing and grinning at him. When the song ended they went back to the table. Harry sang "*Ein prosit*," loosening up a little, trying to put Hess out of his mind for a while. But he wanted to get out of the beer garden. He'd had enough of this Bavarian schmaltz, the oompah band and the cheeky German camaraderie.

They went inside and had dinner: sauerbraten and roast potatoes.

"You're obviously German," Harry said. "But your name isn't and you speak English with a British accent."

"My father, Joe Rizik, was Lebanese. My mother was German. His family emigrated from Beirut in the early twenties and settled in Berlin. My grandfather imported Persian rugs. His clientele were wealthy Germans, mostly Jews."

"How'd your parents meet?"

"My father was in the hospital, with appendicitis. My mother was his nurse. They got on, fell in love. Got married right before he enlisted. He was in the Heer, the regular army, not the SS."

She took a photograph out of her purse, a cracked, faded shot of a good-looking dark-haired guy posing in a coat and tie.

"I never met him. He was a sergeant in the infantry, killed in action on the Eastern Front, 1944. Served with great distinction. One of only twenty-seven men to receive the Knight's Cross with Oak Leaves, Swords and Diamonds. My mother said he was a good man, ashamed of what the Nazis were doing."

She was proud of him, that was obvious, the war hero father she never knew.

"What about your mother?" He cut a piece of sauerbraten and pushed it through the gravy, took a bite, the smell and taste taking him back thirty years.

"She's retired, living outside Bergheim, a village just north of Salzburg." She paused, watching him eat. "You're hungry, yes? Enjoying the sauerbraten, Harry?" she said, smiling, being herself, no pretensions.

She told him about getting a degree in journalism from the University of Berlin, the same school Albert Einstein and Otto von Bismarck had attended. She told him about the building of the Berlin Wall in 1961, the autumn of her senior year, forty-three kilometers long, dividing West and East Berlin.

"Why was it built? I can't remember," Harry said.

"The communists wanted to keep East German professionals from emigrating to the west. They were losing too many doctors, lawyers, and engineers. The manpower losses had been estimated at twenty-five billion marks. I did a story on it when I was hired by the *Berliner Zeitung* after graduating."

"Where'd you get the Brit accent?"

"I lived in London, worked for the *Daily Telegraph* for several years." She paused, sipped her beer. "Harry, I have done all the talking. Tell me about yourself, please. Where do you live?"

"Detroit," Harry said.

"Sure, yes, where the automobiles are made. Is it nice there?"

"The garden spot of the Midwest." Harry grinned to show her he was kidding.

"What is your occupation?"

"Now I'm really going to impress you," Harry said. "I'm a scrap-metal dealer." He explained the basics of the business and she gave him a blank look, chewing a bite of sauerbraten. "Not very interesting, is it?"

"Are you married, Harry?"

"No."

"Were you ever?"

"A long time ago."

"And you don't want to talk about it."

"You're very perceptive."

"What brings you to Munich?"

115

"I read an article in a car magazine about a road trip from Munich to Salzburg. It sounded like fun."

They finished their meal and Harry paid the bill and they walked outside, stood in front of the Augustiner-keller. It was 8:30, a clear warm night.

"I can drive you back to your hotel, Harry, but it is early. Let's go to a club. I'll show you where I live."

"Why not," Harry said.

She hooked her arm around his and they walked to her Volkswagen and drove to Schwabing. It looked different thirty years later. Reminded him of Greenwich Village, same feel, streets lined with cafes, avant-garde shops, clubs and bars, but the look, the architecture was considerably different. She found a space on the street and parked a block from Leopoldstrasse.

"I live right over there, Harry. Two blocks away on Wagnerstrasse 12."

They went to a small dark bar, a Miles Davis track playing in the background, smoke from dozens of cigarettes filling the room. The clientele were young, the men had long hair and beards and dressed in black, the women wore long cotton dresses, or dark tee-shirts and jeans.

They sat next to each other in a booth, facing the room. A waitress in a black miniskirt took their order. She had a tattoo on the side of her calf but it was too dark to tell what it was. Harry ordered bourbon on the rocks. He was full from the beer. Colette ordered schnapps. The waitress walked away from the table.

"Harry, when are you going to the Alps?"

"Are you trying to get rid of me?"

"No, I'm trying to understand you."

"What're you talking about?"

"I don't know, Harry. Something isn't right. You come to Munich to go on this vague trip but you don't have a schedule or an itinerary."

"How do you know?" Harry said.

The waitress brought their drinks. He sipped his bourbon, felt the burn in his throat.

"You were attacked in a restaurant by a group of neo-Nazis," Colette said. "They don't target foreign tourists. That is not how they operate."

"Maybe they were after Cordell Sims, the guy with me. Blackshirts sees a black dude in a claret-colored leisure suit, it sets them off."

"Harry, they ransacked your hotel room and painted a swastika on the wall."

"Maybe it was a coincidence."

"Two times in one night," Colette said. "I think there is something you are not telling me." She sipped the schnapps, eyes on him.

"I think there's something you're not telling me."

She looked surprised, and now eased away from him.

"Who do you work for?"

"I told you, Harry, *Der Spiegel*."

"I phoned the main office in Berlin, nobody seemed to know you."

"I'm a freelance writer," she said, sounding defensive. "I will give you the name and phone number of my editor." She looked angry now, drained her schnapps. "This is crazy. Who do you think I work for?" Calling him out.

Harry sipped his bourbon, studying her face. He was going to say Ernst Hess, get a reaction, but didn't.

"Come on, you can't make such an accusation without explaining yourself."

Now she slid out of the booth, moved across the room toward the door. Harry got up, pulled a five-mark note out of his pocket and put it on the table under Colette's schnapps glass. He walked out of the club and looked down the crowded sidewalk. It took a few seconds to spot her among the nighttime revelers, crossing the street.

She passed her VW and kept going. He followed, hanging back in the shadows, watched her walk up to the brightly lighted front of a modern three-storey building, take a key ring out of her purse and open the door. He

117

waited, saw lights on the second floor. Moved to the door, scanned the directory, saw "C Rizik" and rang the bell.

"Who is it?" she said in German.

"Harry."

"What do you want?" Hard edge to her voice.

"Can we talk?" Harry said.

"About what? You do not trust me, so we have nothing more to talk about."

Harry stepped away from the door, started down the street and heard the buzzer, stepped back, turned the handle and opened the door.

He walked up a flight of stairs and there she was, door open, standing on the threshold, light behind her, blazer off, top two buttons of her blouse undone.

"I want to apologize," Harry said.

She ran her tongue over her front teeth and tucked her hair back behind her ears.

"Then you are welcome to come in."

Colette moved left out of the doorway. Harry moved past her and she closed the door, turned and faced him, waiting for an explanation.

"I've been a little paranoid since last night. Get attacked by six lunatics with ax handles and it might color your point of view."

"Maybe I am with them. Maybe I have been acting, playing a role. Maybe I still am."

She was angry, wasn't finished, wasn't going to let it go just yet. She grinned, came toward him, put her palms on his shoulders. With her heels on they were almost eye level, Harry a little taller. He let her take charge. She kissed him with her red lacquered lips and stuck her tongue in his mouth, blue eyes closed for a few seconds then opening, staring at him.

"You still in character?" Harry said.

"Come with me and find out," Colette said, taking his hand, guiding him through the apartment to her room. They moved to the bed and stood next to it, quietly taking each other's clothes off in the darkness and sliding into bed, doing everything by feel.

Chapter 17

He opened his eyes, saw morning light filtering through the sheer curtains, Colette sleeping next to him on her side, back to him, sheet tucked under her left shoulder, blonde hair spread across the pillow. She'd surprised him, taking him to bed. It was the last thing he expected to happen given his suspicions and her attitude.

He looked at his watch. It was 6:22 a.m. He slid out of bed, picked up his clothes, took everything into the main room, got dressed and looked around. He hadn't noticed much the night before, and hadn't come out of the bedroom until now.

The furniture was simple modern, black leather chairs and couch, chrome and glass tables. There was a framed Toulouse-Lautrec print over the mantel. A man wearing a black hat and black coat, with a red scarf tied around his neck, hanging over his shoulder. The caption said:

AMBASSADEURS aristide BRUANT dans son cabaret.

There was a framed sepia-tone photograph on one of the end tables, a good-looking woman in a nurse's uniform.

"My mother when she was about my age," Colette said, coming in the room, tying the sash on her robe, yawning. She ran her fingers through her hair.

"You look like her," Harry said.

"It was taken in 1945 just before the war ended."

He placed the frame back on the table.

"Harry, I am not exactly sure what happened last night," she said, pulling the top of the robe closed as if she was embarrassed, being modest all of a sudden.

"I am," Harry said, moving toward her. He put his arms around her and kissed her lightly on the mouth. "I'll call you later, check in."

He got back to his hotel room at 7:15. The light on the phone was flashing. He had two messages. Surprised the first one was from Colette. "Harry, I have an idea, call me."

The second one was from Lisa. "Harry, Joyce, the survivor from Palm Beach, wants to talk to you."

Another Dachau Jew who had dug out of the grave that night. He was anxious to talk to her too. Harry ordered room service and took a shower. The food arrived while he was getting dressed. He ate bacon and eggs, and drank his coffee, scanned the Herald Tribune checking baseball scores. The Tigers had beaten Cleveland six to five and were still leading their division going down the stretch, two and a half games ahead of the Yankees.

He finished and phoned Lisa. No answer. Tried Colette.

"Harry, I'm going undercover."

"What're you talking about?"

"A contact I made, this Blackshirt, invited me to meet him at a bar where they hang out. I think he likes me, Harry. Are you jealous?"

"No, I'm worried about you. What are you trying to find out?"

"I don't know. But I'm not going to get a story unless I take some risks."

"What's his name?"

"Werner. And believe me, he's harmless. He has joined them because he has nothing else to do. If you're so worried, you can drive me."

Colette studied her face in the mirror. She applied mascara around her eyes until she looked like a raccoon. Dabbed her cheeks with rouge. Traced her mouth with deep red lipstick.

She dressed in a tight black tee-shirt, breasts on display, tight black jeans and black boots. Slipped rings on her fingers. Let her hair down, combed her bangs until they hung to her eyebrows. Stuffed a pack of cigarettes in the left sleeve of her tee-shirt and practiced making faces in the mirror, psyching herself up. Colette liked her new look, thought she could pass for a neo-Nazi. Her final accessory was a distressed leather jacket. Now she was ready.

Harry drove to Colette's apartment, parked on the street and waited for her to come down. He watched an Audi back into a space in front of him, thinking it was going to slam into him. Just then, his passenger door opened, a girl he'd never seen before got in next to him, cigarette hanging from her mouth. She took it out and grinned.

"Harry, what do you think?"

"Do I know you?"

Colette smiled.

Harry said, "I see what you mean. You look like a neo-Nazi hooker."

"That's what I wanted to hear."

Colette grinned again, rolled down the window and tossed out the cigarette.

"Where to?" Harry said.

They drove to a rundown area on the outskirts of Munich that reminded him of parts of Detroit after the '67 riot.

"It's right there, Harry." Colette pointed. "Across the street."

He slowed down and pulled over. A sign above the door said *Gaststätte*. It was a small pub in the center of a block of vacant storefronts, wind blowing a piece of newspaper along the sidewalk, a couple Blackshirts out front, smoking.

"You still think this is a good idea, huh?"

"No, Harry. That is why I have gone to all this trouble."

"How long is this going to take?"

"If I am not out in one hour call the police."

He didn't like the sound of it.

She read his expression and said, "Take it easy. I am kidding you."

Harry watched neo-Nazis come and go. At the hour mark he was starting to worry in spite of Colette's casual attitude. When she still hadn't appeared twenty minutes later, he got out of the car, crossed the street and went in the bar. When the door opened every skinhead in the place turned and looked at him. The bar was packed shoulder to shoulder with drinkers. Every table occupied. He'd never felt more out of place. He scanned the room, saw Colette subtly shake her head, and felt like a fool, but didn't have time to dwell on it. A tall skinhead with an ax handle came over from the bar.

"What are you doing here? Are you lost?"

"I thought this was a bar. I was going to have a beer."

The skinhead stared at him as if he were an idiot, poked him in the chest with the tapered end of the ax handle. Harry could feel the weight of the .38 in his jacket pocket. Wanted to draw it, put it in the guy's face, but it would be the last dumb thing he ever did.

"I think you've made a mistake. I think you are going to turn around and walk out. Never come back here again."

Harry moved to the door, opened it and went out.

Colette finally came out half an hour later. She glanced in his direction and started down the sidewalk. Harry made a U-turn and picked her up at the end of the block. She got in, looked at him and said, "Are you out of your mind? Harry, what were you thinking?"

"I wasn't. I was reacting. Worried about you. You were in there almost two hours."

"Well, you caused quite a stir."

"Who were you sitting with?"

"Gustav, one of my new friends."

"Where was Werner?"

"Drunk. He introduced me to a few of the guys. Two of them propositioned me in front of him, said they wanted to take me in the toilet and fuck me."

"How romantic," Harry said. "Nice group of guys. What did you say?"

"Nothing."

"Playing hard to get, huh?"

Colette smiled. "I looked at them like they were losers."

"That's a stretch. But in a way you can't blame them," Harry said. "I doubt they see girls like you come in there very often. What was going on in there?"

"The usual. Blackshirts smoking, getting drunk, calling each other out. But I did find out something, Harry. They're having a rally tonight. They were all talking about it. It's at a beer hall not far from here. Rumor has it some high-ranking Third Reich Nazis are going to be there."

"And you're thinking of going?"

"I have to. No outsider has ever photographed one of their rallies."

"And lived to tell about it."

"Harry, you surprise me," Colette said. "If this was your story you wouldn't hesitate. I know you."

It was the last thing he wanted to do, but he couldn't let her go alone.

"What time are you going to pick me up?"

Colette pulled up in front of the hotel at 9:00. He got in, she leaned over, kissed him and smiled.

"You look nice, Harry."

"It's my neo-Nazi rally outfit." He was wearing Levis and a dark-blue jacket. The Colt was in his right side pocket. "I don't have to tell you how dangerous this is, so if you want to change your mind."

She shifted into first, and then second, picking up speed, merging with traffic. They drove to the industrial area they'd been to earlier. Colette went past a beer hall the size of an airplane hangar, and parked down the street. She turned in her seat, facing him.

"If they catch me, Harry, I want you to run."

"They're not going to catch you," Harry said. "We're not going to take any chances, do anything stupid. Okay?"

"Okay."

They got out of the car and walked back through the beer hall parking lot, crouching between cars, getting close to the building. He saw a Blackshirt standing just outside the rear door, smoking a cigarette, three dumpsters lined up against the wall behind him. Harry could hear the muted sounds of cheers, applause inside the hall. The Blackshirt took a final drag, threw his cigarette and went back in.

They hid behind the dumpsters, waited, moved to the door, opened it and went in the kitchen. Harry could hear the amplified voice of someone shouting: "*Sieg Heil. Sieg Heil.*" And then the chorus joining in. "*Sieg Heil. Sieg Heil.*"

Colette led him through the kitchen, up a stairway to the balcony at the back of the hall. They got on their knees, peeking over a solid wood railing. What he saw reminded Harry of photos of Nazi rallies he'd seen, banners with swastikas festooned on the walls, the big room filled with Blackshirts sitting at long tables, drinking beer. At the far end was a dais, a man at the podium in a black suit, three Nazis in uniform on each side of him, sitting at a table, facing the crowd. They were all in their mid-fifties and sixties.

"*Heil Hitler*," the Master of Ceremonies said, raising his arm in the Nazi salute.

The room erupted, Blackshirts screaming, "*Heil Hitler. Heil Hitler*," standing, arms raised, ax handles banging on the wood floor like thunder."

"Who is he?" Harry whispered.

"I don't know." Colette whispered back. She raised her camera and took a couple shots.

"I appreciate your enthusiasm." The MC paused, waiting for the noise to die down. "It is now my pleasure to introduce our distinguished guests. These men are the true heroes of the Reich, men of conviction, men of character. And now, without further ado, let me present Otto Reder, Unterscharführer at Sobibor."

Reder, the first man at the table on the MC's right, stood and took a bow. He was tall, distinguished-looking. The Blackshirts cheered, banged their beer mugs on the table, their ax handles on the floor.

"Wilhelm Hoffman, Sturmbannführer at Buchenwald."

He was on the left, stood and gave the Heil Hitler salute and the skinheads went crazy.

"Gerhard Ulmer from Gusen, Emil Drescher from Treblinka, Kurt Kretschmer from Mauthausen and Ernst Rohm from Auschwitz.

The Blackshirts were standing, shouting: "*Sieg Heil, Sieg Heil, Sieg Heil.*"

The six Nazis on the dais sat. The cheering stopped, and then it was quiet.

"There's someone else on the right side of the dais," Harry said. "You see him?"

"There, in the corner," Colette said.

"Like he wants to see what's going on but doesn't want to be seen. Get him, will you?"

"I'll try but I'm not promising much. I need a longer lens." Colette aimed her camera, took a couple shots.

"In their day," the MC said, "these men did their job and did it well. And now we have to do ours. We are the new rat catchers. The new exterminators. The new patriots. We have to take back the Fatherland."

The cheering started again.

"*Bitte, bitte,*" the MC said. He waited till the room was quiet.

"I am going to be counting on each one of you to do your duty for the New Reich." More cheers, a standing ovation. "Now I want to show you something."

On cue two Blackshirts appeared from behind the dais, escorting a man in a striped concentration-camp uniform, hands tied behind his back, black hood over his head.

The MC said, "Do you know what this is?"

The Blackshirts yelled, "Jew, Jew, Jew."

"Better hold onto your wallet."

The hall erupted in laughter.

"That's right. He wants your money. He wants your car. He wants your house. He wants everything you own. Are you going to let him take it?"

"Nooo," said the Blackshirts, on their feet again.

Colette balanced her camera on top of the railing and pressed the button on the speed winder, taking more shots.

"Who do you think the prisoner is?"

"An actor. Harry, this is drama. They're doing it for effect."

Then the Blackshirts were on their feet, singing:
The street free for the brown battalions,
The street free for the stormtroopers,
Millions full of hope look up at the swastika;
The day breaks for freedom and for bread.

"What's that?" Harry said.

"The 'Horst Wessel Song,'" Colette said. "It's the Nazi theme song."

"It's catchy."

"Harry, we have to go. They always sing it at the end."

They went back downstairs through the kitchen, Blackshirts banging their ax handles and cheering. The smoker had returned, standing just outside the door. They crouched behind a stainless-steel counter. Harry could hear the MC wrapping it up. "I want to thank you for joining us tonight…"

Colette looked worried. "Harry, we have to do something. They'll be coming out any minute."

He glanced around the kitchen, got an idea. Moved to the industrial range against the wall, picked up a heavy cast-iron skillet. Harry moved to the door, went out and hit the Blackshirt on top of the head. He dropped to the ground. Harry tossed the skillet in the dumpster. They dragged the Blackshirt into the parking lot and left him next to an Opel. First impression, he was drunk. It might buy them a little time. Then he heard voices, turned and saw Blackshirts coming out of the hall.

They crouched and ran to Colette's car and got back to her apartment at 10:38. She had a darkroom and was anxious to develop some of the film. Harry made himself a drink, sat at the kitchen table, reading the newspaper.

Half an hour later Colette came out of the darkroom with four still-wet eight-by-ten photos. She put them on the table, each showing part of a face.

"I had to enlarge them four hundred per cent to get anything, that's why there's so much grain." Colette took out scissors, trimmed off the excess and fit the quadrants together on the kitchen table. "Recognize him?"

"Ernst Hess," Harry said.

"Why would he be at a Blackshirt rally?"

"My guess, he's sympathetic to their cause, but with his Christian Social Union affiliation he can't take the chance being seen endorsing them."

"How do you know about the CSU?"

"It's in the paper. Right here." He turned the article around to show her. "They're having a board meeting tomorrow at nine a.m."

She glanced at him and smiled.

"I've seen that look before. You have something in mind, don't you?"

Chapter 18

Harry spent the night at Colette's again. In the morning they drove to Hess' apartment building, arriving at 7:30, parked across the street between two Volkswagens and waited. "Why're you so sure he's here?"

"He was at the rally until after ten last night, and he has to be downtown at nine o'clock. If you had a morning appointment, would you go all the way to Schleissheim, or stay in the city?

"Makes sense," Harry said.

"After the meeting there will be a press conference, so they can tell the media what they talked about, what decisions were made. Hess will be gone for hours."

"How do you know somebody else isn't in the apartment?"

"If somebody is we'll deal with it."

"I like your confidence."

"Harry, if you don't take risks you don't get a story."

"How do we get in?"

"That, I am not sure."

"It's an important detail, don't you think?"

Colette had brought a thermos of coffee, poured them each a cup and handed him a piece of strawberry-cheese strudel on a napkin. They ate breakfast, watching the building.

At 8:20, a black Mercedes sedan pulled up across the street from them. Harry recognized the driver, Hess' bodyguard, and ducked down in his seat. Rausch got out of the car, closed the door, and took his time scanning the the cars parked on both sides of the street. He went in the building and came out ten minutes later, Hess behind him, the big man's eyes moving, alert. He opened the rear door for Hess, then walked around the car, got in behind the wheel and drove off.

Harry sat up, glanced at Colette. "You ready?"

They stood in front of the building. The door was locked. Harry studied the directory. Hess was in apartment 4B. Colette pushed the button, heard the buzzer, but nothing happened, maybe proving that no one was in the apartment. But that didn't help them much.

"How're we going to get in?"

Colette said, "Wait here. I have an idea." She headed down the sidewalk.

"Hey, where're you going?"

She turned the corner and disappeared.

Colette circled around to the rear of the six-storey building that took up a quarter of the block. She went in the employees' entrance and down a staircase into a subterranean room, huge furnace glowing hot, the smell of fuel oil, and a network of pipes. It was dark but she could see a man in a green custodial uniform, wrench in his hands, working on a leaking pipe. She surprised him. Doubted many of the high-rent tenants wandered down into the bowels of the building.

"May I help you, Fräulein?"

He was short, stocky, about her age. Needed a bath and a shave.

"I am looking for the engineer."

"I am the engineer."

"I have a problem," she said, pausing for effect. "I locked my keys in the apartment along with an important file."

"What number?" He seemed shy but willing to assist a woman in distress.

"4B. I work for Herr Hess. He is giving the presentation in one hour. If I don't get it—" She let the custodian imagine what would happen to her. "Do you have a key?"

"Have you talked to the manager, Herr Steiger?"

"This is the second time I have done this. I am embarrassed." She looked at him and smiled. "Could you help me, please?"

Harry waited a few minutes, no idea what happened to her. Went back to the car, sat in the driver's seat, not sure what to do. And then the door to the building opened, Colette standing there looking for him. Harry got out of the car, crossed the street.

She led him to the elevator and up to the fourth floor. The door to Hess' apartment was unlocked. "How'd you do it?"

"I turned on the charm."

Harry grinned. She had it to turn on.

The interior was big and spacious, professionally decorated, with views of the ancient spires of Altstadt on one side and the modern glass office buildings of downtown Munich on the other. They walked through the apartment. There were two bedrooms, one larger than the other, an office, kitchen and living room.

Harry checked the closets and drawers in the bedrooms, looking for a gun, a Nazi uniform, but didn't find anything incriminating. Colette checked the other rooms, went through the utility closet, refrigerator, oven. Nothing. They met in the office. It had a sleek desk with a black granite top on a chrome frame. Behind the desk was a credenza with a matching top and custom wooden file drawers, two banks of three. The drawers on the left were unlocked. Envelopes, stationery, stamps, letter opener in the first one. Pens, paper clips, tape, stapler in the second drawer, and files in the deep third drawer.

The drawers on the other side were locked. He took out the letter opener, jammed the tip in the lock and tried to turn it, but it wouldn't budge. Colette walked out of the room without saying anything, came back a few minutes later with a hammer and a screwdriver.

"Let me try." She got on her knees and pounded the screwdriver into the lock, gripped the handle, turned left and it opened.

Harry said, "Where'd you learn that?"

"A few years ago I wrote an article on how to pick a lock."

He opened the first drawer and found a box of 9 mm Parabellum cartridges. Now they were getting somewhere. The next one was filled with a strange assortment of things. He reached in, taking the stuff out, putting it on the desktop: a couple pairs of eyeglasses, woman's suede gloves, gold Star of David, watches, bracelets, women's panties, necklaces, a diamond ring, a wedding ring, silver locket.

"Harry, what is all of this?"

"I don't know."

Colette opened the third drawer, took out a file folder with several cracked sepia-tone photographs, shuffled through them.

"Harry, look at these."

The first one was a young SS officer in uniform, posing, blank expression. Harry recognized him immediately. Took out the mug shot Taggart had given to him and unfolded it. Now he could see the young Nazi in the older man's face.

"Harry, who is that?"

"Unterscharführer Ernst Hess," Lisa said.

Harry was in her office at the ZOB. He'd dropped Colette off and come right over. Why didn't he recognize Hess before? Sitting across the table from him at Les Halles. Harry showed her another shot, Hess grinning, dead bodies behind him, piled up in a mass grave. "I remember the look of satisfaction on his face," Harry said, "after shooting my father and eleven others with a machine gun, saying, 'This is how you kill Jews.'"

"He looks so ordinary," Lisa said. "He could be a plumber or a taxi driver."

"What did you expect?" Harry said. "He'd have horns and a tail?"

"Hess was only there for a short time," Lisa said, "a few weeks, touring Dachau and its sub-camps."

Martz turned his head a couple times left to right and rubbed his neck. "Harry, don't get old. It's no fun." He paused. "It was very unusual—I would say unheard-of for the SS to murder Jews en masse outside the camp. Why go to the trouble? They would just shoot us in the yard, the *Schiesstand*, sending a message, scaring the hell out of those who saw it or heard about it."

"Maybe they were experimenting," Lisa said. "Dachau was the prototype for other camps, the training ground for the SS. Many well-known Nazis learned their trade there."

"There have been no corroborating accounts that Hess was a mass murderer until now," Martz said. "The voices of the dead can't speak, Harry, but you can."

"What do you know about him?" Harry said.

"His father was a career soldier. His mother was a music teacher," Lisa said. "He was raised in a strict German household. His middle name is Tristan after Wagner's opera."

"Seems appropriate when you realize Wagner was an anti-Semite," Martz said.

Lisa said, "Hess fell out of a tree when he was a boy of nine or ten. His mother heard him crying and beat him with a stick for being weak. Later, a doctor came to the house, examined him, and discovered he had broken his leg."

"Well you can begin to understand why he turned out the way he did," Harry said, moving his chair back from Lisa's desk so he could cross his legs.

"So if you have a bad upbringing murder is justified?" Lisa said, raising her voice.

"My dear, think how sensitive it is for Harry," Martz said. "He is a civilized man, showing compassion."

"The hell I am. He killed my parents," Harry said. "And my daughter. I'm going to get the son of a bitch."

Martz said, "What do you mean, your daughter?"

Harry told them what happened to Sara.

"Harry, I'm so sorry," Lisa paused, eyes holding on him.

"I am, too," Harry said.

"I can't imagine—"

"Tell me more about Hess," Harry said, changing the subject.

Lisa glanced at the open binder on her desk. "He joined the SS in 1939 at age twenty-two. He was on a fast track, an up-and-comer. Everyone thought he was related to Rudolf Hess, Hitler's deputy. It helped his cause until

May 10th, 1941, when Rudy flew a plane to Scotland to negotiate peace with the British. Then, of course, Ernst tried to distance himself from his famous namesake." Lisa took off her glasses, rubbed her eyes. "After Dachau, he was transferred to Berlin. Assisted Adolf Eichmann in organizing the Wannsee Conference. Reinhard Heydrich brought top Nazi leaders to a villa in Wannsee, a suburb of Berlin. He wanted their buy-in on deporting all the Jews of Europe to extermination camps like Auschwitz." She paused, put her glasses back on. "After the war he started a construction company to rebuild the cities that were bombed by the Allies."

"And profited handsomely," Martz said.

"He sold the company in 1967 for thirty-six million marks," Lisa said. "And then bought an airship factory, started building Zeppelins."

Harry said, "Tell me more about this Dachau survivor."

"She saw an SS officer murder dozens of Jews. That's why she's anxious to talk to you."

"Where does she live?" Harry said.

"Palm Beach, Florida," Lisa said. "I'll set up a phone call for today at 5:30. We'll do it at the house. Harry, can you be there?"

"Of course."

"With the photographs and your testimony we have a strong case against Hess."

"Harry, do you remember where they took you in the forest the day of the massacre?" Martz said.

"It was a few miles outside Dachau."

Martz looked at him. "Do you think you could find it?"

"I don't know," Harry said. "It's been a long time. I don't know if I can trust my memory. Let me think about it."

Martz dabbed his wet eyes with a Kleenex.

"Were you at the camp during the liberation?" Harry said.

"I had been transferred to Ampfing to work in the munitions factory, but was brought back to Dachau in the autumn of 1944. I was in a barracks with Léon Blum."

"The premier of France?" Harry said.

"The very same," Martz said. "The Americans liberated us on April 29, 1945. They were so horrified by the conditions, they made the citizens of Dachau feed and clothe us. Made them come to the camp to see the naked, emaciated bodies of the dead piled up in the mortuary room next to the crematorium."

"What did you do after?"

"I went home," Martz said. "Whoever had been living there was gone."

Just then, a bear of a man, mid-thirties, came in the room. He had dark curly hair and a full beard. Wore black horn rims and a white yarmulke.

"What did I miss?"

"Meet Harry Levin, Dachau survivor. Harry, this is Leon Lukiski, our other partner."

"It's an honor, sir," he said.

"Harry has identified Ernst Hess, and has agreed to help prosecute him."

"Great news," Leon said. "Mazel tov."

"I'll fill you in," Lisa said. "Harry, is there anything else?"

"Yeah. Do you have a shovel I can borrow?"

Chapter 19

Harry went back to his hotel, showered, changed and called Cordell.

"Yo, Harry, where you been at? Thought the 'shirts came back for a three-peat."

"I had a date."

"You sly dog. She got any friends?"

"I'll ask." He paused. "Doing anything today, want to go on a field trip?"

"Field trip? We back in middle school?"

"Dachau," Harry said. "The concentration camp."

"Why you want to go there?"

He picked Cordell up at the Pension Jedermann on Bayerstrasse at 11:30. Cordell in a powder-blue leisure suit with beige stitching and a beige polyester shirt with musical notes scattered all over the front. "Man, you're a dresser, aren't you?" he said when Cordell got in the car.

"I'm fly, Harry. Got my fly on."

"You sure do."

"You know what fly mean, Harry?" Cordell said, grinning.

"Let me guess. Fashion-conscious. Am I in the ball-park?"

"OK, you in the right direction," Cordell said. "I can hook you up with some cloth, style you."

"Guys selling scrap don't dress like that."

"You be the first. They be looking at you with envy and shit."

Harry wondered what Michalski, the buyer at the steel mill, would say if he showed up in a powder-blue leisure suit. It wouldn't be pretty.

135

Peter Leonard

Harry drove through Altstadt, and once he had cleared the ancient spires he saw a Zeppelin hovering high above. "Look up there." He pointed to the top edge of the windshield. "See it?"

"Yeah. More Nazis, Harry? Think it's following us?"

"I don't know. I guess we'll find out."

They got on the highway and drove northwest out of the city, Cordell looking through the windows, checking to see if the Zeppelin was still up there. "Don't see nothing, Harry. We cool." Cordell took a red Nazi armband out of his pocket. "Souvenir from the other night. Check it out."

"Hitler said the red symbolized the social idea of the movement. White was the nationalistic idea, and the swastika represented the mission of the struggle for the victory of the Aryan man, that was a victory of the idea of creative work, which always has been and always will be anti-Semitic."

"Huh? What was the Führer smoking he wrote that? Must've been some good shit."

"All of them were smoking it." Harry paused. "They listened to the lunatic, believed him. Hitler thought Jewish men purposely seduced German girls to pollute the Aryan race."

"What would he'd a thought about brothers doin' the fräuleins?"

A few minutes later they were cruising along the northern perimeter of Dachau concentration camp. "When I was here there were thirty-four barracks. There's only one left."

"When was that?"

"Got here in November 1941, escaped in April 1942." He pulled the BMW over on the side of the road, looking past Cordell at the entrance gate. "There's the guardhouse, and that brick building with the chimney is the crematorium."

"Hold on, Harry, rewind."

"It was the beginning of November. The Nazis came to our house, ten armed men, banging on the door, seven in the morning. I got out of bed, looked out the window

136

and saw them in front of the house. An SS sergeant told us to get dressed and come downstairs, bring what we could carry but no food.

"We started walking through Altstadt, joined now by other families, friends and neighbors forced out of their homes. Fifty of us, I counted. People were stumbling along, weighted down by layers of clothing, carrying suitcases and duffel bags. We walked through town and then we were outside of the city. I was thirteen, no idea what was happening. None of us did. They marched us sixteen kilometers to Dachau. I knew we were in trouble when I saw the walls and towers of the camp."

"What's that mean: *Arbeit Macht Frei*," Cordell said, trying to pronounce it, pointing to the words on the gate.

"Work makes you free. That was the irony," Harry said. "The harder you worked the weaker you got. Only way to be free was to die."

"What you do, they put you in here?"

Harry turned his head, held Cordell in his gaze. "I was a Jew."

"You got a tat?"

"They didn't do that here. They put your number on your uniform." He paused. "Morning roll call was four a.m. in the summer and five thirty in the winter. After going to the bathroom we were given a cup of black coffee, then marched to the assembly area for roll call. After roll call the work commander, a prisoner, called out names for work details. If your name was called you were given a slice of bread and maybe a little piece of sausage. We worked, usually in the Plantage, farmland near the camp until eleven thirty. Marched back to the barracks for dinner, a small serving of cabbage or carrots and a small piece of potato. At twelve thirty we marched back to work until six, then back to camp for roll call, and back to the barracks for supper: watery soup, sometimes a bit of cheese.

"I saw a man beaten to death by a guard for stealing potato peelings, stuffing them in his pockets 'cause he was starving. I remember bodies that looked like skeletons stacked on top of each other outside the crematorium.

"Waking to the sounds of rifle shots, firing squads shooting prisoners who had broken the rules. I remember naked prisoners sprayed with a hose in January and left to die."

"Why we here? This some kind of cathartic experience, got to purge this from your soul?"

"I'm getting my bearings."

"Your bearings? What's that mean?"

Harry told him about the mass execution, the mass grave, digging his way out and going to the farmhouse and being helped by the woman.

"Harry, you got some dark secrets. But I got to ask, you really think you gonna find this grave in the woods after all this time?"

"I don't know." Harry checked the side mirror, shifted into first gear and got back on the road, thinking about that day almost thirty years ago. "We went right out of the gate and got on the two-lane road heading to Munich, just like we're doing now. I could see SS guards, eight men in two kubelwagens driving close behind the truck. I remember looking through the slit in the tarp, seeing forest, walls of trees on both sides of the road. Prisoners packed together, the heat from the bodies. The Nazis called it *sardinpackung*, packed like sardines. I remember seeing a concrete marker: *Dachau 4 km*, on the other side of the road. And then the truck slowing and turning into the woods, the back end bucking, going through the trees, and then panic because all at once we knew we weren't being transferred to a sub-camp."

"What'd you think?"

"I knew."

They rode in silence for a few minutes, Harry clocking four kilometers on the odometer. They passed stands of trees, and a couple factories, and houses built in the green hills to the east. Everything looked different. The road was wider and there were billboards now, advertising beer and lodging, the 1972 Olympics coming to Munich. He drove a little farther—it was just by feel now, pulled over next to a wooded area, glanced at Cordell.

"This the place, Harry?"

"We'll see." It was just over four kilometers from Dachau. But Harry admitted to himself they could've been off by a hundred yards or half a mile. He got out of the car and went to the trunk, opened it and took out the shovel, leaned the handle against the fender, closed the lid. Cordell was standing next to the BMW, watching him, lighting a thin brown Davidoff.

"Ready?" Harry said.

They went in the woods, Harry picturing what it looked like that day thirty years ago, seeing the scene in his memory, seeing himself moving uphill through the trees behind the truck and the kubelwagens, running for a few minutes until the truck stopped. He remembered the clearing, thinking at the time how odd it was. The trees just ended, and he was looking out at flat hectares of farmland.

They walked due west from the highway for fifteen minutes, Cordell next to him, saying, "Anything look familiar?"

"Trees," Harry said.

"Trees, huh? That suppose to be funny? I'm gettin' eaten alive. These Kraut skeeters like dark meat."

Harry said, "Why don't you go back sit in the car, I'll look around a little longer."

"What am I going to do in the car?"

"Listen to the radio. You like yodeling?" Harry said it straight.

"Huh?"

"Find yourself a nice yodeling station." He grinned. "Do me a favor, will you? Get the car and drive back toward Dachau a kilometer or so. I'll walk through the woods and meet you." He handed Cordell the keys.

Cordell liked the idea. Get away from the skeeters. He was no Boy Scout, didn't like communing with nature. He wanted to help Harry but this idea was fucking crazy. He got in the car, adjusted the seat, looked in the rearview mirror, looked through the windshield, saw a car coming toward him on the other side of the road, let it pass and made a U-turn, on the highway now, moving. Watched the odometer and when the number rolled over he slowed down and made another U-turn, pulled off the road and waited, left the motor running, turned on the radio, something classical, turned the dial, heard yodeling, no shit. Man, it was funny. He tried it, no fucking way. Dude singing:

Yodel-oh-ee-dee-yodel-oh-ee-dee,

Diddly-odel-oh-ee-dee,

Yodel-oh-ee-dee-ay-dee...

Cordell thought he could bring yodeling back to the D, give it some attitude, see what the brothers thought. He took the sterling silver cigarette case out of his shirt pocket, opened it, took out a Davidoff, tapped it on top of the case, lit up, wished it was a joint, but liked the look of it, skinny bad-ass cigarette.

He turned off the car, rolled down the window and waited. Heard the clock ticking. Felt the wind shake the BMW when a car passed by. Sat there twenty minutes, then thirty, saw something out of the corner of his eye, looked like Harry coming out of the woods. He watched him all the way, watched him open the door, get in with the shovel. Man looked stressed. "What's up, Harry? Want to keep going?"

Shook his head. "This is crazy," Harry said.

Cordell was right there with him on that. "What you want to do?"

"Go back to Munich."

Cordell checked the mirror, put it in gear, got on the road. He was hungry, thinking about some food, and then some poon, in that order. He'd gone maybe a klick when he saw Harry look at him.

"Pull over, will you?" Harry said.

He did, noticed they were back where they started, saw tire tracks in the gravel.

"This is it. I'm going to give it one more shot." Harry said, like he apologizing.

"Whatever you want to do."

Harry got out with the shovel and Cordell watched him walk to the woods, disappear in the trees. Wished him luck even if it was some grisly shit he doing. Cordell thinking how they met, and now how they were friends. Sure, part of it was circumstances. Two strangers from the D, meeting in a strange motherfucking land. But was more than that. Cordell liked the dude.

Cordell drove south this time, went exactly a kilometer, pulled over and waited. Same drill as before. Put the seat back as far as it would go, got comfortable. He was thinking about his situation: out of the army, almost out of money, had to go back to Detroit get his stash. Thirty thousand dollars hid at his momma's house. Only problem, he wasn't in the service no more. Go home, they make him do his time? But first they got to find him.

He saw something in the mirror, car coming. It slowed down and pulled up behind him.

141

Chapter 20

Harry drove the curved tip of the shovel into the soft ground, levered the handle back and brought out a shovel full of dirt. Dug down a foot or so, didn't find anything, and moved along the edge of the clearing covered with grass, leaves and pine needles. Was he in the right place? There was no way to be sure. The scenery looked different than he remembered it. The trees, mostly pines, were taller, and far in the distance was a factory, a series of low-slung buildings and an asphalt parking lot filled with cars, spread out on what might've once been farmland. It was the open angle, the view beyond the forest that seemed vaguely familiar. One hundred yards from where he was standing was a steel chain-link fence marking the perimeter of the property.

He tried to picture the pit, tried to calculate where it was in relation to the tree line. Harry moved along the edge of the clearing, went ten feet out and sunk the shovel in the soil again. Dug a hole a foot and a half deep. Nothing. Now he went out farther from the tree line, drove the shovelhead into the ground, dug down and hit something. It felt like a root. He cleared the earth around it, and wedged the tip of the shovel under it and it came up, a stick caked with dirt. He bent down and picked it up. But it wasn't a stick. He wiped it on the grass to clean it and now recognized it as a human bone, a piece of a leg, one end brittle, decayed.

Harry dug around the hole, clearing more dirt, making it bigger and deeper, found a stained, tattered piece of cloth, part of a striped Dachau uniform—the number 027 still legible. But now he felt guilty for disturbing the grave of his parents and so many others. Filled in the hole and scattered leaves and pine needles over it.

He moved back toward the tree line, heard the hum of a motor, looked up, saw the Zeppelin coming in just over the treetops, casting a shadow, man with a gun in the open window of the gondola. He dropped the shovel and ran.

Rausch told the pilot to go in as low as he could. He saw Harry Levin at the edge of the trees, a clearing behind him, holding a shovel, and fired a burst from the silenced machine gun, rounds chewing up bark, blowing off branches, Levin running and disappearing in the forest.

The airship spun around, hovering and then gliding back the way they had come, Rausch scanning the ground, looking for any sign of movement. The gun felt good in his hands like it was part of him. He saw Levin appear from behind a tree, emptied the magazine, ejected it, popped in a fresh one, racked it and kept firing, pieces of bark and branches flying. They hovered and waited. He looked down, the floor of the gondola littered with shell casings.

They glided south fifty meters, Rausch and a spotter next to him with binoculars, looking for any sign of movement. He did not see anything. The Zeppelin drifted east and then north, circling back around to where they had started.

He directed the pilot to go west and south this time, making another circle, gliding over treetops. Nothing moved. And now Rausch believed he had shot Harry Levin and Levin was somewhere down there wounded, or more likely, dead. The only way to be sure of course was to land the airship and search the area. They flew back to the clearing. The airship went down close to the ground. Rausch jumped out with the machine gun and went into the woods.

Harry had been lucky, that's all there was to it. There were trees to take cover behind, trees to hide him as high-velocity rounds tore up everything around him. It had all happened so fast he hardly had enough time to react. The Zeppelin circled around a couple of times, Harry burrowing half under a fallen tree trunk. It continued on, going north, and disappeared. He got up and hid behind a giant oak tree, gripping the Colt in his right hand.

He looked in the direction the Zeppelin had gone and thought he saw something, and then did, someone coming toward him, moving through the trees, a dark shape carrying a machine gun on a strap around his neck, holding it with two hands across his chest. Harry went down on his knees. The man, dressed in casual attire, like he was going out to dinner and a movie, passed right by, and Harry recognized Rausch.

When the bodyguard disappeared from view Harry took off, went back toward the clearing, taking cover just inside the tree line. He saw the Zeppelin hovering about ten feet off the ground over the grave site.

Twenty minutes later the bodyguard returned, got back on the airship, and Harry watched it rise up over the trees, heading for Munich. This time he was reasonably sure it wasn't coming back.

Harry came out of the woods, sweating and filthy, clothes covered with dirt. He stood on the side of the highway, looking down the empty road in both directions. Cordell was gone, of course he was. Probably saw the Zeppelin and took off. Harry didn't blame him. This wasn't his fight, but there was another possibility. He'd been kidnapped. The Zeppelin had radioed their position, and Hess dispatched a gang of Blackshirts. That seemed more likely.

He checked his watch. 4:30. He was supposed to be at Martz' house in an hour for the phone call with Joyce. He wasn't going to make it. Looked at his options, realized he didn't have any. Walked on the side of the road, ducking back in the trees when he heard a car. Made it to Dachau in thirty-two minutes, looking around, nervous, studying everyone he passed. He stopped at the Hofgarten, needed time to think, compose himself, and he was dying of thirst. He stood at the dark bar, ordered a beer, and drank it fast, men lined up on both sides of him, holding the handles of their mugs, talking and drinking.

He had to go to the police station, tell them what happened. They were going to think he was crazy. He recited the lines in his head. "I was in the forest looking for a mass grave of Jews killed by Ernst Hess and his SS guards on April 2, 1942. His bodyguard came in a Zeppelin to kill me with a machine gun. Oh, and my friend and rental car disappeared." He told them that, they'd put him in a padded cell. And yet, it was all true.

Harry walked in the police station that was as quaint and Bavarian as the town, and talked to a cop sitting behind a heavy desk. He had dark hair, a dark mustache, and wore a blue uniform with matching tie and epaulets, the word Polizei over the left pocket in white letters. Harry spoke German, told him he'd been with his friend, Cordell Sims, in a rented BMW. He stopped to take a leak in the woods, and when he came out the car and Mr. Sims were gone. Harry took out his wallet and showed him his driver's license.

As it turned out, Herr Sims—who had no identification—was in a jail cell. The police thought he had stolen the vehicle and were holding him until an investigation could be completed. Another bizarre turn of events. The BMW was in the police-station parking lot. Harry told him to check the rental agreement in the glove box and that should clear things up.

It did, but an hour passed before Cordell was released. He didn't say anything till they got in the car and were pulling out of the station parking lot.

"Didn't mean to leave you there, Harry. But didn't have a choice in the matter." He opened his cigarette case, took one out and lit up. "Question is, how'd you know where I was at?"

"I didn't," Harry said. "When I came out and the car was gone, I figured you'd been kidnapped. There was no place else to go."

"It was a mind fuck, Harry."

"I hear you. Had one of my own." He told him what happened, Cordell's eyes on him, blowing smoke out the side of his mouth against the windshield, holding the cigarette with his thumb and index finger like a comrade from Minsk.

"You like livin', Harry? 'Cause you want to continue, I suggest you get the fuck out of here."

"I can't."

"You can't, huh? Why's that?"

"Something I have to take care of."

Chapter 21

The uniform was tight through the shoulders but fit good enough. The cap hid his face and he had shaven off the mustache and goatee to further disguise himself for the occasion. His daughter Katya had said, "Papa, you look so different, so much younger." Hess carried a square box filled with newspapers to give it weight, plus a couple items he would need, the box wrapped in brown paper, an ordinary parcel delivered by an ordinary postman. Nothing to call attention to himself, or arouse suspicion in this quiet neighborhood.

The package was addressed to Wilhelm Martz, Kreuzstrasse 47. Hess rang the doorbell and waited. The door opened a few inches. A woman with dark hair and round glasses stood back in the shadows of the interior, eyeing him with suspicion, as if postmen were not to be trusted.

"Special delivery for Herr Martz." He smiled like a friendly jovial uncle. "It looks important. Maybe filled with money, you never know." He smiled again.

"Will you leave it there on the stoop, please?"

"Herr Martz himself must sign for the package. New postal regulations. Is he at home?"

"Please, wait there, I will tell him." She closed the door, but not all the way.

Hess waited a few seconds, gave her time to move into the house, pushed the door open, slipped into the dark foyer. There were rooms on both sides. Straight ahead, down a short hallway was a staircase that led to the second floor. He didn't see or hear anyone. Rausch had been watching the house and was sure only Herr Martz and his daughter were there.

He put the package down, leaned it against the wall in plain view, knowing it would confuse them. Now he pushed the door and heard it click as it closed and locked. He moved to his left out of the foyer into an elegantly furnished room with a view of the street. Hess sat on one of the comfortable upholstered chairs and waited. A few minutes later he heard them talking, coming toward him down the hall, he could feel his pulse quicken.

"What is it?" a man's voice said. "I'm not expecting anything."

"I don't know. You have to sign for it."

"That's crazy. Anyone can sign for a package."

"It's what he told me."

Hess saw them walk past him into the foyer, footsteps on the hardwood floor.

"That's strange," the daughter said. "It's the package."

"I thought I had to sign for it."

This was perfect. They had no idea what was happening. Hess was grinning, enjoying their confusion. He almost laughed. He could hear Herr Martz shaking the box.

"What do you think it is?"

"I don't know," Herr Martz said.

"Why don't you open it?"

They came into the room, the old man ripping the paper off it. Hess stood, drew his Luger, aimed it at them and said, "It's just some old newspapers."

"Ernst Hess," the old man said, catching him by surprise.

"Have we met?"

"Not formally. But I remember you."

"I am flattered," Hess said.

"Don't be. It isn't a compliment."

"You still think this is Nazi Germany? You can walk into our home?" the daughter said with considerable umbrage and hostility. "What do you want?"

Hess grinned. She was tough. If they had all been as tough as her exterminating them would have been a lot more difficult. But then, her generation had learned from the mistakes of their elders. "Where is Harry Levin?"

"How do we know?" the daughter said.

"But you know him."

The old man said, "His parents were my friends before you murdered them."

Hess wasn't expecting that. "Why was he in the forest outside Dachau with a shovel? What was he looking for?"

"Why don't you ask him?" the daughter said.

"I am asking you."

"We have no idea what you are talking about," Herr Martz said.

"Let me help you." Hess took a black-and-white photo out of his shirt pocket and handed it to him. "Harry Levin drove here yesterday. You gave him a shovel." He pointed with the barrel of the Luger.

The old man said, "He is doing this for me. Digging up lilacs in the forest to transplant in my garden."

He was digging up something. The mass grave of Jews was in that general vicinity, but how would Harry Levin know about it unless he was there? Was this possible?

Hess took them down to the cellar, made them undress and kneel on the brick floor. He tied their hands behind their backs with the rope he had brought in the box. The daughter had a remarkable body, full breasts, and slender waist, round hips, a high backside. He could feel himself getting aroused. That was part of the pleasure. "Was Harry Levin at Dachau?" He would have been a teenager and there were not many that young.

The old man said, "I remember one day prisoners were packed in the back of trucks and taken somewhere. The trucks would return for more. Almost six hundred people disappeared that day. We were told they were being transferred to a sub-camp to work in the factory."

Hess said, "Were Harry Levin and his parents on those trucks?"

"You didn't kill everyone," the daughter said. "You weren't paying attention. That was your mistake. There are witnesses. Survivors. They came out of the grave and now they are coming after you."

Hess walked up and placed the barrel tip of the Luger against the old man's temple. "Tell me the names of these witnesses." He said it looking at the daughter, eyes moving down to her beautiful breasts, making the old man's life or death her responsibility.

It was 6:27 in the evening when Harry dropped Cordell off. Sorry he'd missed the 5:30 phone call with Joyce. But they could reschedule. He went back to his hotel and phoned Martz. No answer. He was probably out to dinner. Martz was seventy-six. He had some quirks. Liked to eat early. If he ate too late he couldn't sleep. That seemed reasonable. Harry showered, dressed and tried him again. Still gone. He called Colette and told her he had to stop by and see Martz. He'd be over as soon as he could.

Harry took the elevator down, went to the bar and ordered a Dewar's and soda, nursed it and tried Martz again at 7:45, let it ring a dozen times. Nothing. Now Harry was concerned. According to Martz, he was a creature of habit. Got up at the same time every day. Had his meals at the same time. Went to bed at the same time.

Harry paid for the drink and took a taxi to Martz' house on Kreuzstrasse. The house was dark, but as he walked to the front door he could see a light on in the salon. He rang the bell. No one came. He heard the phone ring inside. No one answered it. Harry walked around the house, through the garden to the back door. Looked at his watch. It was 8:10. Again, his gut told him something wasn't right. Martz had a weak heart. Maybe he'd had a heart attack.

He looked around for a key. Checked under the doormat, under the copper planters that flanked the brick entryway, and realized Martz wouldn't leave a key. He was too paranoid. Harry scanned the back of the house and noticed Martz' bedroom window was open a couple inches. Under the window was a metal trellis crisscrossed with vines that extended seven feet up the back wall of the house. Harry grabbed the frame and pulled. It felt secure, bolted to the stucco wall of the house.

It was dark but there was enough light from a full moon to see what he was doing. Harry climbed to the top of the trellis, reached up and pulled the sides of the window open. He boosted himself up on the sill and climbed in. The bed was made, the room, like Martz himself, neat and tidy.

There were two more bedrooms down the hall, Lisa's and a guest room. He checked them, went downstairs. There was a box filled with newspapers on the living-room floor, the label addressed to Wilhelm Martz. He knew one thing, Martz wouldn't leave the place like this.

Harry went down the hall to his office. Martz' desk had been ransacked, drawers pulled out, papers strewn across the antique rug and hardwood floor. He left everything where it was, walked out and checked the rest of the first-floor rooms. Nothing appeared to be out of place.

The only part of the house he hadn't seen was the basement. He opened the door, turned on the light and went down the stairs. It was damp and musty, the only light coming from a single bulb hanging from the ceiling on a wire, but it was enough to see them, Martz and Lisa, on their stomachs on the floor. It startled him, took his breath away.

Harry stood next to them, felt sick to his stomach. They were naked. Both had been shot in the back of the head, blood pooling under their faces, running in dark lines like tributaries, disappearing under boxes stacked in the back corners of the room.

It looked a lot like the crime-scene photographs Harry had seen on Taggart's desk at the Washington DC police station. The bodies shot and positioned in a similar way, the bloodstains suggesting that Martz had fallen a foot to his right and was dragged next to Lisa. Harry wondered if there was some connection between Martz and Lisa and the Washington couple. Were they related? Harry went upstairs, called the police, asking for Detective Huber, and when Huber got on the phone, told him who he was and what had happened.

Harry could hear the sirens. He sat in an overstuffed chair staring out the front windows of Martz' house.

Within a few minutes, three police cars and an ambulance pulled up in front. He met the police at the door, Huber and three detectives. Harry led the way to the cellar, and stood off to the side with Huber six feet from the bodies. The medical examiner was squatting next to Martz and Lisa, measuring and chalking lines around them. Another detective was shooting photographs from different angles.

Harry stared at the bodies, noticed the locket Lisa wore on a chain around her neck was missing. He asked Huber if anything had been taken off the bodies. He shook his head. The missing locket got him thinking about the random items they'd found earlier at Hess' apartment.

Huber's gaze was fixed on the floor. He moved toward Martz, bent over and picked up a shell casing with the tip of his pen, turned it upside down studying the imprint on the bottom.

"What caliber?" Harry said.

"Nine-millimeter Parabellum."

Same kind he'd found at Hess' apartment. "What kind of gun fires a cartridge like that?"

Huber glanced at him but didn't answer. He brought out a small spiral notebook and a pen, made a few notes.

"What time did you discover the bodies?"

"About 8:20."

He was shorter than Harry had remembered, five eight maybe, with narrow shoulders, heavier from the waist down.

"Who are they?"

"Martz, an old friend of my family, and his daughter, Lisa."

Huber wrote in the notebook. "They live here?"

"Yes." He reminded Harry of photographs he'd seen of Himmler, same beady eyes and thin lips. Pictured Huber in an SS uniform.

"Why were you here?"

"I was worried about Martz. He had a weak heart. I phoned him a number of times and he didn't answer. I thought maybe he'd had a heart attack."

Two medical orderlies picked up the bodies and put them in black bags, zipped them closed and took them upstairs, one at a time on a gurney. All that was left was the chalk outlines of their bodies and the blood.

"Do you know who did this?"

"It was an execution," Harry said. "Reminds me of how the Nazis used to kill Jews. One shot to the back of the head."

"So you think the killer was a Nazi?"

"Or a neo-Nazi. Lisa works for the ZOB."

"I am familiar with the organization." Huber wrote in the notebook. "Why did you not mention this earlier?"

"I didn't think of it."

"This could shed a different light on the homicides."

"You think?"

"What is your purpose here in Munich?"

"Do I need a purpose? I was born here. I wanted to come back and look around, see my old house, check out the neighborhood."

"There is no reason to be defensive. It is a simple question." He paused. "You are staying at the Bayerischer Hof?"

"I moved. I'm now at the Königshof."

"If you think of anything else, call me." He took a card out of his pocket.

"I've already got one," Harry said, looking at the chalk lines on the floor. "What are you going to do about this?"

"Examine the evidence and see where it leads us."

Chapter 22

Harry went back to his hotel. It was 11:40. He was tired, sat on the bed and called the Washington DC Police Department, asked for Detective Taggart.

"Taggart," he said, coming on the line.

"It's Harry Levin."

"Harry, what's going on?"

"That couple murdered the night Sara died, were they Jewish?"

"Whoa. You trying to solve that one now? I can't give you information about a homicide investigation."

"These two cases might be related."

"Yeah, they were Jewish."

"How old?"

"He was mid-forties. She was ten years younger."

"Were they born in Germany?"

"How the hell do I know where they were born?"

"You found shell casings at the scene, didn't you?"

"How do you know that?"

"What caliber?"

"You're pressing your luck."

"What're you worried about?"

"Nine-millimeter Parabellum," Taggart said. "Two of them."

Harry could hear him drawing on a cigarette, blowing out smoke.

"What kind of gun?"

"Luger. That's all you get till you give me something."

"Anything taken off the bodies? Personal possessions: a ring, watch, bracelet, earrings, glasses?"

"Who told you that?"

"I'm guessing," Harry said.

"The dentist had a gold chain. It was broken. What-ever was hanging from it is missing." Taggart's voice sounding faint all of a sudden like the connection was fading. "Hey, where you at?"

"Munich," Harry said.

"Don't even tell me. Are you out of your fucking mind?"

"Hess shot the couple in Georgetown."

"Yeah? Why would he do that?"

"I don't know."

"The Krauts were right about you, Harry. You should see someone. Seriously. You're fucked up."

He heard static. Taggart had hung up.

He got to Colette's just before midnight. Stood in front of her apartment building, felt a cool breeze blow-ing up the street, saw a light on in her apartment. He moved to the door and pressed the button. A few seconds later she appeared in the window, looking down at him. She buzzed him in. He took the stairs. She was standing in the doorway when he got there, wearing a robe and tor-toiseshell glasses, hair up, looking sexier than ever. Harry kissed her hard and long, backing her into the apartment and closing the door while he was doing it.

When they finally broke for air Colette was smiling and Harry was too.

"Where have you been? Did you get a better offer?"

He told her about Martz and Lisa.

"My God, Harry, I'm so sorry." She put her arms around him. "What are the police doing? Do they have any suspects?"

"If they do, they aren't saying."

"Come in, have a drink, I'll make you something to eat."

Colette took him in the kitchen, sat him at the table and poured him a glass of chilled pinot gris. She cracked two eggs in a bowl and made him a ham and cheese om-elet, served it with a little salt and pepper sprinkled on top. She sat across the table and watched him eat, devour-ing the omelet in six bites, guzzling the wine.

"Harry, you were starving. Can I get you anything else?"

"What about your photographs?"

"You have to see them."

She walked out of the room and came back with two stacks of prints. Handed Harry the first one, stood by his side while he shuffled through them. There were a couple long shots of the MC and the uniformed Nazis on the dais.

"I showed these to a former teacher this afternoon. Dr. Ritmeier, an expert on Nazis past and present. The MC is Franz Stigler, head of a local Blackshirt faction. By day he's an electrician." She paused. "Dr. Ritmeier doesn't think the men on the dais are real Nazis. He tried to match the names and faces with known SS personnel at the camps and couldn't."

"These neo-Nazi idiots are being duped, huh?"

"Isn't it amazing."

"What about Hess?"

"Dr. Ritmeier has no information or evidence of Hess being sympathetic to their cause. It would be a serious conflict of interest."

Knowing it and proving it were two different things. The other photos showed the Nazi banners, cheering Blackshirts on their feet, raising their ax handles, showing Nazism was alive and well in Munich. He glanced up at her.

"What do you think?"

"They're great. You really captured it," Harry said. "Let me see the others?"

She handed him the second stack and sat next to him. Individual tabletop shots of the things they'd found in the drawer at Hess' apartment. Souvenirs Hess had taken from the people he'd killed. He'd bet the gold Star of David in the photograph he was looking at matched the chain the dentist in D.C. was wearing.

She got up, stood next to him and put her hands on his shoulders. He untied the sash and opened the robe. She was naked underneath. He kissed her white creamy stomach, moving up to her breasts, lingered there for a while, stood, kissed her mouth and she led him to the bedroom.

She took off her robe and kissed him and helped him off with his jacket and sat on the edge of the bed, naked, grabbed his belt, pulling him toward her and unbuckling it. He unbuttoned his shirt and took it off, slipped out of his pants and underwear and sat next to her. Now she got on her knees, sexy blue eyes looking up at him behind the tortoiseshell frames, and he forgot about everything that had happened earlier.

Chapter 23

In the morning, Harry took a cab back to his hotel. He got out at Königsplatz, stopped at a newsstand to buy a paper and that's when they got him. He was glancing at the front page when the car pulled up and the doors opened. He heard the quick beat of footsteps on the sidewalk, and then he was lifted off the ground before he had a chance to react. Two Blackshirts carried him to the back of a Mercedes sedan, threw him in the trunk and closed the lid. He heard the tires squeal, felt the car take off, Harry on his side, trying to hold his position.

There was a lot of stopping and starting as they drove through the city, and then he could feel the big sedan accelerate and maintain a constant speed.

He knew who they were and who they worked for and it didn't look good. But Harry had one thing going for him—a .38 Colt with a five-shot load tucked in his belt behind his back. They'd missed it or hadn't thought to look.

At 9:28 he felt the Mercedes slow down and turn to the right. Harry drew the revolver, put the hammer on a loaded chamber. Turned his body, legs bent, feet on the bumper side, gripping the Colt with both hands. The Mercedes hit a stretch of irregular ground and bucked up and down for a while before it stopped. Harry's guess, they were in the woods somewhere and his time was up. He heard two doors open and close and movement on both sides of the car. The trunk lid sprang up. He saw two of them, eyes squinting, trying to adjust from darkness to bright light, seeing trees behind them.

They reached in to grab him. Harry pointed the Colt, fired. Shot one and then the other, both in the upper chest.

They staggered back and went down. He climbed out of the trunk, shot the driver as he was getting out of the car, turning with a shotgun in his hands. Went down and didn't move. Harry slipped the Colt in his pants pocket, picked up the shotgun, and racked it.

He was in the woods surrounded by pine trees. Stood over the two Blackshirts behind the car, aiming the shotgun. Both alive, staring up at him, but not for long based on the amount of blood. Both looking at him surprised. Where'd he get the gun? In German Harry asked who'd sent them. Neither one answered. He could see blood bubbling out of their mouths, and then they were gone.

He tossed the shotgun in the trees, stepped over the third Blackshirt, and got in behind the wheel. The keys were in the ignition. He started the car and drove out of the woods, spun around on the shoulder and went right on the highway. He saw a sign for Munich, 10 km. Harry knew that everyone connected to him was at risk now. He stopped at a gas station on the highway, called Colette. No answer. And remembered her saying she was going to Nuremberg to interview a Jewish couple that had been attacked by Blackshirts two days earlier. He hung up, tried Cordell's hotel, asked for him, let it ring a while and hung up.

Cordell had slept late, window open, cool night air coming in, all snuggly and such under the eiderdown comforter. Germans might be cold, but they knew how to stay warm. Didn't want to get up. But at 10:04, he forced himself, got in the shower, stood under the hot water for fifteen minutes, thought he heard the phone.

Got out, dried himself, stood at the sink, towel around his waist, shaved, checked himself out in the mirror. Brown eyes, nice straight teeth, chocolate-colored skin. Afro coming back, had like two inches up there. He turned his face right and then left, admiring his jaw line, his profile.

Ladies grooved on him. Before the service he'd been bangin' LaDonna, M'shell, Tifany, Bernita and Rochelle, shuffling them in and out of his crib, each thinking she the one. Now thinking back, it had been a lot of work.

Maybe he didn't need five at once. Did one, had to get ready for the next. Once, done all five the same day. Was so sore Mr. Johnson had to lay low, take some time off, Cordell horny all of a sudden, thinking about it.

He heard Marvin in his head, danced into the bedroom, took off the towel, threw it on the bed, reached in his duffel, grabbed a pair of boxers, slipped them on, singing:

Ain't that peculiar?

A peculiar ality...

Now he was trying to decide what to wear, checking out his four leisure suits hanging in the closet. Wore powder blue yesterday. How about, go with the dark green today? Match it with the light green shirt had palm trees all over it.

Cordell had been thinking about leaving Munich. Had to get away from Harry, man was bad luck. Like upside-down horseshoes, broken mirror and a black cat all in one. Man needed a rabbit's foot in a bad way. Was thinkin' of takin' the train to Amsterdam, smoke some of that high-powered hootch was everywhere. Check out the red-light district, see what the Dutch ladies was all about. Sample some Netherland pussy.

Phone started ringing, and then a knock on the door. He looked through the peephole, saw a white dude, face distorted. "Still in here. Come back later." Phone kept ringing. He moved to get it, heard an explosion. Bullet blew through the door and the window behind him. Cordell ducked down behind the bed, got as low as he could. Two more rounds punched holes through the door. The phone was still ringing. Now the dude was banging against the door, putting his shoulder into it, molding splintering.

Cordell moved to the window, opened both sides all the way, got up on the sill in his boxer drawers. Door sounded like it was going to give. He bent down and squeezed through the window, standing on a narrow concrete ledge, looking down at the dumpsters below him in the alley behind the hotel, holding onto the window, afraid of heights, knees weak and rubbery. But he couldn't stop, moved across the ledge, taking little bitty steps to the end of the building and reached around the corner, tried to grab the downspout but was too far.

Harry was driving like a maniac through the city, traffic surprisingly heavy for a Saturday morning. Cordell's hotel was on Bayerstrasse just south of the train station. A few minutes later he pulled up across the street from Pensione Jedermann, a five-story building with a mansard roof, and saw four Blackshirts getting out of an Audi sedan parked in front.

Harry left the Mercedes at the curb, ran across the street and into the hotel. Saw the Blackshirts getting in an elevator. Harry crossed the small lobby, picked up a house phone, asked the operator to connect him to Cordell Sims' room. It rang a dozen times. He put the phone down, ran back to the Mercedes, got in and drove around the block. He didn't know what room Cordell was in or what floor he was on, or if he was even in the hotel at that time, but remembered him saying he had a great view of the alley. Harry drove behind the place, and there was a black guy in his underwear, standing on a narrow second-storey ledge. Behind him a Blackshirt with a gun was coming through the window. Cordell looked back at the guy, looked down at the dumpsters lined up below him and jumped. Harry heard him hit, saw him disappear under the trash. The Blackshirt aiming at the open dumpster, firing rounds that pinged off the metal.

Cordell rose up out of the garbage, flipped over the side, landed on his feet and ran down the alley out of the line of fire. He was fast. Harry followed in the Mercedes, clocked him doing twenty, pulled up next to him, side window down.

"Man, what you doing?" Cordell said, slowing down, stopping, body bent over, holding his knees, breathing hard.

"Need a lift?" Harry said.

Cordell went around the front end of the car and got in next to him, grinning. "Harry, you never cease to amaze me. Where the fuck you come from?"

"I was in the neighborhood."

Peter Leonard

"In the neighborhood, huh? Where'd you get this?" Cordell said, nodding, eyes moving across the dash.

"I borrowed it," Harry said, accelerating down the alley.

Cordell shook his head. "You somethin' else, Harry."

He glanced at Cordell's boxers. "That a new look you're trying out?"

"It's part of my new Save Your Ass line. Like when crazed neo-Nazi motherfuckers try to bust down your door, don't have time to get dressed."

"I wouldn't have thought you were a boxer man."

"Why is that?"

Harry said, "They don't seem fly enough."

"Oh, fly, huh? 'Cause you now an expert? Got nothing to do with fly, Harry. Got to do with comfort. Freedom. Understand what I'm talking about?"

"I had my boxer period," Harry said. "Switched back to briefs. I look better in them."

"Better for who?"

"Whoever I'm with."

"Listen to Mr. Vain himself."

He took a left and a right on Bayerstrasse. Cordell's hotel was behind them about a quarter mile. "We better go to the police."

"We tried that," Cordell said. "What do you think they gonna do?"

"Then we're going to have to pick up an outfit for you. Head over to Maximilianstrasse."

"Ever since I run into you, it's been an adventure," Cordell said.

Harry parked, took a business card out of his wallet and handed it to Cordell along with a pen.

"Yeah, Harry, I know where you work at."

"Write your sizes down. Shirt, pants, shoes. I know what you like. I'll see if I can find a Louis the Hatter. Pick you up a leisure suit, rhymes with pleasure, right?" Harry said, having a little fun with him. "Don't go anywhere." He was grinning when he got out of the car and walked down the street.

162

Hard to explain, Harry'd get him in trouble, show up get him out. Cordell didn't know what he'd a done, Harry hadn't come when he did. He checked the glove box, found the owner's manual and car papers, Benz was registered to Friedrich Acker. Wondered if it was reported stolen? Wondered if the police were going to show up like they did last time? Cordell promised himself he got out of this mess today he would leave town, not look back. He sunk down in the seat watched people walk by the car, no one really paying much attention to him, brother sitting there practically naked.

When Harry finally came back, he was carrying two shopping bags, got in the car, slid them over to Cordell.

"Here you go," Harry said.

He opened the first bag, looking at green suede knickers and a white shirt. "The fuck is this?"

"Selection wasn't good," Harry said. "It was the best thing I could find."

"Best thing you could find? You go to a costume shop?" Second bag had hiking boots and green knee-highs. "This some kind of a joke?"

"Try it on," Harry said. "It's temporary. Just till we get your clothes."

Cordell slid the shirt out, unfolded it, took all the pins out and put it on. Now he grabbed the shorts, slid into them. Put on the knee-highs and the boots. Saw Harry look over with a grin. Met his gaze. "Don't say nothing." He leaned forward, grabbed the rearview mirror, tilted it to the right and looked at himself. "Who am I suppose to be Harry, Hans the mountain boy? Feel like I'm in a Shirley Temple picture."

Harry started the car, checked the mirrors and pulled out of the parking space, punched it and they were moving in traffic.

"Where we going now?"

Chapter 24

"Lisa's office," Harry said. He parked, took the Colt out of his pants pocket and turned the cylinder to a live chamber. Two rounds left. He could feel Cordell's eyes on him.

"What're you going to do with that?"

He glanced at Cordell. "Defend myself."

"What am I supposed to do? Where's my gun at?"

"Stay behind me."

"Harry, you a bad-ass now. That right?"

He had two rounds in the Colt and five more in the safe in his hotel room.

They took the elevator up to the fourth floor, room 412, ZOB in black type, all caps, stenciled on the frosted glass panel in the door.

"What's ZOB mean?" Cordell said.

"It was named after a Polish resistance group during World War Two, the Żydowska Organizacja Bojowa. They fought the Nazis." Harry knocked on the door. No one came. He turned the knob. It opened. He stepped in, turned on the lights, saw something was different immediately. The bookcases were empty. The photos of at-large Nazis had disappeared from the wall. The top of Irena's desk that had been covered with stacks of files and paper was now bare, nothing on it. He took the Colt out of his pocket, holding it with two hands, Cordell to his right but behind him, crowding him a little.

"Sure this's the right place?" Cordell whispered. "Looks like they moved."

Harry turned to him, put his index finger over his mouth and walked into Lisa's office, aiming the Colt. It was in the same condition, no pictures on the walls, desktop clean, drawers empty. Not a piece of paper anywhere. Everything was gone.

He checked the other offices, checked closets and under desks, checked file cabinets. Everything had been cleaned out. Except for the sign on the outer door, it looked like the ZOB had never been there, never existed. Harry wondered how they did it, the manpower it must have taken to pack and move all that stuff so quickly. No sign of Leon and Irena either, but it was Saturday. Maybe they hadn't come in to the office. He knew they lived together, had their address back at the hotel.

"Now what?" Cordell said.

Rausch had watched his men surprise the Jew, pick him up and drop him in the trunk of the stolen Mercedes, and slam the lid closed. Over in ten seconds. Exactly the way he had planned it. He had phoned Hess mid-morning, telling him the situation had been handled, taken care of. "Forget about Harry Levin. He is gone."

"You are sure?" Hess said. "You saw the body?"

He was always skeptical unless he was involved. "I wouldn't be calling you unless I was," Rausch had said.

But now it was after 3:00, more than six hours since the Jew had been abducted and he had not heard from Trometer or any of them. He guessed they were in a ratskeller, getting drunk. He thought back, remembered exactly what he had told them. "Take the Jew in the woods, shoot him, bury him. Call me when you are finished." What did they not understand? The outcome seemed certain, foregone. But then, they were not trained soldiers, and Levin was unpredictable.

Rausch recalled the scuffle at the restaurant in Washington DC. He had underestimated him and look what happened. He glanced in the rearview mirror, ran his fingertip over the scar on his cheek, the cut that required four stitches to close, remembered the unassuming Jew throwing him over the table, plates and glasses shattering, landing on the floor.

Rausch had never lost a fight in his life. Harry Levin from Detroit had made him look like an amateur, embarrassed him. He remembered Hess, angry, questioning him on the way back to the embassy.

"What happened?" Hess had said. Make a mistake and he would rub your face in it, make you feel like a fool. "Maybe I need a new bodyguard, Someone younger, more capable."

"Maybe you do." Rausch wasn't going to play the game. He had just turned fifty-one. It sounded old, but he was in shape, ran a couple miles every day, lifted weights, boxed and spent time every week at the shooting range.

Then Hess smiled and patted his shoulder. "Arno, of course I am joking."

Rausch wasn't so sure.

The black man, Cordell Sims, was another story. He had jumped out a second-floor window into a trash bin and disappeared. What were the odds of doing that without sustaining injury? According to their contact at the Munich police, Sims had been a soldier stationed in Heidelberg before being dishonorably discharged for striking his platoon sergeant. The thought of it infuriated Rausch. Soldiers followed orders, you did what you were told. They should have put him in prison, or shot him. He would do it for them when the opportunity presented itself.

It was starting to get dark. The hotel lights popped on. Rausch sat in the Volkswagen, watching the activity in front of the hotel. Earlier he had gone to the lobby and used the house phone, asking for Herr Levin. Herr Levin did not answer, but it proved he was still registered.

Rausch had gone to the concierge's desk and said, "A friend of mine, Herr Levin, is a guest in the hotel. I want to surprise him. Can you tell me his room number?"

The concierge said he was not permitted to give that information.

Rausch placed a fifty-Deutschmark note flat on the desk in front of him. The man stared at the money.

"You are a friend," the concierge said, trying to rationalize taking it.

"*Ja*." Rausch forced a smile.

The concierge put his hand over the bill, scooped it up and put it in his pocket.

"Herr Levin is in Suite 7F."

Rausch found it and knocked on the door, waited thirty seconds, picked the lock, went in and closed the door. He stood and listened and heard the muffled drone of an airplane somewhere overhead, the faint sound of a horn honking on the street below. He walked through the salon into the bedroom. The bed was made. There were receipts on the desk: a beer garden in Dachau, car rental in Munich, an airplane ticket, Pan Am flight, Munich to Detroit but no date. He opened the closet. There were shirts, trousers and a sport jacket on hangers, a pair of brown shoes on the floor. There was a shelf with a safe on it. He tried with all his strength to pull it free but he could not budge it.

There was a shaving kit in the washroom, a bottle of aspirin, comb, toothbrush, and toothpaste, eye drops. He walked back through the bedroom, sat on a couch in the salon and waited.

They were walking toward the Mercedes when Harry noticed a police car double-parked next to it, two cops looking in the windows. He grabbed Cordell's biceps, steering him in another direction.

"Man, what you doing?" Then Cordell tuned in, saw what was happening. "Yeah, okay, I'm with you. Let's go this way."

They had walked a couple of blocks, hailed a cab and took it to Harry's hotel. They entered from the rear side, boosted themselves up on the loading dock, walked through the stockroom, moving past floor-to-ceiling shelves. Saw a couple of maids filling their carts with room supplies. No one said anything or seemed to notice them.

He turned a light on when they walked in the suite, Cordell trailing behind, wide-eyed, looking around the living room. Harry pointed to a cabinet under the TV. "Help yourself to the mini-bar. I think it has Courvoisier and I know it's got Coke." He sat on the couch, watching Cordell open the cabinet, staring at all the bottles:

167

soft drinks, water, juice, beer, and little airline bottles of whisky, vodka, gin, and assorted liqueurs. Cordell turned and looked at him.

"Want something, Harry?"

"Scotch and soda."

"Dewar's cool?"

Harry nodded. Cordell mixed the drinks in heavy lowball glasses, came over and handed him his Scotch and he took a sip. "Perfect." He looked at his watch. 5:15. "I've got to make a few calls," he said to Cordell. "Relax, turn on the TV. You can watch *Hogan's Heroes* in German. I'll be in the bedroom."

He walked in with his drink, sat on the bed, put his glass on the end table, picked up the phone and called Colette, assumed she'd be back from Nuremberg by now, but got her answering machine. "It's Harry. Meet me at Odeonsplatz at 6:00." He'd tell her what happened later.

Next he dialed the operator. Although he had never talked to her he felt an obligation to call Joyce, tell her what had happened. He asked for a US operator and then a listing in Palm Beach, Florida for Joyce Cantor. There was a J. Cantor but the number was unlisted. Harry told the operator it was an emergency and she told him to call the police.

His second call was to Lisa's partners, Irena and Leon. Harry tried the number, let it ring ten times and hung up. He went in the closet, opened the safe, picked up his passport, and slid it in his shirt pocket. He grabbed the extra ammunition, took out the Colt, opened the cylinder, ejected the spent shell casings and loaded three rounds in the empty chambers. He snapped the cylinder back in position, slid the gun in the waistband of his khakis behind his back. He went in the bathroom, threw the spent casings in the toilet and flushed it.

Chapter 25

Hess stood in front of the house at 64 Kaulbachstrasse at 4:52 p.m., holding the package under his right arm. He rang the buzzer and waited, brushed dandruff off the shoulder of the uniform, looked at his reflection in the glass, adjusted the cap, straightened it over his face.

A woman's voice said, "Who is it?" She spoke with a pronounced Polish accent.

"The postman." He liked saying it, thinking of himself as a common man everyone trusted. "Special delivery for Herr Lukiski."

"He is not expecting anything. Who is it from?"

"The name is Martz, a Munich address."

"What would Lisa be sending him?"

"Fräulein, I have no idea."

"No, I'm sorry. I'm thinking out loud. Leon is in the shower and I am cooking dinner. Will you leave it inside the door, please."

Hess found it interesting she would offer this information about what they were doing. It was because he was the postman. She trusted him. "No, I am sorry, you have to sign for it."

"Can you bring it up?"

That was what he was hoping she would ask. "Yes, of course."

She buzzed him in and he walked up the narrow staircase. She was standing in the doorway when he reached the top, an attractive woman with blonde hair, wearing an apron over a dark skirt and white blouse. He could smell onions cooking, he could hear music. Hess gave her an avuncular smile. Now he could hear a phone

169

ringing somewhere inside. She glanced back but made no move to answer it.

"You are working late," Irena Pronicheva said.

"The packages must be delivered." It sounded like something a friendly postman would say. He was surprised the Jews were still so gullible after all that had happened to them. It was difficult to comprehend.

"Do you have a pen?"

He patted his shirt pocket. "No, I'm sorry. Someone on my route forgot to give it back."

"I will get one, please come in.

He stood just inside the flat, watched her walk into another room and disappear before closing the door. If she recognized him Hess saw no sign of it. The grilled onion smell was stronger and it made him hungry. The music was Mozart, good old Wolfie, his opera *Don Giovanni*. He wondered if the average postman could distinguish one Mozart opera from another. He glanced around. A framed Picasso print over the fireplace mantel caught his eye, *Les Demoiselles d'Avignon*, from his proto-Cubist period. These Polish Jews were surprisingly cultured.

When she came back in the room his arms were raised, fingers pointed up as if conducting the orchestra, a nice touch for a postman.

"So you enjoy Mozart, I see."

He brought his arms down to his sides. "Very much."

"My favorite opera is *Die Entführung aus dem Serail*," she said smiling, animated now.

"I can understand why."

"I have a pen," she said, holding it up, showing it to him.

"Herr Lukiski must sign. The package is addressed to him."

She turned toward the darkness of the other rooms. "Leon, you have to sign for it."

Hess said, "Something smells like it is burning."

She swore in Polish. "Excuse me."

She turned and moved into the kitchen. He heard her shake a skillet on the stovetop. He shifted the package from his right arm to his left, and saw a man coming toward him from another room. Lukiski was big, bearish, long dark hair still wet from the shower and a full beard. Hess was surprised, expected someone more handsome and fit to be living with such an attractive woman. The idea of it annoyed him.

"For me, are you sure? What would Lisa possibly be sending?" He seemed to sniff the air. "Irena, something is burning."

From the kitchen she said, "I am taking care of it."

Lukiski glanced at him. "Where do I sign?"

"Right here." Hess pointed to the signature line.

He signed his name and Hess handed him the package. The woman came in from the kitchen as he was shaking it.

"Leon, what is it?"

"How do I know?"

"Open it, will you." She glanced at Hess. "Thank you very much. We won't keep you."

He drew the Luger from under his jacket. "I can't leave just yet. I must ask you some questions."

The phone rang. The woman looked over at it on the table next to the couch.

"What is this about?" Lukiski said.

"The witness," Hess said. "Is there somewhere we can go and talk?"

He brought a desk chair in from the bedroom, sitting with his legs crossed, Luger resting in his lap. He was looking at their backs, the two of them kneeling in front of him on the white tile floor, facing the tub. She was even more attractive without clothes, flawless white skin, and red nipples. Leon was short-limbed, covered with hair and looked to Hess like photographs he had seen of early man.

"Why are you doing this?" Her tiny voice echoed off the tile.

He was tying up loose ends. She turned her head, trying to look at him. They all did. In the face of death they did whatever they had to do to survive. "Turn your head back. Look straight." It had always been more difficult to kill someone who was looking at you. It became

171

too personal if you were making eye contact. It threw off your concentration. "Do you know who I am?"

"Hess," Irena Pronicheva said, voice accusatory. "I thought you looked familiar when I saw you come up the stairs but the uniform fooled me."

"Where is the woman, the survivor?" He knew she lived in Palm Beach, Florida, but not her address. He had gone through some of the confiscated files from the ZOB. He had listened to the illuminating conversation between Lisa Martz and Frau Cantor, the American Jewess explaining how they were going to prosecute that Nazi murderer and bring him to justice.

He was surprised to learn that five Jews had dug their way out of the mass grave. It did not speak well of their skill as marksmen. But there had been extenuating circumstances. Half of his men were drunk on schnapps. He should have waited until the job was finished before passing out the bottles, but the mass killings had disturbed a number of them, some became physically ill.

They had caught and shot three survivors the next morning, during the Jew hunt. He remembered finding the little kikes, thinking they had escaped and then realizing they were going to die. Seeing that had been one of his more pleasurable memories of Dachau.

And now, if he could believe what Rausch had told him about Harry Levin, there was only one witness left, and of course the journalist.

"Tell me about Frau Cantor. How did she survive?"

"A farmer took her in."

A traitor, Hess was thinking.

"She lived within a few kilometers of Dachau until the war ended."

Unbelievable. He had probably visited the farm, talked to the farmer. "Do you, by chance, know his name?"

"I do not."

"Would you tell me if you did?"

"No."

They were both moving, trying to ease the pressure on their knees. "I know you are uncomfortable. It will not be much longer."

172

"What do you have against us? The war ended twenty-seven years ago. We were not even born."

It was more complicated than that. But he wasn't going to try to explain it. He raised the Luger, aimed at the back of Leon Lukiski's head and felt a rush of adrenalin.

It was still pumping ten minutes later. He could feel his heart bouncing in his chest. Nothing like this pure high, this surge of power, fingers shaking as he wiped the blood off Leon's eyeglasses and slid them in his shirt pocket. He found a bottle of schnapps in a cabinet in the kitchen, poured a glass and drank it, trying to calm down.

Chapter 26

Harry called the valet and asked to have his car brought up and driven to a *gaststätte* down the street. He wasn't taking any chances. There was a sizable tip in it for someone. He and Cordell took the elevator down, walked out through the stockroom and down an alley. They came out on Königsplatz a block from the hotel. He scanned the street, didn't see any Blackshirts hanging around. They walked down to the beer garden and met the valet in the parking lot. Harry gave him twenty-five Deutschmarks and they got in the car.

"Harry, that was some slick shit. You like a spy or something?"

"Looking out for you," Harry said.

"Since when?" Cordell flashed a smile. "No offense, Harry, but I've got to get away from you."

"I don't blame you," Harry said.

"Always tell it like it is, don't you?" Cordell grinned. "Don't get me wrong, you cool, but you bad luck."

"I can't disagree with you," Harry said.

He drove to Odeonsplatz, parked and waited. It was 5:50 p.m. "I told Colette to meet us here."

At 6:15 Cordell said, "I don't think she got the message."

"She may not be back yet," Harry said. "I'm going to try her again." He could see a familiar yellow phone booth across the plaza. He opened the door and got out of the car.

Harry dialed Colette's number, got her answering machine again and hung up. He called the hotel, asked if he had any messages. Nothing. Went back to the car and got in.

"What's up?"

"Colette still isn't there."

"Try her later."

He drove to 64 Kaulbachstrasse, a tree-lined street in a university neighborhood, slowed down, pulled over and parked.

"What's this?"

"I have to stop here and see someone. It'll just take a few minutes." Harry glanced across the front seat at him. "Want to come with me?"

"Think I'll wait here."

Irena and Leon were in 2A, the upper floor of an old house. He stood at the door, pressed the buzzer. It didn't make a sound and he wondered if it was working. He tried the door. It was closed but not all the way. He pushed it open. The foyer was dark. He turned on a light and walked up the stairs. It reminded him of his parents' house, stucco walls, wood beam ceiling, simple architecture. He knocked on the door. "Irena, it's Harry Levin." He waited. Tried the handle, the door opened. He walked in, stood in the living room, faint smell of sautéed onions. "Anyone home?" The stereo was turned on but no music was playing.

He went in the kitchen, saw a frying pan on the stovetop, overcooked onions stuck to the bottom. He went back through the living room, down a hallway, wood floor, into a bedroom, green carpet, double bed, framed prints on stucco walls, TV on a pedestal table at the foot of the bed.

The bathroom door was closed halfway. He didn't want to barge in if she was taking a bath. "Irena, it's Harry Levin." As he got closer he could see a stream of blood on the white tile floor. He took another step, saw feet and legs, the naked bodies of Leon and Irena. He drew the Colt, cocked the hammer and went in. The tub and surrounding walls and ceiling were spattered with blood. He studied the scene, bodies positioned the way Martz and Lisa were, two shell casings on the white tile, lingering odor of dead meat, like the smell of a butcher shop. He heard footsteps in the hall behind him.

175

"Don't move," a voice said in German.

Harry looked over his shoulder at two Munich police officers, guns drawn, aimed at him.

"Place your weapon on the floor."

Harry bent down, laid the Colt on the white tile.

"Place your hands on your head."

Harry did, and one of the cops approached him, kicked his gun skidding across the floor, and cuffed his hands behind his back. The two cops escorted him through the apartment, down the stairs and out the door. Almost dark, sun fading, red highlights over the rooftops. There were two patrol cars parked on the street and more uniformed police standing in the yard. A crowd from the neighborhood had gathered, people staring at Harry as he came out. He walked past the first patrol car and saw Cordell in the backseat. Their eyes met, Cordell shook his head.

"You have a gun," Huber said.

"I better," Harry said. "The way things have been going."

"Do you know the penalty for carrying a concealed weapon in Germany?"

They were in an interrogation room, Huber sitting to his right, putting on his glasses, blank expression.

"We will come back to this. Why don't you tell me what happened."

"I was visiting friends," Harry said, stretching the truth a little.

"The people you visit do not seem to live very long." Eyes looking at him over the black frames of the glasses.

"They were dead when I found them."

Huber said, "Who do you think is killing these people?"

Harry didn't know if he could trust him, didn't know how much to tell him. Huber could have been a Nazi sympathizer for all he knew. "If I tell you, you won't believe it."

"The situation you are in, I think you had better."

"Ernst Hess," Harry said, letting the name hang. Huber kept his eyes on him, brow furrowed, serious, and

176

then a hint of a smile. More emotion than Harry had ever seen from him. "He's trying to cover up what he did during the war."

"What are you talking about?"

Harry told him.

"If this were true," Huber said, "why was he not prosecuted?"

"There were no witnesses," Harry said.

"But now you have come forward." He paused. "You make these accusations. What proof do you have?"

"Go to the morgue," Harry said. "The bodies are piling up. A few days ago you found an auto dealer and his wife, the Lachmanns, shot the same way as the others, but you haven't connected the dots."

"Maybe the dots lead to you."

Colette got back to her apartment at 6:30 Saturday evening, listened to Harry's message. She went to Odeonsplatz to meet him, arriving at 6:45. Walked around, didn't see him. Tried his hotel from the pay phone. He didn't answer. She went back to her apartment, checked her messages again, nothing from Harry. She called his hotel and left a message. Maybe he was out with his friend.

She tried him again first thing in the morning. He was still checked in but didn't answer. Now Colette was worried. She phoned Bernd Kramer, her contact with the police, and found out Harry was in custody at Stadelheim. Arrested for carrying a concealed weapon, awaiting arraignment.

Chapter 27

Monday afternoon, Colette was on the phone with her editor, Gunter, in Berlin, discussing the risks of running her story about Hess. "You'll get the photos and the article on Wednesday. Incriminating stuff. This should put a wrench in Hess' political future."

"I'm more concerned about your future as a journalist. Hess is popular, well liked. There will be a backlash. You could be a target. I'm not even sure Max will agree to publish it."

"Can you hang on?" Colette said. "Someone is ringing the bell." She put the phone down, crossed the living room and looked out the window, saw him and went back to the phone. "Gunter, just a minute, the postman is delivering a package." She buzzed him in and opened the door. Heard him coming up the stairs. "Thank you so much," Colette said as he approached, face partially hidden under the brim of the cap. He was carrying a small rectangular package, his shoes making a snapping sound on the tile floor.

She was wondering who it was from, glanced at the label on the box. "*Der Spiegel.*"

He looked at her and said, "The magazine?"

"I am a journalist."

"You have to sign." He patted his shirt pocket and the front of his uniform jacket. "Forgive me, I have misplaced my pen."

She noticed his manicured nails and shoes, handmade black leather like Max wore, her editor-in-chief in Berlin, the shoes contrasting the plainness of the uniform. "I'll be right back." She walked quickly through the apartment, glanced at the phone on the table, Gunter still on the line, went into her bedroom, closed the door and locked it. Knew she had only a minute or two before Hess came after her. The photos from the rally were in an envelope on her desk, Colette regretting now she hadn't sent them earlier. She tucked the envelope in her purse, grabbed her passport.

There was a sliding door that opened onto a small balcony. All the apartments had them. She slid the door open and went out. She had two chairs and a table and would sit there in the evenings and watch the sun set over the city. Colette slid a chair over to the edge of the railing, stood on it and jumped half a meter over onto the Steigerwalds' balcony. She knew they weren't home, tried their door, it was locked. She jumped to the Dauschers, looked back and saw Hess on her balcony. She tried the door. It opened and she went in and ran through the apartment. Opened the door, looked down the empty hall, and ran for the stairs.

Hess was wondering what she saw, what tipped her off. He didn't go after her. She was too young, too fast. He walked into the kitchen, noticed the phone off the hook and hung it up. A light was blinking on the answering machine next to it. He pressed the message button and listened:

"Colette, where are you? Call your mother."

"It's Gunter. How are you coming on the article? Call me."

"It's Harry. Meet me at Odeonsplatz at six." This one was dated the day before.

Now the phone was ringing. He let it ring and listened to the message: "Colette, Gunter, I was cut off. Get back to me."

Hess ejected the tape and put it in his pocket. He walked through the kitchen. Like the rest of the apartment, it was clean, spotless, nothing out of place. He admired the discipline required to maintain an orderly life. There was an address book on the counter. He put it in his pocket.

Off the kitchen where he expected a pantry was a windowless room with photographic developing equipment on a long counter: enlarger, safelight, timer, a plastic tub of processing chemicals and next to it a tub of water. Half a dozen black-and-white photographs were clipped to a drying rack with clothespins.

The photographs had been taken the night of the rally, high angles from the rear of the hall, capturing the frenzy and energy of the Blackshirts. His face peeking around the banner was featured in three of the pictures. They were extreme long shots, difficult if not impossible to identify him. There was a binder on the counter that had plastic sheets of 35 mm negatives organized in rows. There were individual photographs of the mementos locked in the drawer in his apartment, Jewveniers, as he thought of them, items he'd taken from the Jews he'd killed. Hess was shocked they'd broken into his apartment. He took everything. But the important question—had she made a duplicate set, and sent them to her publisher?

Harry had been in solitary confinement for two days, going crazy in the six-by-eight-foot cell that had a bunk, sink and toilet, and a barred, grime-stained window with a dim view of industrial Munich. Harry doing push-ups and sit-ups to burn off his anxiety. He'd been out once in thirty-six hours to shower and walk around a small concrete enclosure, the exercise yard, a guard standing by the door, keeping an eye on him. Harry had it to himself in the early evening, sun fading over chainlink fence topped with razor wire. The only other time Harry had been in jail was overnight in Washington DC. It was tough then and even tougher now. Not knowing what was going to happen, Harry assuming the worst, seeing himself going to trial, sentenced, doing time.

He heard a key scrape the lock. The door opened, a guard handed him a pile of clothes and told him to get dressed. The clothes were his, pale blue shirt, navy pants, navy blazer, black shoes and belt. Whoever had gone to his hotel room had a sense of style. The guard waited while he changed, cuffed his hands and escorted him upstairs. From there a detective took him outside and put him in the backseat of an unmarked Audi sedan.

Harry surprised to see Huber sitting next to him, wearing a tweed sport coat, looking over black horn rims, a large manila envelope in his hand. Huber leaned over, unlocked the cuffs, put them in his sport-coat pocket. The driver's door opened, the detective got in behind the wheel, started the car and they took off.

"What's going on?" Harry said.

"You leave Germany, I make the weapons charge disappear. This is the best offer you are going to get."

"What if I don't want to leave?"

"You go to trial. If the judge is lenient you are sentenced to three years in prison and given a fine. Tell me what you want to do."

"I see your point."

"I thought you would."

Huber handed Harry the envelope. Harry opened it and took out his wallet, passport and watch. He fastened the watch on his wrist. It was 3:45 p.m., Monday.

Huber took a Pan Am ticket out of his inside sport-coat pocket and handed it to him.

"What about my clothes?" He saw signs for the airport. Saw a plane take off, rising through the clouds, its turbines whining.

"Your bag will be there when you arrive in Detroit."

"Why're you doing this?" Huber continued to surprise him.

"You can't stay here stalking one of Bavaria's leading citizens. We have bodies, yes, but nothing to connect them to Herr Hess. You may have been a witness to murder thirty years ago, but proving it is another matter."

"He's going to keep doing it," Harry said. "I hope you know that."

"Let me worry about it."

They pulled up in front of the terminal. Huber escorted Harry to the gate, showed his ID to the gate agent and walked him outside, across the tarmac to the plane, a big blue-and-white Pan Am 747, the two of them standing at the bottom of the stairway. He glanced up and saw a silver Zeppelin drifting in the clouds overhead.

181

"Do not come back to Munich, Herr Levin. This time I could help you but I will not be able to again."

Harry walked up the gangway, and went in the plane. Showed his ticket to a stewardess and she pointed down an aisle. He was in 15A. Sitting in 15B, in the empty plane, was Cordell Sims, grinning in a claret-colored leisure suit.

"I wondered what happened to you." Harry took off his sport coat, folded it and put it in the overhead compartment, sat in the aisle seat. He looked out the window and saw a catering truck parked next to the plane.

"I got to tell you, Harry, sitting in lock-up I had my doubts."

"You're not alone," Harry said.

"And look at us now. So it's finally over, huh?"

"I don't know."

"You don't know? They kicking you out of the country. How many countries you been kicked out of?"

"Two. Both of them Germany." Harry paused. "They couldn't wait to get rid of us. Americans making trouble, reminding people the Nazis are still at it."

"But you want to stay, don't you? Get Hess. I see it on your face. I see you sneakin' off the plane. How they do in movies. Go through the galley while they loadin' the food on, hide in the caterin' truck."

"That's not a bad idea," Harry said.

"Whatever you do just don't involve me, okay?"

"I'm not going to do anything," Harry said. "I'm going home." That was the truth. He felt like he was letting Sara down, but what could he do?

People were getting on the plane now, coming down the aisles, carrying their bags, lifting them into the overhead compartments, squeezing into their seats.

"What's the first thing you're going to do when you get home?" Harry said.

Cordell flashed a megawatt grin. "Get me some trim pussy, fresh gash beef. Been three months. Not like you, Harry, man about town, banging the fräuleins."

"One," Harry said.

"What happened, you all break up, or what?"

"That's a good question. I'll have to get back to you on that."

He thought about Colette, had strong feelings for her, but what was going to come of it? Especially since he couldn't come back to Munich without risking jail time.

"Got one back home?"

Harry grinned, picturing Galina draping her trench coat over the banister, walking up the stairs naked, turning at the last second, looking over her shoulder at him, saying, "Harry, are you coming?"

"You do, don't you. Harry, you old hound dog."

"How about you?"

"Had five when I left. See where they at."

They flew to London, had a two-hour layover, and got on another plane to Detroit. Harry upgraded to first class, only saw Cordell one time when he walked up to the front of the 747 to check it out, see how the other half lived. Harry was sipping champagne, eating shrimp cocktail.

"Looks nice up here, Harry."

"It's not that good," Harry said, trying to make him feel better.

"No? Wanna trade seats? I'm back with the chickens and goats. Had something for supper didn't know what it was. Could not identify it."

Harry didn't see Cordell again until they landed and went through customs. They got their bags, walked outside. It was busy, crowded at 4:30 in the afternoon, cars stopping in front of the terminal to pick people up. Harry was taking everything in, happy to be home. He'd been gone eight days but it felt like a month. "You want to get together sometime, come out have dinner, give me a call. You've got my card, right?"

"S&H Recycling Metals on Mt. Elliot just east of Hamtramck."

"I'm impressed."

"Live on Hendrie in Huntington Woods," Cordell said.

"What if I want to reach you?"

"Yeah, for what?"

"Who knows," Harry said.

"Don't know my mom's still in the house, or if the house still there. Better let me do the contacting."

Harry offered his hand and Cordell shook it. "Till we meet again."

"Be cool," Cordell said, hoisting his duffel up on his shoulder. He crossed the street, heading for a bus that had just pulled up.

Chapter 28

Bergheim, Austria. 1971.

Colette had run out the rear door of the apartment building, got in her car and drove 150 kilometers south out of Munich her mother's chalet in Bergheim, arriving Monday evening at 6:45. Colette knocked on the door. Gretchen Rizik opened it, screamed, and hugged her for five minutes saying, "It is so good to see you. I can't believe you are here." Colette told her she had a couple days off and wanted to surprise her. Didn't mention Hess or what happened in Munich. Why scare her mother, make her worry? She would stay in Austria and lie low until the article appeared. Colette had mailed everything to Gunter on her way out of town.

When they were sitting at the kitchen table having dinner—Wiener schnitzel, roast potatoes and sauerkraut—Colette told her mother about Harry. "He's American, born in Munich."

"How did you meet?" Her mother excited, dying to know all the details.

"I interviewed him for the story I just wrote."

"How romantic," Gretchen said, holding up a forkful of sauerkraut but too busy talking to eat. "What is his name?"

"Harry Levin."

"That's a good German name. How old is he?"

"Forty-three, but seems younger," Colette said. "Eat your dinner."

"The food can wait, this is more important. What does he look like?"

185

"Handsome, mother. He has dark hair, good shoulders, and he's about this much taller than me." She raised her hand a few inches over her head. "He's a Holocaust survivor. Escaped from Dachau when he was fourteen."

"He is a Jew?"

"Yes, a Jew. Is that all right? You married an Arab."

"Of course. Is he rich?" Her mother smiled and ate the forkful of sauerkraut, finally.

"I didn't ask." Colette cut a piece of schnitzel. "The only problem is I'm here, he's in Detroit." Bernd had phoned her late morning to say Harry was going to be released in a few hours and deported.

Her mother finished chewing and dabbed her mouth with a napkin. "When are you going to visit him?"

"When he invites me."

"He makes you happy. I can see it in your eyes."

Her mother had purchased the chalet after the war, one of the thousands of refugees fleeing Germany. Her father had been a successful importer. He had left enough money, if invested properly, for Colette and her mother to live comfortably the rest of their lives. The chalet was three kilometers outside Bergheim, built on a hill with a northern view of the Bavarian Alps.

In the morning, Colette went to the village to buy groceries. She was going to make her mother spaghetti and meatballs for dinner. She walked out of the market and put her grocery bag on the front passenger seat. Drove out of the village and saw the Basilica of Maria Plain, with its black onion-domed spires against brilliant blue sky. She crossed the bridge over the Salzach and wound through the rolling hills.

Colette could see her mother's house perched on a hill from a kilometer away, snow-capped peaks rising up behind it. There was a dark Audi sedan parked in front of the chalet as she made her way up the long gravel road.

She parked and got out with the groceries, went inside and put the bag on the antique wooden table in the kitchen.

Rausch was sitting with Frau Rizik, talking and drinking coffee when he saw a dark-green VW drive up, then heard someone in the kitchen.

"Colette has returned. Dear, there is someone I want you to meet."

Just then, a younger, more attractive version of the mother came in the room. Rausch stood. Tried to hold back the smile.

"Colette, this is Herr Zundel. He was in the Heer with your father."

"How do you do," he said. "It is a pleasure to finally meet you." She stopped ten feet from him, seemed hesitant to come any closer. Hess had supplied the background on the father. He had been a lieutenant in the Heer, killed on the Eastern Front. "Your father was a brave man and a good soldier," Rausch said. "It was an honor to serve with him."

"Dear, come in and join us."

"In a minute," Colette said. "Excuse me. I will be right back."

She walked out of the room, seemed anxious to leave. Did she suspect something?

"Colette is a journalist," Frau Rizik said. "Works for *Der Spiegel*."

"Ahh, Der Spiegel, our most respected magazine. Impressive. She must be very good."

"I have all her articles. Would you like to see them?"

Colette had seen him somewhere, she was sure of it. And then he appeared like a snapshot in her head: getting out of the Mercedes in front of Hess' apartment building. He was the bodyguard.

She went through the kitchen and up the stairs to her mother's room, saw the city of Salzburg spread out through the picture window. On a shelf in the closet was a gray metal box. She opened it, slid her father's military sidearm out of a worn leather holster, remembering her mother had shown it to her years ago, saying she felt safer having it because she was living alone. Colette ejected the magazine, filled with bullets and snapped it back in.

She went down the stairs, the gun hidden behind her back, walked into the salon. They were gone. She looked out the rear windows and saw them on the deck, her mother pointing to the mountains. Probably telling him where she skied. Colette sat on the couch, holding the Luger under a pillow in her lap.

They came back in a few minutes later. Her mother saw her and smiled.

"So you decided to join us. I was just telling Herr Zundel your first article about the Berlin Wall won an award."

Colette said, "His name isn't Herr Zundel. He wasn't in the Heer with Father. He's a Nazi." She stood, pointing the gun at his chest fifteen feet away, nervous, trying to keep her hands steady.

"I am nothing of the sort," the Nazi said. "Put the weapon down, please. I have papers in the car that will prove what I am saying is the truth."

She saw his right hand slide inside his jacket. "Keep your hands where I can see them. I am nervous. I don't want to shoot you, but believe me I will." She glanced at her mother, who seemed frozen. "Call the police."

"You are making a mistake," the Nazi said.

"Dear, what are you doing?"

"He came here to kill us."

He smiled. "I will show you my identification."

"Keep your hands where I can see them. Mother, call the police." This time she raised her voice.

Gretchen Rizik moved toward the kitchen, keeping her distance from the Nazi. But he lunged at her, got his arm around her neck, hand going into the jacket, coming out with a matte-black gun which he pressed against her cheek.

"Put down the weapon," he said.

Colette had to do something, and do it fast. Focused on the bodyguard's big foot in a brown leather shoe, aimed at it—hands shaking, squeezed the trigger, the Luger jumping, her ears ringing. The Nazi was hobbling now, trying to stay on his feet, firing, her mother moving left, diving for the couch, Colette moving left, aiming at his chest, squeezing the trigger. The Nazi going backward, looking at her, trying to raise the gun and then he was on the floor.

Colette kicked the pistol out of his hand, but he was dead, eyes staring up at the ceiling. She searched him and found his billfold, opened it and took out his driver's license. His name was Arno Rausch, fifty-one, a Munich address. What was she going to do with him? Saw herself putting him in the trunk of his car and driving it into the Wallersee, a lake not far to the north.

Her mother was sitting on the couch. She didn't look good, face drained of color. "Are you all right?" Colette laid her down on the couch, tried to make her comfortable. "You're going to be okay," Colette said, wondering if she'd had a heart attack. She got up and called an ambulance.

Chapter 29

Detroit, Michigan. 1971.

First thing Harry did when he got home, he mixed a drink, bourbon and soda, sat at the kitchen table, listening to the messages on his answering machine, skipping through them until he heard Colette's voice.

"I have been so worried about you. My friend with the police told me what happened. I tried to visit but they would not let me see you. I am staying with my mother in Bergheim. Call me as soon as you can. I miss you."

Harry picked up the phone and got an overseas operator. He gave her the number and listened to it ring a long time before he hung up. He tried her apartment and got her answering machine. He had a bad feeling. It was 11:20 p.m. in Munich. He thought about calling Huber but decided against it.

Cordell got home at 5:25, opened the front door and went in the house. Looked the same as the day he enlisted, maybe worse. Shit everywhere in the living room, empty Popeye buckets, liquor bottles: pints and fifths scattered on the floor. Plaid sofa, fabric all tore, lamps without shades, holes in the plaster walls, ashtray overflowing with tan filtered cigarette butts, electric fan on, blade out of line. He could hear it scraping the mesh cover.

"Momma, you home? Where you at?" Dropped his army duffel on the floor in the hall, walked down to the kitchen, saw more of the same. Lightbulb hanging from a wire in the ceiling, dishes piled in the sink, bottles on the floor, empty refrigerator. His momma was some kind of fucked-up homemaker.

Cordell went upstairs, checked the bedrooms, found her lying next to some raggedy-ass nigger snoring loud like somebody working a jackhammer. She surprised him, opened her eyes, pulled the sheet up to cover herself. He moved to the foot of the bed, her eyes following him.

"Spook, what you doin here?" She'd been calling him that since he was a little boy afraid of the dark, fuckin' with him, makin' fun of him. "What you doin' home?" she said, slurring. "Suppose to be in the army."

"Got kicked out."

"Know what they goin' do to you?"

"No, what? You a lawyer?"

"Don't get smart."

"Not going to be around long enough to worry about it."

"Where you goin'?"

"Who's that?" Cordell nodded at the brother. Big man with a full 'fro.

"Reginald."

"Reginald, huh? Sounds like royalty, looks like a street trash."

"What you 'spect?"

He turned, walked out. Went to his old room, sat on the bed, stained mattress on a gray metal frame, no sheets or blanket. Sat, looked around. Had a desk and chair. Old beat-up dresser. Cracked shade covering the window. He pulled it up, saw the house next door, look about five feet away. He went to the closet, opened the door, all his clothes and shoes were gone. Must've sold everything to keep herself high.

Cordell brought the desk chair into the closet, positioned it against the back wall and stood on it. Pushed up on a two-by-six board in the ceiling until it moved. Loosened it, pulled it out, put it on the floor.

He got back on the chair, reached through the opening into the attic, felt around till his hand touched the shoebox. Slid it toward him and lifted it out. Took the top off, lookin at $32,550 and a nickel-plate .45. Proceeds from his time with Chill. Spent a lot on the bitches. Saved a lot, too.

Cordell ejected the clip, checked the load and popped it back in. Next, he counted out five thousand, split the pile in two, folded the bills and put them in the front pockets of his pants, wads bulging a little under stretch polyester.

He put the box back in the attic and replaced the board. He was in the hall on his way downstairs when his mother came out her room.

"What you doin', scratchin' around in there."

"Lookin' for my shit. Where's it at?"

"Gone, honey chile."

"So am I." He wondered if she'd seen him in the closet, could figure out what was happening? Looked in her eyes, saw she was still fucked-up. "Can I trust you not to sell anything else?" He'd brought the duffel up and changed into the dark-green leisure suit with the matching shirt.

"Can't promise nothin'."

"Well, Momma, thank you very much."

She flashed a stoned grin. "Just playin' with you. Your things be okay."

Cordell walked down 14th to the Boulevard, stood in front of the GM building, got a cab, took it to the Ponch, got a suite with a river view, could see the Ambassador Bridge and the Detroit city buildings. He went in the bedroom, stretched out on the bed, biggest one he'd ever seen, picked up the phone, called Bernita.

"Hello." Soft voice kind of sleepy like she was takin' a nap.

"How you doin', baby?"

"Who this?"

"Who you think it is?"

"Cordell?" Surprise in her voice. "You suppose to be in the army, ain't you? Germany or some such place."

"No, I in Dee-troit or some such place."

"What you doin' home?"

"Came back to check on my sweet potato girl."

"I seein' Pony now," she said, her voice sounding like she wasn't sure.

"What you doin' with that midget nigger?" Pony was like five five, little sawed-off nigger worked for Chilly.

"He around," Bernita said. "Takes me places, buys me things."

Why was he wasting his time? She started to say something else and he hung up the phone. Fuck Bernita.

Next he tried Rochelle. No answer. Tried LaDonna. Her voice said, "That you, sugar plum?"

How'd she know he was back? "You got me."

"Cordell?" Straight-up surprise.

"Who you think it was?"

"No one."

"No one you callin' sugar plum?"

"What you doin' home?"

"Ain't spendin' nothin' on no two-timin' bitches is what I'm doin'." He slammed the phone down. Called M'shell and Tifany. No answer. Nobody happy to see him. Leave town for two months, everyone forget about you. He called room service, ordered fried chicken, the whole dinner with yams and cornbread and two Courvoisier and cokes, feeling better, like his shit was comin' back together now.

"Way I see it you've got a couple major obstacles," Stark said. "Number one, he killed your daughter, so you're going to be perceived as a distraught father out for revenge."

"I told you about the woman, the other survivor."

"What's her name?"

"Joyce Cantor." Harry picked up his Stroh's and drank from the bottle.

"She credible?"

"I've never talked to her but from what I've heard her story's accurate, believable. She was there."

"You better get her on the phone, tell her what's going on."

"I've tried. Her number isn't listed."

"Where's she live?"

"Palm Beach."

Peter Leonard

"I'll get it for you."

They were at the Lindell AC having lunch, burgers and fries, Harry glancing occasionally at the Detroit sports memorabilia on the walls. It was crowded and loud. Jimmy Butsicaris, the owner, making his rounds, talking to four guys in suits a couple tables away.

Stark wiped his mouth with a napkin, took his cigarettes out, tapped one out of the pack and lighted it and left the pack on the table. Benson & Hedges 100s.

"My biggest concern from a legal point of view," Stark said, blowing out smoke, "you bring charges against Hess, a solid citizen, politician, successful businessman, Huber could tie you to the three neo-Nazis you shot. And he's got the murder weapon." Stark placed his cigarette on the edge of the glass ashtray.

"How do you know they found the bodies? And what connects them to the gun?" Harry said.

"That's the chance you take."

"What about the mass grave?"

"How do you put Hess at the scene?"

"Joyce and me."

"It's been thirty years. How can you be sure he's the right guy?" Stark picked up his hamburger and took a bite.

"I remember him."

"But you didn't recognize him when the DC cop gave you the mug shot," Stark chewing while he talked. Stuck his finger in his mouth and dislodged a piece of hamburger, looked at it and put it on his plate. "And you didn't recognize him in the restaurant, sitting at the table."

"I was distracted," Harry said. "Had a few things on my mind."

"You went to Munich to the man's house and didn't recognize him," Stark said. "When did this light bulb of recognition go on?"

"There was something familiar about him, but I didn't put it together till I saw him in a Nazi uniform."

"I have to tell you, it doesn't sound very persuasive." Stark put his napkin over what was left of the hamburger

194

and picked up his cigarette. "And since we're on the subject, here's another concern. Hess is a war criminal. He's supposedly killed or had killed anyone with a connection to his past. Am I right? You think he's just going to forget about you?"

"It's crossed my mind."

"I hope so."

Harry brought the Colt Python out and laid it on the table next to his plate.

"Jesus, put that away. Are you fucking nuts?"

He picked up the gun, slid it back in his sport-coat pocket. "Here's something I didn't tell you. The night Sara was killed a Jewish couple were murdered in Georgetown, shot in the back of the head. I saw photographs on Taggart's desk. Martz and Lisa were killed the same way. Nine-millimeter Parabellum shell casings next to the bodies. Fired from a Luger."

"What're you saying, Harry?"

"Hang on, it gets better. Before Hess hit Sara he'd been at a strip joint called Archibald's. Dancer named Coco said she was sitting next to him, touched his leg."

"Probably copping his joint," Stark cut in.

"Hess had blood on the front of his pants."

"Spatter from the Georgetown couple?"

"That's what I thought."

"You tell Taggart?"

"Yeah. He thinks I'm crazy."

"I can see why."

"It wouldn't have mattered. Hess has diplomatic immunity."

A waitress came and took their plates, asked if they wanted anything else, another beer? Stark shook his head. "Just the check," Harry said. "It's on me."

"Okay, big spender, thanks." Stark lit another cigarette. "Were the Georgetown couple survivors?"

"Taggart didn't know."

"How old were they?"

"He was forty-five. She was thirty-six."

"Maybe the parents crossed paths with Hess at one time. Knows their names?"

"Why would he go after the son or daughter? Doesn't make sense."

"When did it happen?" Stark said, flicking his cigarette ash.

"August 2nd, the night Sara was killed."

"All right. Let me see what I can find out."

Stark called him at the scrap yard the next day. "The Georgetown couple are Mitchell Goldman and Sherri Shore. He was a dentist, successful practice, recently divorced and engaged. She was his fiancée and former receptionist."

"Why would he get remarried so fast?"

"Maybe she was pregnant. Or maybe he's a glutton for punishment. I don't know. Both the dentist and the fiancée were born and raised in Baltimore. Both sets of parents also born and raised there. I dug a little deeper. Mitch Goldman's ex moved to Florida after the divorce and took her maiden name."

"What's so unusual about that?"

"Nothing unless her name happens to be Joyce Cantor. That the connection you're looking for?" He paused. "She works for Sunset Realty, lives in the Winthrop House. Condo, corner of Worth Avenue and South Ocean Boulevard. Trendy neighborhood. Phone number's 407-642-3655."

"She saw Hess coming out of a restaurant in Munich, recognized him, and went after him," Harry said.

"How come she recognized him, you didn't?"

"I don't know."

"Hess flew to DC to kill her. Shot the fiancée by mistake. Did the dentist, I'm guessing, 'cause he happened to be there. I wouldn't be surprised if he's got the same thing in mind for you, Harry."

"We know Hess is good at shooting unarmed people," Harry said. "Let's see how he does against someone with a gun."

Chapter 30

Hess flew first class Munich–London, London–Detroit with a passport identifying him as Gerd Klaus from Stuttgart. Going through United States customs, a dark-skinned agent—Hess would have guessed was Hispanic—studied his passport, taking his time, in no hurry even though there were many people in line behind him.

"What is your purpose for coming to the United States, Mr. Klaus?"

"Business," Hess said, friendly and polite even though it was demeaning to be interrogated by this Mexican.

"What type of business are you in?"

"Automotive parts."

"Do you have a business card?"

"Sure do," he said in his best American English. Hess had come prepared, handed the man one of his freshly printed cards that said he was Midwest sales manager. He had been speaking English for thirty years. He loved American cinema and had even perfected a Southern accent.

"Welcome to America," the Mexican said, stamping his passport and handing it back to him.

He had reserved an automobile at Avis, waiting for a bus outside the terminal with the other salesmen in suits and ties. He rented a silver Chevrolet Malibu, two doors and a long hood, that drove like a truck, the steering sloppy and loose. If this car was any indication of American innovation, they had a long way to go before they would catch up to the Germans.

He drove to Detroit. He had booked a room at the Statler Hotel on Washington Boulevard, handed his car keys to the valet, checked in and was escorted to a room on the seventh floor. He made an overseas phone call to his secretary, Ingrid, asking if Rausch had phoned. Rausch had gone to Bergheim the day before to dispose of Colette Rizik and her mother.

"No, I am sorry, Herr Hess, he has not."

That was unusual. But lately, Arno had seemed to lose his concentration. Hess gave her his phone number at the hotel.

At 4:00 p.m. Hess drove to a bar in a town called Allen Park, a gray single-storey cinderblock building, paint peeling, pickup trucks outnumbering cars in the parking lot. The inside was dark and crowded, men lining the bar, loud rock music playing. He was approached by a man in his mid-thirties, long hair pulled back and tied in a ponytail, muscular arms exposed in a sleeveless denim jacket.

"You Mr. Klaws?" he said, pronouncing the name wrong.

Hess nodded. He could see *Sieg Heil* tattooed on his right forearm.

"How was your flight over? I'm Buddy." He extended his hand and Hess shook it. "So you're the genuine article, huh? Never met a real Nazi before. Sir, this a real honor, I mean it."

He reminded Ernst of the Blackshirts, his own neo-Nazis, a generation that was missing something, a generation that would never measure up to the high standards or the high achievers of the Third Reich.

"Ever meet Adolf Hitler?"

"I was fortunate enough to make the Führer's acquaintance, yes."

"What was he like?"

"Charismatic, mesmerizing, a born leader."

"I'll bet. He's one of the greatest men that ever lived. I read *Mein Kampf*. Talk about a page-turner, I couldn't put it down." He glanced at the bar. "Want a beer or something?"

"Do you have the weapon?"

"Well, you bet. No time like the present, huh?"

Hess followed him outside to a red pickup truck parked in the lot.

"Step into my office," Buddy said, grinning.

Hess opened the passenger door and sat on the bench seat. Buddy got in and reached for the glove box, opened it and took out a blue steel semiautomatic with a suppressor on the end of the barrel.

"Here she is," Buddy said. "Silenced Walther PPK, exposed hammer, double-action trigger mechanism. Reliable and concealable. Magazine release button is on the left side of the frame, but as a former military man I bet you knew that. Holds seven plus one in the throat. And a box of extra rounds like your man Mr. Rausch specified. I myself prefer a higher-caliber weapon, something with knockdown power. What're you huntin', small game?" Buddy smiled again. "Extra ammo's in the glove box. Total for everything's eight hundred dollars."

More than twice what the gun was worth, the American Nazi taking advantage of him. Hess reached for his billfold in the inside pocket of his sport jacket, opened it, counted eight hundred-dollar bills out of a thick stack and handed the money to Buddy. He slid the gun in his right side pocket and put the box of cartridges in his left pocket. "Do you know a secluded area where I can fire the weapon?"

"Sure do. Tell you what, you can follow me or ride with me. Your choice."

Hess followed him out of Allen Park on a two-lane road to a rural area with farms on both sides of the road. Buddy turned left on a dirt road that went straight into woods, slowed down and parked on the side of the road. They walked through the trees, reminding him of the Vonderer Forest in Bavaria, big mature trees, high canopy of leaves. They walked in deeper and came to a clearing, a stretch of open grass that was fifty meters wide.

"Here you go. This is about as secluded as you're going to get."

Hess was going to try the Walther out on Buddy. Kill anyone who could identify him. But he might need another weapon or even the man's assistance with something. Keep your options open, Hess said to himself.

Buddy'd read about the Blackshirts this neo-Nazi organization in Munich, Germany and wrote a letter: *To whom it may concern*, saying he would like to start a Blackshirt chapter in Detroit, Michigan, USA. And if any of them were ever planning a visit to the...f A, he'd be honored to show them around. He'd even put some Blackshirts up at his house in Hazel Park, a suburb of Detroit.

He didn't hear anything for months, then got a letter from some guy named Arno Rausch saying a famous Nazi, Gerd Klaus, was coming to town and he could use some help procuring a firearm, a Walther PPK fitted with a suppressor.

Buddy knew just where to get it. He'd met Ed Stannard at the Gun & Knife Show at the Light Guard Armory a few years back. Ed, who everyone called "Ed the Head," dealt guns both legally and under the table. Buddy'd called him, told him what he needed and drove out to his farmhouse in Saline that had tall bushy marijuana plants growing around the outside, looking like overgrown shrubs.

The inside smelled like weed and Ed had guns spread out across the carpet of the empty living room. Ed'd screwed the silencer on the end of the barrel of the Walther and handed it to him.

"Here you go, bro." Ed'd said. "Don't get caught with the suppressor, they give you like ten years."

"Don't worry," Buddy said.

"Need any assault rifles? I can give you a real good deal."

"I'm all set," Buddy said. "But how about some ammo for the Walther?"

"No problem."

Buddy'd been a member of the Viking Youth Corps and the Imperial Aryan Alliance but was between organizations at that time. He had 88, neo-Nazi code for *Heil Hitler* tattooed on his left shoulder, and *Arbeit Macht Frei* on his right biceps, German for: "work makes you free." What was on the gates at concentration camps. And *Seig Heil* on his right forearm.

Buddy's dad, Herb, had been a member of the American Nazi Party and used to goose-step around the house in his Nazi uniform: brown shirt, black tie and pants, red, black and white swastika arm band, peaked cap with the Totenkopf emblem on it. His dad preached racial purity to Buddy and his sister Tanya. He'd said, "Immigrants, homosexuals, nigs and Jews were polluting our society." His dad and his buds would burn Mexican flags they called buzzard rags, and Israeli flags they called kike Kleenexes.

His dad used to get in arguments with the other Nazi Party higher-ups, and they even tried to kick him out. His dad had said, "I am a member of the American Nazi Party in perpetuity until voluntarily, or by natural or unnatural means I am so relieved." Whatever that meant.

In truth, Buddy thought his dad looked like a clown walking around, saying *Seig Heil!* And *Heil Hitler!* But Buddy liked the Nazis. Had read everything he could get his hands on about them. He loved the swastika and their uniforms and their cool black boots. He agreed with their ideology too about Aryan purity.

The next morning Hess drove by the scrap yard, a mountain of metal behind a warehouse and a small cinderblock building. He stopped on the side of the road and watched a crane with a grapple hook load metal scrap into the back of huge semi-trailers.

Hess turned around and drove through Hamtramck, a predominantly Polish town. He didn't have much respect for Poles. Germany had invaded Poland in 1939, taking over the country in a couple weeks. He remembered seeing newsprint photographs of German troops goose-stepping through Warsaw. He stopped at a pay phone, dialing the number for S&H Recycling Metals, getting ready to use a Southern accent and a name he had seen in the *Detroit News*.

A woman's voice said, "S&H, how may I direct your call?"

Hess said, "Is Harry there?"

"Who's calling please?"

"This is Ray Meade."

"I'm sorry, Mr. Levin's out of town. Sir, what did you say your name was?"

"Ray Meade, darlin'. When do you expect him?"

"Tomorrow afternoon. He's driving back from Pittsburgh."

Hess hung up the phone.

Fifteen minutes later he was parked on Lothrop near 14th Street in front of a brown two-storey brick house, the address Rausch had received from their contact at police headquarters in Munich. Hess was looking at a black-and-white photograph of Cordell Sims taken the night he was arrested. A big American sedan passed by him, moving slowly, three Negros in the front seat all turning, studying him.

He opened the door, stepped out of the Malibu, walked to the house and knocked on the door. Hess waited several seconds and knocked again. He peered in one of the front windows on the left, saw the decrepit condition of the interior and wondered if anyone was living there. He knocked on the door again and this time it opened. A hostile black woman, whose age he would have guessed at fifty, stared at him before she said anything.

"What do you want, get me out of bed I'm trying to sleep?"

"I'm looking for Cor-dell," Hess said. The Southern accent to his ear sounding effortless, authentic.

"Ain't here. You the dude he met over to Germany?"

"I am," Hess said, using the information to his advantage. "Do you know where I can find him?"

"No, but he gonna come back later get his things and go."

"Tell him Harry Levin stopped by, will you?"

"Yeah, you the dude he was talking about. Jewish fella, huh?"

"That's me," Hess said, smiling.

"Where you from with that accent?"

"Chattanooga, Tennessee originally."

"Dint think they had no Jews livin' down there."

"There are a few of us."

"Man name Harry Levin come by lookin' for you," Cordell's momma said, wearin' her stained light-blue robe, curlers in her hair.

"Harry Levin, you sure?" Harry didn't know where he lived.

"That's what the man said. You think I'm making this up?"

"What'd he want?"

"Asking for you. Did I know where you was at?"

It was strange. They'd only been back a few days, why would Harry be lookin' for him? Cordell opened his wallet, took out Harry's card, went in the kitchen, called the number and got the answering machine. A lady's voice said, 'You have reached S&H Recycling Metals. Our office hours are Monday through Friday seven a.m. to four p.m.' He left a message.

Cordell went upstairs, got his things, put the shoe-box in his duffel, told his momma he was leavin'. He'd picked up a Dodge Dart at a used car lot on Gratiot earlier that afternoon. Paid cash. $1,500. Ran like a top.

She said, "Leavin' for where?"

"Don't know that yet." But in the morning he was going to head toward Chicago. Start over.

The Negro, Cordell Sims, got out of a dark-blue automobile at 6:30 that evening. He entered the house on Lothrop and came out ten minutes later carrying a green military duffel. Hess followed him on Woodward Avenue to the Pontchartrain Hotel. Sims went in with the bag and appeared thirty minutes later. It was 7:20 p.m.

The next stop was Sportree's Bar. After that, a nightclub called the Parizian on Linwood. Hess parked across the street, watching the blacks, reminding him of an African tribe with their bright-colored clothing, high Afros, neck chains and jewelry. He watched them strut around like peacocks. Groups of them standing outside, men and women, smoking and talking, shaking hands in some ritual motion. A parade of automobiles stopping, two or three at a time, Negros getting out, moving toward the

Peter Leonard

door, and when it opened he could hear the high-pitched scream of a trumpet or the thumping of drums.

Cordell Sims entered the club at 9:30 and came out at 11:15, escorting a woman with an Afro, short dress accentuating her long legs. Hess opened the door and got out of the Malibu, waited for traffic to clear, crossed the street and followed them, the sidewalk deserted. He saw them get into Cordell's dark-blue Dodge. Hess drew the weapon, holding it at arm's length down his leg, approaching the car from behind, crouching along the driver's side, looking through the window. Cordell and the woman were kissing. He brought the Walther up and fired five times through the windscreen, shattering the glass.

Headlights were approaching. He slid the gun in his pocket and crossed the street.

Chapter 31

Harry got back from a meeting with his US steel client in Pittsburgh at 3:30 in the afternoon, stopped at the yard on his way home. He walked in the office and Phyllis told him there was a message for him on the answering machine.

"Here, want to listen to it?" She pressed the button.

"Harry, Cordell. What's going on? I hear you came by. Miss me already? I'll get back to you."

It was Cordell's voice but Harry had no idea what he was talking about, had expected him to call back but he didn't.

"And some guy named Ray Meade," Phyllis said. "Southern accent."

"Never heard of him."

"He sounded like you were friends."

"That's what salesmen do."

That evening, Harry was going through the main section of the *Detroit News* and saw a one-column article with a headline that said:

Gunman Sought in Shooting Outside Detroit Nightclub

The article went on to explain how the victims, Cordell Sims, twenty-one, and Rochelle Campbell, twenty, both from Detroit, had walked out of the Parizian nightclub on Linwood Avenue, entered Mr. Sims' 1970 Dodge, and, according to witnesses, were shot by a lone gunman. Ms. Campbell was dead on arrival at Henry Ford Hospital. Mr. Sims remained in critical condition. Police were investigating.

Harry figured the shooting might be payback for something in Cordell's past, his days selling heroin. Still, it made him uneasy. Made him think of Hess. He took the Colt out of his coat. Walked around the house checking the windows and doors, making sure they were locked. Looked out at the front yard from his bedroom. There was a Chevy he'd never seen before parked on the street. It wasn't one of the neighbors'. Was he being paranoid?

He checked the back of the house, glancing down at the patio, and the back yard that had a five-foot-high wooden fence around the perimeter. It was too dark to see anything. He went downstairs, moved through the dining room to the French doors and saw someone on the patio, looking in the kitchen windows.

He drew the Colt, went out the side door on the driveway, came around the back of the house and saw Galina in a trench coat, warm September night. He lowered the gun, she hadn't seen it, slipped it in his pants pocket. "Galina, what're you doing?"

"I want to surprise you, Harry."

"You did."

She stepped toward him, wrapped her arms around him. He stood rigid.

"What's the matter? I think you would be happy to see me."

"I thought you were a burglar."

"Harry, you don't even lock your door." She frowned. "And you are not glad to see me. I can see it in your face."

He wasn't in the mood. "I have something I have to do tonight. Can I call you tomorrow?"

She opened her trench coat and flashed him. "What you are missing."

He knew what he was missing. He watched her walk across the backyard. She went through the gate in the fence and disappeared. He walked back around the house to the front, scanned the street. The Chevy was gone.

Harry decided it was time to call Joyce, tell her what was going on. He dialed the number Stark had given him.

Heard a soft, quiet voice say, "Hello."

"Joyce, it's Harry Levin."

Silence for a beat. "Harry, my God, what is going on, where are you?" She sounded upset.

"Detroit."

"I've tried calling Lisa Martz like thirty times. It just rings. I've been going crazy. I contacted the Munich police, they wouldn't tell me anything. Harry, I've been dying to talk to you."

He decided to give it to her straight. "The Nazi you saw on Leopoldstrasse, his name is Ernst Hess. He was in charge of the killing squad that day in the woods outside Dachau. And he's now a politician in Bavaria." Harry paused. "Hess killed your ex-husband and his fiancée, thinking she was you."

"My God." She paused. "It never occurred to me."

"Why would it?" He took a breath. "Hess killed Lisa, her father and her partners."

"Do you think he's coming for us?"

"I don't know. But it wouldn't surprise me."

"We'll go to the police."

"And tell them what? Have you seen Hess? Has he threatened you?"

"This is crazy. No one can help us? What are we going to do?"

"Do you have a friend you can stay with? Somewhere you can go till I can get down there?"

"I'm a realtor. I have listings and appointments."

"Have someone cover for you. You've got to get out of there. Pack a bag and leave as soon as you can. Don't tell anyone where you're going. Don't go near your office."

Harry slept with the Colt on the table next to his bed. Thought it was preferable to putting it under his pillow, squeeze the trigger in the middle of the night, blow his head off. He took it in the bathroom the next morning when he showered, needed to get used to having it with him.

He got to the yard early. Talked to Jerry Dubuque. Jerry ran the operation, made sure they had enough scrap to keep up with demand, made sure the trucks were loaded and the deliveries were on time. Harry ran the business, handled the clients, took care of the payables and receivables, made sure they had enough cash to buy what they needed.

Jerry came in the office, sat across the desk from him. He had started dressing like Harry, wearing khakis and blue button-down-collar shirts, black loafers and Wayfarer sunglasses. Phyllis had noticed too and mentioned it.

"Hey, I haven't had a chance to ask, how was your vacation? Went to Germany, right? What'd you do?"

Harry said, "Visited my old neighborhood."

"I was toying with the idea of going to the Olympics next year. What do you think?"

"Better get your tickets." Harry sipped his coffee out of a Styrofoam cup. "Let me ask you something. See anything suspicious the past couple days?"

Jerry frowned. "Like what?"

"Like seeing the same car keep driving by." It sounded lame. He should've thought this through a little better.

"Where're you going with this?"

"Like somebody stopping out front, looking around." That didn't sound much better.

"Harry, what the hell're you talking about?"

Phyllis opened the door, came in, closed it and whispered, "Harry, there's a detective out here wants to talk to you."

"Send him in."

Jerry got up with his coffee, gave him a puzzled look. "You in some kind of trouble, Harry?"

Good question.

Jerry and Phyllis walked out of the room and a short dark-haired guy walked in, tan wash-and-wear suit looking out of season in October, striped tie, scuffed brown shoes. He had a lot of hair parted low on the side, combed across his forehead, and wide, heavy sideburns to the bottom of his ears.

"Detective Frank Mazza, Mr. Levin." He took out his badge, flashed it in diminished formality. Didn't offer to shake hands. Suit coat coming open as he came toward the desk, a revolver in a holster on his right hip.

"Have a seat," Harry said. Arm outstretched, indicating the chair.

Without expression Mazza said, "You know why I'm here?"

"You found my business card in Cordell Sims' wallet. You talked to his mother, she said I stopped by the house the other day, but it wasn't me."

"No, who was it?"

"I don't know."

"But you know Mr. Sims?"

"I read in the paper he's in critical condition," Harry said. "What's the story, is he going to make it?"

"You own a firearm, Mr. Levin?"

"I've got a license to carry a Colt Python .357 Magnum." It had expired about six weeks earlier. No reason to mention that.

"That's a lot of gun."

"I carry a lot of money. Scrapping's a cash business."

"How do you know Mr. Sims?" He pushed his hair back off his forehead.

"We're friends. I see him occasionally."

"Do you shoot heroin?"

"Do I look like I shoot heroin?"

"You'd be surprised."

"Never in my life."

"Do you use drugs, Mr. Levin?"

"I smoked weed one time at an Allman Brothers concert. Got home, ate everything in the refrigerator." He paused. "Where's Cordell?"

"You know who shot him?" Frank Mazza said.

"No idea," Harry said. "You didn't happen to find nine-millimeter Parabellum shell casings at the scene, did you?"

"Why would you ask that?"

"Just curious."

Mazza combed his hair back with his fingertips. "But you don't know who shot him, huh?"

Harry shook his head.

"Maybe you should come down to 1300, see if we can jog your memory."

209

"You'd be wasting your time," Harry said.

Bob Stark got him Cordell's mother's address on Lothrop. "Her name's Gladys Jackson. Divorced Sims, married Melvin Jackson. Divorced him."

"She gets around, huh?"

"You could say. Cordell's at Detroit Receiving, where most of the inner-city shooting victims are taken, room 308, still listed as critical, but doing well considering he was shot three times."

Harry took Woodward to Grand Boulevard, passed the GM Building on his left and Fisher Building on his right, two Detroit landmarks. Drove to 14th Street, went right on Lothrop, found the address, parked and knocked on the door. The house was a mess and so was the woman who lived there. Bags, half-moon shapes under her eyes that were darker than her skin. Looked like she'd been in a prizefight and lost. She was wearing a stained terrycloth robe, and had curlers in her hair. "Mrs. Jackson, I'm Harry Levin." He took out his driver's license and handed it to her. She glanced at the photograph, seemed to study his face and gave it back to him.

"'Nother white dude come by here saying he was you. Spoke Southern. Saying he from Chattanooga."

Harry still had the mug shot of Hess that Taggart had given him. He took out the paper, unfolded it and handed it to her. "Is this the man?"

Her eyes opened wide. "That him," she said. "Who is he?"

"Could be the one shot Cordell."

"Why he do that? Shoot my boy three times. Kill the sister was with him." She gave the mug shot back to him. "He gonna try again?"

Harry drove downtown to Detroit Receiving on St Antoine behind the police station. Parked, went in and took the elevator to the third floor. The hospital was old and overcrowded. Not enough beds so patients on gurneys were lined up in the hall under gloomy fluorescent lights that cast a yellow glow. Nurses and orderlies running around amid the chaos. Harry had never seen anything like it.

He walked around till he found room 308. Expected a cop in uniform to be sitting in a chair in the hallway the way he'd seen in movies. There to protect Cordell in case the assassin returned. He went in. A gray-haired black man was sleeping in the first bed. Cordell was in the second one, IVs in both arms. The machine behind him against the wall was making a whooshing noise. Cordell sensed his presence, glanced at him and grinned.

"The fuck you doin' here, Harry?"

"Good to see you, too. How you feeling?"

"Ever been shot?"

"No," Harry said. "You see who did it?"

"Shape outside the car is all. Then metal was flying at us through the glass. I'm moving, ducking, tryin' not to get hit. Five shots. Little sounds like *pufft, pufft*. Man had his gun silenced. Hit me here." Pointed to his left forearm. "Here." Pointing to the upper left side of his chest near the collarbone, a bandage bulging under the hospital gown.

"Rochelle came out to smoke one, got smoked."

"She your girlfriend?"

"Not any more." He reached for a plastic cup on the table next to him, picked it up and sucked water through the straw.

"Remember anything about the shooter?"

Cordell closed his eyes for a few seconds and opened them looking at Harry. "Wore a hat. Just saw it like a blip, flash in my head."

"What kind of hat?"

"Little motherfucker with a brim. Had a feather on the side?"

"Sounds Tyrolean."

"Can see him now," Cordell said. "Was a white dude."

Harry showed him the mug shot of Hess.

"Might be," Cordell said. "The Nazi, huh?"

Harry nodded. "He stopped by your mother's, told her he was me."

"Let me ax you something. You the star witness. Why's he coming after me?" Cordell said.

"He's tying up loose ends. Taking out anyone knows something about him."

"Loose ends? Man, I don't know nothin'. Don't know shit."

Harry was wondering if Hess had come to Detroit first. Take care of them and go to Palm Beach? He had to call Joyce again and warn her. He saw Cordell's right foot come out from under the blanket. His ankle had a leg-iron on it, chained to the side rail. "What's that? They think you're going to run out, skip your medication?"

"Warrant for my arrest. Check it out. Charging me with felony firearm. Guess you can relate, huh? And I was just about to leave town."

"Maybe I can help with your legal problems."

"How you gonna do that? You a lawyer?"

"I know one and he's good."

"Tell him to work fast. Few more days, I heard a nurse sayin', they gonna move me to the jail infirmary. Wayne County. Trust me, you don't want to do time in there."

"I'll see what I can do," Harry said.

Harry went back to the yard. Galina had called. She was cooking a brisket, and insisted on dropping some off for his dinner.

"Don't worry, Harry. If door is locked, I know where to find spare key."

He was going to call Galina and tell her not to bother, but he didn't want to talk to her, get in a conversation. He was trying to avoid her.

212

Chapter 32

Hess pushed the button and heard the bell ring inside, waited, knocked on the door. The time was 4:57 p.m.

He had parked the Chevrolet Malibu down the street. The sky was overcast and getting dark as he walked along the driveway to the rear of the house, glancing at the neighbor's property. He didn't see anyone in the yard. Harry's garage was built on the north end of the property, a fence around the perimeter, empty slate patio directly behind the house. French doors that opened onto the patio were locked. He kicked in a glass pane near the handle, reached his hand through, unlocked the door and went inside.

Hess stood in the dining room and listened. He heard a dog barking somewhere outside. He moved through the house, studying the furnishings in the salon, sleek leather chairs and sofa, chrome and glass end tables, antique rugs, Ushak and Tabriz, Mondrian reproductions framed in black metal, Bang & Olufsen sound system, antique deco clock on the fireplace mantel. White lacquered bookshelves built along the wall that met the fireplace, filled with encyclopedias, hardcover books. He moved to the Steinway grand piano that was positioned in front of the windows with a view of the street. A woman on the sidewalk passed by the house, walking a dog, a breed of poodle. A heavy truck rumbled by shaking the foundation.

He went back through the dining room into the kitchen. There was a table in front of the windows that looked out on the back yard, an island counter with three high-back chairs behind it on one side. Across the room was

213

a small television on another counter built into the wall. Next to the TV was a phone and answering machine.

Hess pushed the message button and listened, skipping past sales solicitations until he heard a woman's voice. "Harry, I did as you suggested. I'm still on the island but in a safe place. When are you coming to Florida?" Very soon, Hess said to himself.

He walked into the foyer, stairs to the left, front-door alcove to the right. Behind him was a small wood-paneled room with a fireplace. He walked up the stairs to the second floor, photographs in frames on the wall, Hess stopping, studying them, the daughter, he guessed, in a series of pictures from a baby to a young woman. He entered the room at the top of the stairs. Still enough light to see this was where the daughter had slept. Thinking about her, the irony of it, the automobile accident bringing Hess and Harry Levin back together.

He heard something and moved to the window. He looked down and saw a car, lights on, in the driveway, stopping next to the house. A woman got out carrying something, approached the side door and rang the bell.

Hess ran down the stairs to the foyer. He heard the bell ring a second time and then the sound of a key in the lock. He was in the hallway moving toward the kitchen when the door opened and closed.

"Harry, it's me, are you here?" The accent sounded Russian. "I bring dinner."

He was in the foyer, looking through a doorway down a short hall into the kitchen. He saw her walk past him, carrying a tray covered with aluminum foil. She placed the tray on the island counter in the center of the room, removed her coat and draped it on the back of a chair. She moved to the left and disappeared from view. He heard a cupboard door open and close, and heard the clinking of glass bottles. She reappeared with a bottle in one hand and a cocktail glass in the other. She placed them on the island counter next to the tray.

He heard the refrigerator door open and the rattle of ice. She came back to the counter and dropped a handful of ice cubes into the cocktail glass. She unscrewed the cap on the bottle and poured what appeared to be vodka over the ice.

Hess had admired Harry Levin's taste in automobiles, his furnishings and now his taste in women. In another situation he would have liked to join her for an evening cocktail, but whisky, not vodka. What was he going to do? She appeared to be settling in, expecting Harry Levin's imminent arrival.

The foyer was dark, he moved, bumped the open door with his hip and it hit the wall with a dull thud. The woman turned and glanced through the doorway in his direction.

"Harry, is that you?"

She placed her drink on the counter and walked toward the foyer as Hess retreated into the salon.

"Is someone there?"

She came into the room. It was dark but not completely. Sitting in a leather chair, he reached over and turned on a lamp that was on the table next to him.

"I must have fallen asleep," Hess said, using his Southern accent. "I thought I heard someone."

"You scare the hell out of me," the woman said. "Who are you?"

"I was going to ask you the same thing. I'm Ray, friend of Harry's, staying here for a few days. I'm in the scrap business. Yard down in Ohio."

"Harry did not mention you were here."

"He didn't mention you either."

"Come have a drink with me."

"I don't mind if I do," Hess said, hands on the armrests, pushing himself out of the chair.

"You hungry? I have a nice brisket and roast potatoes."

"Well this is my lucky night, isn't it?" Hess said.

Harry borrowed a bolt cutter from Jerry Dubuque, Jerry saying, "What the hell're you going to do with that?"

"Cut some bolts," Harry said. "What do you think?"

"Aren't you the same guy that said the only Jew you know who uses tools is your dentist?"

"This is an exception."

"You need help, call me."

When Phyllis left for the day Harry wrapped the bolt cutter in brown paper and put it in Jerry's car. He had talked to Bob Stark earlier about Cordell's legal problems.

"Harry, it's complicated. He was arrested for selling heroin, looking at five years. Would've ended up doing two and a half. But Cordell's attorney was smart. He told the judge his client's father had taken off and his mother was a drug addict. Cordell was a victim of circumstances. Wants to make something of himself. Offered to enlist in the army in lieu of incarceration. The judge agreed. But the felony remains on his record. When the police found him outside the nightclub he was carrying a concealed weapon, so they've got him on the weapon charge. And since he was arrested for selling heroin, which is a felony, they've also got him on felon in possession of a firearm. If convicted he's looking at five to seven and a half."

"Can you get him out on bond in the meantime?"

"That's what I'm looking into. It's going to take a little time. The court thinks he's a flight risk. You would be too, you had that hanging over your head."

He drove to Lelli's on Woodward for a late dinner. Had a bowl of their wonderful minestrone, spaghetti and meatballs, a green salad and two glasses of house red, lingered over coffee, paid his check and walked out at 10:45. He drove to Detroit Receiving, parked on St Antoine, the street quiet, deserted. Got out with the bolt cutter wrapped in brown paper, about three feet long, hoped it looked like a gift. And now wished he'd thought to put a bow on it. Would've been a nice touch.

A black security guard was smoking a cigarette outside the main entrance. Harry walked in the lobby, nobody at the reception counter. A sign said, *Admittance*, with an arrow pointing down a hallway. He walked thirty yards and came to a reception area with chairs and couches. To the left was a bank of four elevators. He got in one and rode up to the third floor.

The hall was dark. The only sound he heard was his shoes on the tile floor. The nurses' station was straight ahead, three RNs standing there, one in front of the counter, two behind it. He ducked into the waiting room on his left. It was dark. The TV was on, a Western starring John Wayne, low volume. Black man stretched out on one of the couches, sleeping. Harry could hear him snoring. He sat in a chair with the bolt cutter in his lap, watching the nurses' station. One by one the nurses disappeared, checking patients, going on rounds.

Harry got up and made his move, crossed the hallway. There were half a dozen wheelchairs lined up. He grabbed one, put the bolt cutter on the seat and wheeled it down the dark hall lined with patients sleeping on gurneys. He opened the door to 308, pushed the chair in and closed it. The man in the first bed was on his back asleep.

Harry stood over Cordell, touched his arm, and shook him. "Wake up," he whispered. Cordell opened his eyes, blinked and yawned, staring up at him.

"Harry, what time is it?"

"Eleven thirty."

"What're you doing here?"

"I brought you a present." Harry held up the package.

"What's that?"

Harry ripped the paper off and held the bolt cutter up by the rubber grips, dull gray handles that had once been red.

Cordell's eyes sparkled, he grinned. "Harry Levin takin' the law in his own hands. I see it, I don't believe it."

"I've got to get you out of here before the shooter comes back." Harry opened the blades of the cutter head, centered them on the chain hooked to the leg-iron, gripped the handles and pushed them together, felt resistance from the hardened steel, pushed through it and heard the metal snap as the blades cut the chain.

"Harry, you never cease to amaze me. Suppose you were in the neighborhood again, huh?"

There was a bandage wrapped around his left forearm where he'd been shot, and a plastic hospital bracelet on his wrist. Harry lowered the bedrail, brought Cordell's legs over the side, Cordell wincing in pain, holding his bandaged thigh, exposed now as the hospital gown gathered and bunched at the top of his leg.

"Round hit me banged around in there, surgeon had to go in find it," Cordell said, face straining to get the words out.

He was hurt bad. Harry doubted he could walk. How was he going to get him to the car? How was he going to take care of him? Harry slid Cordell off the bed and got him in the wheelchair, Cordell groaning. Pulled the blanket off the bed, wrapped it around him and wheeled him out of the room.

Buddy was surprised when the real Nazi, Gerd Klaus, called saying he needed his help. Had a job for him, he didn't mind shooting a coon. Mind? Be a pleasure. They met at Nemo's over by Tiger Stadium, sat at the crowded bar, had a beer while Mr. Klaus told Buddy what to do and handed him an envelope with ten one hundred dollar bills in it. Buddy would've done it for nothing but could definitely use the money. Mr. Klaus said he'd do it himself but he had a nosey Jew to take care of. "I can help you with that too you need me." But Mr. Klaus said he didn't.

Buddy'd said, "Miss the Third Reich? Those were the good old days I bet." Mr. Klaus looked at him but didn't say anything. He wasn't the most talkative person Buddy'd ever met. "You guys were so close, but you have to admit, you got a little greedy. Going for England and Russia at the same time. Spread yourselves a little thin, don't you think?" Mr. Klaus seemed pissed now, wouldn't look at him, stared straight ahead. "Subject's still a little sensitive, huh? I understand. You don't want to talk, that's okay. It's not a crime yet?" He grinned, thinking it was funny, but the Nazi didn't react.

That had happened earlier. He parked on the street, took the .44 Mag out of the glove box. Got out and locked the pickup. He went in the main entrance, boon security guard inside the door. "Evening officer," he said, grinning at the rent-a-cop.

Buddy walked down a hall to the elevators, went up to three, nobody around, walked to the end of the hall, the nurses' station, opened a door and started down another hall that was dark and hard to see, walking by all these sick people sleeping on gurneys lined up against the wall. He passed a white dude pushing a colored guy in a wheelchair. "How you doing?" The white dude nodded at him.

Buddy opened the door to 308—he'd asked an orderly what room his good friend Cordell Sims was in—saw an old colored guy asleep in the first bed. The privacy curtain between the beds was pulled closed. He opened it and saw the second bed was empty, bolt cutter lying on the mattress. He went to the bathroom, opened the door, nobody there. And then it hit him. Cordell Sims was in the wheelchair. Had to be, right?

At first Harry thought he was a male nurse. Who else would be walking around a hospital at close to midnight? Wasn't part of the janitorial staff either. Not in jeans and a sleeveless denim jacket. Young, about thirty. Harry's height, trim build, long hair pulled back in a ponytail. Harry looked over his shoulder and saw him go into Cordell's room.

He leaned into the wheelchair, pushing it, got it moving, started running. Got to the end of the hall, went through the door, picking up speed again, racing past the nurses' station, down another hall to the elevators, pushed the button. He looked back, saw someone running down the hall toward them. Saw the elevator coming up from the first floor. The doors opened. The runner was halfway down the hall. Harry rolled Cordell in and pushed the button. The runner, the young guy he'd passed earlier, had a gun in his hand, getting closer. The doors were closing as he got there, but he was too late. They were already on their way down.

Buddy took the stairs to the first floor, lobby empty, rent-a-cop outside having a smoke. They wouldn't have come this way, have to get by the guard. So where in the hell were they? Maybe down on the lower level, sneaking out another way. But the jig was in a wheelchair and that meant he couldn't walk or he'd be walking.

He took the hall the opposite way, ran all the way to Emergency, big room packed, crazy, out of control, people moaning, bodies on stretchers. Ambulances and black-and-gold Detroit police cars were pulling up outside. Orderlies wheeled a white guy in on a gurney, blood all over him, dude yelling.

And then he thought—wait a goddamned minute—with all this going on, who's going to notice somebody leaving in a wheelchair? Following his hunch he went outside, walked down the concrete ramp past the police cars to the sidewalk, looked right. Nothing. He walked around the corner to St. Antoine, looked left and saw them—suck my balls—just down the block, white guy helpin' the colored guy into a car but couldn't tell what kind.

Buddy took off running but was still thirty yards away when the car started moving, picking up speed. He drew the .44, held it with two hands, aimed down the sight and squeezed the trigger, the big gun making a racket, fired four times but couldn't tell he hit the car or not. It kept going.

What the hell was he going to tell Mr. Klaus? Then he got to thinking. Why was it his problem? Far as he was concerned he'd taken the risk, earned the money. Fuck Mr. Gerd Klaus, the Nazi.

Chapter 33

Harry heard the gunshots and floored it. He got a brief glimpse of the shooter, a dark shape in the rearview mirror, before he turned the steering wheel right and then left, zigzagging out of the line of fire. Cordell was in the seat next to him leaning back against the door, letting out a breath.

"You OK?"

"Better now that I'm out of there. Harry Levin to the rescue once again. Not a moment too soon. How you do it? You clairvoyant? See the future, Harry? Tell me what the fuck's gonna happen next. 'Less you see something bad."

"I had a feeling whoever shot you was coming back. But who was that? I wondered if he was someone from your days selling."

"Never seen him in my life."

"Maybe he works for Hess. But we know he isn't German. You hear him say 'How you doing' when he passed us in the hall?"

"Must've missed that."

"You can stay at my place tonight," Harry said, "we'll figure out what to do in the morning."

"Don't have to figure out nothin', I know what I got to do."

"Let's see what my lawyer says."

"That's OK but I'm goin' to see it from somewhere else."

"The way things are going I might be in the cell next to you."

"I doubt it. Nothin' touches you, Harry. Shit slides right off your back." He paused. "You don't mind, got to run by the Ponch get my clothes."

221

Harry cut over to Jefferson, the Motor City dark and quiet just after midnight on a Wednesday night, parked in front of the hotel, turned in his seat. "Need some help?"

"I need more than that. Listen, I'm hurtin', you mind gettin' my stuff? Best I stay here." He let out a breath. "Go to the desk tell 'em you Mr. Sims, 521. Suite with a river view. You look presentable, Harry. They ain't gonna say nothin'." He closed his eyes.

"You all right?"

"Put my clothes in the duffel." He paused. Harry could see he was in pain. "One more thing. I got money in the safe. Combination: right seven, left seven, right seven."

"Your lucky number, huh?"

"I hope so."

Forty minutes later he pulled up in his driveway, stopping behind Galina's Nova. Pictured her upstairs in his bed, naked, waiting for him. It was the last thing he wanted to deal with right now. He shook Cordell and his eyes opened. "We're here." Harry got out of the car, went around and helped Cordell in the house, Cordell's arm over his shoulder, taking short steps down the hallway into the foyer, and into the den, sat him on the couch. Cordell groaning, making faces till he got settled. "Can I get you something?"

"Water, Harry, you don't mind."

It smelled like cooked meat in the kitchen, oven on warm. He could see a roasting pan on a rack inside covered with foil. Bottle of vodka on the island counter, and next to it a low-ball cocktail glass with red lipstick on the rim. He turned off the oven, left the pan where it was. Filled a glass of water and took it to Cordell, watched him drink it down without stopping. He put the glass on the coffee table, helped Cordell stretch out on the couch, and covered him with the hospital blanket.

Harry went upstairs, his room was dark, bed made. No sign of Galina.

He went down the hall into Sara's room, turned on the light. imagined her standing in front of the full length mirror, getting ready to go out, trying on shoes.

"Hey, Pops, which one do you think?" She said, pointing at a black flat on her left foot and a wedge sandal on her right.

"The sandal," Harry said, looking at her outfit.

"Me too. Great minds, huh?"

"Yeah," Harry said, wishing he could see her again.

He went downstairs, walked through the house, checked every room. Saw the broken pane in the French door, and drew the Colt from the waistband of his khakis. Harry moved through the dining room and kitchen to the back hall, opened the basement door and went down the stairs, holding the gun in front of him with both hands, expecting Hess to jump out.

He moved through the basement rooms, eyes adjusting to the darkness, hearing the creak and groan of the furnace kicking on. Harry squatting, looking under the ping pong table in the rec room, checking the dark corners of the laundry and furnace rooms. He went back upstairs to the kitchen, theorizing that Hess had come, waited for Galina to leave, broke the pane and entered through the French doors. Hess then waited for Harry, gave up and left.

But why did Galina leave her car? Maybe she'd had one too many. She wasn't much of a drinker. Harry phoned her house. No answer. He'd try her again in the morning. Harry checked the answering machine, expected one from Colette. No messages. He turned off the lights in the kitchen. Checked on Cordell, eyes closed, sound asleep. He went up to his bedroom, laid on the bed. He had to be at the office early, set his alarm, put the Colt on the end table, and closed his eyes.

Hess was thinking about the woman, attractive, well proportioned. He liked a woman with ample hips and breasts he could grab onto. Imagined the big woman on her knees, ramming her from behind.

They talked and had a cocktail. She was from Riga, Latvia, a Jewess, not surprisingly. Her parents had been killed by the Nazis. Hess pretended to be sympathetic, furrowed his brow, patted her arm. "The Third Reich was a brutal regime. From what I've read on the subject, the Nazis were sadistic murderers."

She looked into his eyes. "You are a Jew?"

Hess shook his head, trying not to smile, give himself away.

"Do you know how many Jews were killed?"

Hess was thinking, Not enough.

"More than six million."

"Beyond comprehension," Hess said. This could not have worked out better. Harry would come home and see her car in the driveway. He would walk in the house and smell the food. Seeing the woman would distract him. Hess would step back out of sight, pull the weapon and shoot them.

They sat on high-back chairs at the island counter, drinking their cocktails. An hour later when Harry Levin had still not arrived he could see signs the woman was getting impatient. She glanced at the clock a couple times.

"This is not like Harry. He should be home by now."

Hess, smiling, said, "Don't worry. He will walk through the door any minute. Have another cocktail."

"One more," she said. "But you must join me."

Hess took her glass and filled it with ice, poured vodka almost to the top and handed it to her. He refilled his glass with Canadian Club whisky.

She frowned staring at the drink.

"Ray, you trying to get me drunk?"

"I am enjoying your company. Promise me you will not leave until Harry arrives." He couldn't let her leave, and hoped the alcohol would relax her.

"Did Harry tell you about me?"

"He spoke of you in the most complimentary way."

Her face lit up. "What did he say?"

"You are a remarkable woman," Hess said. "I can see that myself."

Now she was smiling. "Harry say that, really?" She sipped her drink, and glanced at the clock on the oven. The time was 8:45. "I don't want to, but if he is not coming here in fifteen minutes I have to go."

"Do you have children?" Hess said, trying to change the subject.

"Two girls, teenagers. Visiting their father in London." She paused to drink her vodka and said, "You are married?"

"Twenty-two years." An eternity, Hess was thinking. Married in name only. They slept in separate bedrooms, rarely socialized together. What had he seen in Elfriede, a big unpolished, unsophisticated farm girl? He had married her because the sex was good and, at the time, he didn't know any better.

She finished the vodka and glanced at the clock again, slid off her chair, and stood leaning against the counter. She seemed intoxicated, unsteady.

"Tell Harry I was here. Brisket is in the oven. Nice to meet you."

"No one is expecting you. Why do you have to leave?"

At 1:22 a.m., Hess was in his car creeping along West Jarvis Avenue, a quiet tree-lined street in Hazel Park, a middle-class community with small cookie-cutter houses built in even rows. He found the address he was looking for, parked on the street and walked to the rear entrance of the house. The sliding glass door was unlocked. He entered a small room with mismatched furniture, empty pizza cartons and beer cans on a coffee table, an ashtray overflowing with cigarette butts. He walked through the house checking the rooms. Buddy was asleep on a mattress on the floor of a small cluttered bedroom that smelled of cigarettes and stale beer. The money he had given him was on top of the dresser still in the envelope. He picked it up and counted the bills. One was missing. He folded the money and slipped it in his shirt pocket. There was a beer can on the dresser next to car keys, billfold and cigarettes. He shook the can and heard beer slosh inside.

Buddy was on his back, snoring. Hess stood over him, pouring beer on his face. Buddy thrashed and flipped over, and sat up rubbing his eyes.

"What the fuck's going on?" Surprised, angry until he saw Hess standing over him. "Mr. Klaus, that you? Jesus H Christ, you scared the shit out of me."

"Were you successful?"

"Was I successful?" He smiled. "Let me put it this way—there's one less coon you got to worry about." He yawned, rubbed his jaw. "What're you doing here in the middle of the night? Got another job you need done?" Buddy coughed. "Hey, hand me my smokes, will you?"

"You don't have time."

"Yeah. Why's that?"

Hess raised the Walther and shot him in the chest.

The sun was coming up when Hess arrived at the scrap yard. Levin's silver Mercedes was parked behind the building. He drove past the yard and parked on Luce, a side street, and crossed Mt. Elliot. He walked through the entrance past the scales into the empty yard. A semi rumbled in behind him, turning around, backing up next to the mountain of scrap metal.

The door to the building was unlocked. He opened it and walked through the entryway and through another door, and down a short hallway, two small cramped offices on one side, an office and toilet room on the other side. There was another office at the end of the hall, this one appreciably larger than the others. It had a desk and furniture grouping behind it. The room was dark, shades drawn over the two windows. His eyes adjusted and he noticed someone asleep on the couch. Hess pulled the Walther, flipped the safety off, crossed the room and stood over Harry Levin on his stomach, asleep. He heard a car drive by, raised the weapon, finger squeezing the trigger.

A woman's voice startled him. "Harry, what are you doing here so early? Harry—"

It came from the intercom on the desk behind him. Hess walked out of the office and moved down the hall. He heard the woman's voice again and stepped inside the toilet room. He heard footsteps in the hallway and ducked against the wall, and saw the woman walk by. He closed the door, opened the window and hoisted himself up and through it to the ground.

Hess was in the car when he heard the siren.

Chapter 34

"My God, Harry. I thought it was you," Phyllis said when
he came in the office, 6:30 in the morning.

"What happened?"

"Somebody shot Jerry." Phyllis started crying. "He
wanted to be you, Harry. Even dressed like you." She
dried her eyes with a tissue. "What was he doing with
your car?"

"We traded. Jerry was supposed to take it in for a
tune-up. Lives right near the dealership. He was doing
me a favor."

"Police want to talk to you, the Eye-talian detective
with the hair." There were two Detroit Police cruisers and
an unmarked Plymouth sedan in the lot when he pulled
in, wondering what the hell was going on. Phyllis handed him a black coffee. He sipped it and walked down
the hall, two uniformed cops standing outside his office.
Went in, shades up, bright sunlight coming through the
window on the east wall. Somebody was taking photographs of Jerry Dubuque dead on the leather couch,
blood pooled on the beige industrial carpeting under him,
two shell casings on the floor. Harry felt bad, he liked
Jerry, felt responsible. Knew Hess had done it. Who else?

"If I didn't know better I'd say you were the intend-
ed victim, Mr. Levin," Detective Mazza said, standing on
the other side of his desk in the tan wash-and-wear suit
he'd had on last time.

"You sound disappointed," Harry said.

"You going to tell me what's going on?"

"If I could," Harry said.

"Why don't you try."

228

"Want me to make something up? 'Cause that's what I'd be doing."

"First an acquaintance of yours, Cordell Sims is shot and now one of your employees." Mazza took a pen out of his shirt pocket, squatted and picked up a shell casing with it, holding it up so Harry could see it. "But you don't know anything."

Mazza smelled like a smoker and had nicotine stains on the index and middle fingers of his right hand.

"What was Jerry Dubuque doing in your office?"

"By the look of it, sleeping one off," Harry said. "It's happened before. Jerry occasionally hits the bars in Hamtramck after work. Has a few too many, comes back to the office. It's the only couch in the place. I'd rather have him sleep here than get on the road."

"Mr. Dubuque have a drinking problem?"

"He did, he doesn't any more," Harry said.

"No sign of forced entry."

"Jerry wouldn't have worried about locking the door. Wouldn't have crossed his mind. The gate out front is locked at night. I've got a security man who keeps an eye on the yard, sits in his car and listens to music."

"What's his name?"

"Columbus Fletcher. Phyllis, Miss Wampler can tell you how to get in touch with him."

"What time's he leave?"

"Between six fifteen and six thirty."

"What time do you usually get here?"

"Seven."

"Shooter must've parked in front or on a side street across Mt. Elliot, waited for your security man to go. Came through the gate saw your Mercedes in the lot, saw Mr. Dubuque on your couch and shot him. Miss Wampler said she arrived at six fifteen, and I believe the perp was still here. Heard her and went out the bathroom window. It was still open."

The photographer finished and nodded at Mazza. "All set." He put the camera in a black bag with a strap, and walked out of the room.

"You keep money around, Mr. Levin?"

229

"There's ten thousand dollars in the safe. I told you the last time you were here, it's a cash business."

"Do me a favor, check and make sure it's all there."

Harry had a vintage Mosler bolted to the floor behind his desk. He turned the chair around, sat leaning forward and opened it. Saw banded stacks of fifties and hundreds. "Looks like it is."

"So," Mazza said, "we can rule out robbery as a motive."

"Unless whoever it was tried to open the safe and couldn't."

Mazza took out a pack of Camels, tapped one out, put it between his teeth and lit it. "I think it was planned. Perp comes here sees your car in the lot, sees someone on the couch in your office, thinks it's you. Same type of gun used on Cordell Sims. There's something you aren't telling me. Quite a bit I'd say." Mazza paused, taking a deep drag on the Camel, blowing out smoke. "This a dope deal gone wrong? You and Cordell in business together?"

"Not even close."

"Laundering money through the scrap yard?"

Harry frowned, let that one go.

Mazza ran his tongue over his teeth and spit out a loose piece of tobacco. "Where were you last night?"

"Home watching TV, *Columbo* and Johnny Carson."

"Anyone with you?"

"Why?"

"Mr. Sims decided to check out of Detroit Receiving about midnight," Mazza said, stubbing his cigarette out in an ashtray on Harry's desk.

"Can't say I blame him. Whoever shot him was probably coming back to finish the job."

"Know anything about it?"

"Why would I?"

"Security guard described you in detail."

"I doubt it."

"Then we'll have you come down, appear in a lineup. How's that sound?"

"Like you don't have anything and you're trying to force it."

230

"Any idea the penalty for harboring a fugitive?" Mazza said, pushing his hair off his forehead.

"No, but you're going to tell me, aren't you?"

Harry did have one thing going for him. Hess thought he was dead.

Cordell felt pain in his shoulder and leg before he opened his eyes and saw her, cute little white girl sitting in a chair, smiling at him. "Who're you?"

"Franny, Harry's niece. He asked me to check on you, see how you're doing."

"Been better."

"I'm a nurse. Let me see your wounds."

She got up, came over to the couch. Took three aspirin out a bottle on the end table, put them in his hand and gave him a glass of water.

"This should help take the edge off."

He swallowed the aspirin and drank some water, handed her the glass. "What hospital you work at?"

"Providence, but I'm still in school. Not registered yet."

"Know what you're doing?" Cordell said.

She gave him a look like, pardon me? Pulled the blue hospital blanket down, lifted his gown and pulled the bandage off his thigh. Stared at it, poked the skin around it. Pulled the bandage off his forearm, looked at the little hole, was black 'n' blue around it. Lifted his arm, checked the other side where the bullet came out. She slipped his right arm out of the gown and checked his shoulder and nodded.

"Am I gonna make it, Doc?"

She grinned. "Looks good. You're healing well."

"Motherfucker itches."

"That's normal. I want to take you upstairs, put you in a hot tub."

She helped him up to the bathroom, filled the tub with warm water and Epsom salt, and helped him in.

"Just soak for a while."

Girl was cool. Didn't seem nervous seein' a naked brother. "Want to go out some time?"

"I've got a boyfriend."

"I'll teach you how to do the Freaky Deaky."

"I already know it," Franny said. "If you don't keep your freak clean you might get shot."

"How you know about that?"

"I read it in the paper. Call me when you want to get out," she said, stepped into the hall and closed the door.

When the police left Harry paged through a stack of transaction reports and shippers Jerry had put on his desk the day before. Without Jerry he'd have to put Phyllis in charge for a few days. She could handle it. He gave her a couple blank checks and told her to get more money when she needed it.

"Harry." Phyllis on the intercom. "Someone named Joyce is on the phone for you."

"Put her through." He picked up the receiver. "How you doing?"

"Going out of my mind."

"Where are you?"

"I'm staying at a friend's house on the island. Let me give you the address and phone number."

Harry wrote it down.

"Have you seen Hess? Is he there?"

"No." He didn't want to worry her.

"When are you coming down?"

"Tomorrow. Hang in there."

It was 10:37 a.m. when he got home. Galina's car was gone. Harry was now convinced that she'd had one too many and walked home. Cordell was on the couch in the den, watching TV, eating a bowl of cereal.

"You're looking good."

"Feelin' better, thanks to your niece. She's something, Harry."

"You see a woman come by and get her car that was parked in the driveway?"

"No, but I've been noddin' off."

"I don't want to ruin your day but the police are looking for you. And unless I'm wrong they're going to be coming here with a warrant."

"What do got in mind?" Cordell said.

"You up to traveling?"

"Depends on where you talkin'."

"Palm Beach."

"I can get next to that." Cordell said. "Already packed. One question. How we getting there?"

Harry checked his messages, one from Colette.

"I'm still in Bergheim. My mother is in the hospital. Call me when you can. I'll explain everything."

He tried her again. No answer.

Hess could feel the hot humid air as he stepped out of the aircraft into the jet way at 3:30 p.m. He had had a window seat, and enjoyed seeing the blue ocean, the green palm trees, and the orange tile roofs of Palm Beach as the plane came in for a landing. He had checked out of the Statler Hotel in Detroit, driven to the airport, returned the Chevrolet Malibu to Avis. Three hours later he was in Florida. No customs agents asking questions this time.

He walked through the terminal to baggage claim and waited for his suitcase. He had disassembled the Walther and wrapped each piece in an article of clothing. He waited outside for a bus to take him to the Hertz lot, surprised how warm and bright it was after being in Detroit.

He rented a Lincoln Town Car that drove like a bus, cruising with the windows down to Palm Beach, checking in at the Breakers, a lavish architectural gem on the Atlantic Ocean. He insisted on a room with an ocean view and stood staring out the window, watching waves roll onto the shore.

Hess unpacked his suitcase and assembled the Walther, locking the weapon in a safe in the closet. His clothes were inappropriate, too heavy for the warm climate. He had seen a men's shop downstairs off the lobby, and went there, purchasing golf shirts, one red, the other yellow, a pair of aviator sunglasses, khaki trousers, sandals and a black golf cap with the Breakers logotype on the front. He returned to the room, changing into the red golf shirt, the khaki trousers, the cap and sunglasses, studying himself in the mirror, amazed at the transformation, seeing a pale fifty-year-old American tourist.

233

Worth Avenue was one-way. He parked on the north side twenty meters from Cocoanut Row. It was 5:15. Sunset Realty was on the corner next to an Italian restaurant. He studied color photographs of homes for sale in the windows of the real-estate office. He could see a dozen desks through the glass but only three were occupied— all by women on the phone. He opened the door and went inside, saw a stack of elegant brochures in a metal display rack. *Take one*, it said. He did, and walked out.

Hess sat in the Town Car, studying a map of Palm Beach. He turned right on Cocoanut Row and right on Peruvian Avenue, and drove all the way to South Ocean Boulevard, gazing out at the ocean, feeling an easterly breeze, whitecaps breaking out to sea. He turned right again, passed the Winthrop House, Frau Cantor's residence, driving along the water, glancing at the oceanfront estates, trying not to drive off the road.

He turned around and went back to Worth Avenue, parked next to the seawall, smelled the salty breeze. The Winthrop House was across the street. The apartments had balconies. Hess wondered if he would see her, wondered would he recognize her if he did. He had seen her the one time on Leopoldstrasse in Munich. At first he thought she was drunk, coming at him the way she did. People on the street had stopped and taken notice. How could they not? A crazy woman was raising her voice, accusing him of being a Nazi murderer. Instead of confronting her he had walked away, hailed a taxi.

Rausch had followed her and found out her name and where she lived. Hess was certain he had killed her that night in Washington DC, and was surprised weeks later when he discovered she was still alive.

Hess went back to the Breakers, sat in the bar sipping a Martini, cold gin and vermouth, two olives. He was paging through the real-estate brochure, glancing at photographs of premium properties.

Mediterranean-style waterfront compound, stunning white stucco with red tile roof, 387 feet of ocean frontage, 10,287 square feet, 8 bedrooms, 10 bathrooms, pool, tennis court. Listing #1137.

The next one:

Oceanfront Estate, 288 feet of frontage, 8,940 square feet, 2-bedroom pool house, 60-foot Italian marble pool, 7 bedrooms, 11 bathrooms. Listing #1089. Listing Agent: Joyce Cantor

A color photograph of her, head and shoulders, pretty face and radiant smile, late forties. No sign of the ranting lunatic accusing him on Leopoldstrasse.

After the listings was a profile of Frau Cantor under the heading: Integrity, Experience, Professionalism.

The text read:

Whether Joyce is representing an oceanfront buyer or listing a 2-bedroom condo she treats her clients with equal commitment.

Nobody maintains a higher level of ethics and professionalism.

Hess grinned, amused by the lie, feeling the warmth of the gin settling over him. He dipped his thumb and index finger into the liquid, pinched an olive and popped it in his mouth. Hess finished his martini, paid the check and took the elevator to his room.

Harry pulled into a motor court outside Valdosta, Georgia just before midnight, eleven and a half hours straight, stopping for the first time in Knoxville when Cordell said he couldn't hold it any longer, was going to go on the floor of the car if Harry didn't find a rest stop. Now he was stretched across the backseat asleep. The only interesting part of the trip was driving through the Smoky Mountains in Tennessee.

The room had twin beds and smelled of disinfectant. Harry carried the bags in, helped Cordell and fell asleep with his clothes on as soon as his head hit the pillow. It was still dark when he opened his eyes at 5:20 a.m. He took a shower, woke Cordell and got back in the car.

"Sure you never been in the military?" Cordell said to Harry. "What the hell kind of schedule you on?"

"I'm doing all the heavy lifting," Harry said. "All you have to do is get in back and sleep."

"Sir, yes sir," Cordell said, saluting.

"I'm trying to get to this survivor before Hess does."

"How you know he's going after her?"

"I don't. But Hess thinks he got me and she's the only one left. Am I getting through to you?"

"Harry, lose your sense of humor somewhere back in Tennessee?"

"Ohio," Harry said. "Most boring state I've ever driven through."

"You think so, huh? Try Nebraska sometime, you go out of your mind."

"What were you doing in Nebraska?"

"Taking a load to LA for Chilly."

Cordell was in back, snoring when they crossed the Florida state line.

Hess phoned Sunrise Realty at 10:00 a.m., asking for Joyce Cantor.

"I am sorry, sir, Ms. Cantor has taken a temporary leave of absence to address some family issues."

Hess grinned at the woman's choice of words, but decided that getting shot could be considered a family issue.

"May I ask who's calling?"

"Mr. Emile Landau," Hess said, using his Southern accent. "Joyce has come highly recommended by a mutual friend. I am from Atlanta, here for a few days. I was planning to look at oceanfront estates today." He sipped his coffee waiting for a response.

"Lenore Deutsch, our top-selling agent, is handling Joyce's listings in the interim. No one knows more about Palm Beach real estate than Lenore."

"Is she ethical and professional?" Hess said, thinking of Joyce Cantor's real-estate profile.

"Extremely, sir. Lenore always has her clients' best interests in mind."

"How can I disagree with that? Tell Lenore I will meet her at 1160 South Ocean Boulevard, one this afternoon—and I will have my checkbook with me." A nice touch, Hess thought. How could she resist such an invitation?

Chapter 35

The estate was the ultimate in luxury. In fact, the listing in the brochure had used those very words. Ten bedrooms, Italian marble pool, gourmet kitchen and private spa, views of the ocean and intercoastal, private beach and boat dock, every amenity imaginable.

People would have given their first-born to stay there, and would never want to leave, but Joyce felt like a prisoner. The situation was pure madness. A lunatic Nazi was coming to kill her and there was nothing she could do about it, no way to stop him. She had gone to the Palm Beach police station yesterday after talking to Harry. Met with a detective, man about her age named George Morris, dark hair, short-sleeve white shirt, coffee stain on the pocket, dark eyes, flat Midwest accent. She told him she was a survivor, told him about seeing Hess, the Nazi, in Munich six weeks before. She saw a grin form on his thin lips. He looked at her like she was a college kid on spring break who'd had too many shots of tequila.

"I'm sorry," Detective Morris said, "the police can't do anything unless there's a threat. By that I mean, you see this Nazi in Palm Beach, he starts harassing you—" Morris started to grin and covered his mouth with his hand. "I want you to call me."

Joyce would've loved to hear what he said about her when she left. He obviously thought she had a screw loose.

The estate was owned by the Frankels, Abe and Millie. Joyce had sold them the property a month earlier, her first big sale at Sunset Realty, and they had become good friends. The Frankels were going to be in New York at their Fifth Avenue apartment until early January. Joyce said she was having her condo painted. Millie said the estate was hers for as long as she needed it. That solved one problem. Harry was on his way, and that made her feel better, but what could Harry do if Hess showed up?

Joyce tried to keep busy, checked her messages, watched TV, exercised, sat by the pool, but nothing took her mind off Hess. The estate had an alarm system, and Josefina, the Costa Rican caretaker, lived there part-time. Security guards checked the house and grounds at night, and she locked the door to her suite on the second floor, but none of it relieved her anxiety, this feeling of foreboding.

She was thinking back on her life: escaping from the mass grave in the woods outside Dachau, taken in by the Muellers, the farm couple who had risked their lives for a Jewish girl, fed and protected her until the end of the war. Joyce's aunt Sima and uncle Stanley had sent her a visa and money for passage to New York and invited her to live with them in Baltimore. Joyce didn't have anyone else. She was twenty-one. Stan owned a real-estate company and offered her a job.

Four years later she met Mitch. Life couldn't have been much better. He was smart and good-looking, had just graduated dental school. He was, as Joyce's aunt had said, a catch. They got married. Mitch bought into a practice with five other dentists, specializing in root canals. That's all they did. He talked about swollen gums and abscessed teeth and dead roots at the dinner table, eyes lit up with excitement.

He made a good living and Joyce didn't do badly herself. With two incomes they were able to afford the house in Georgetown. They were married eighteen years when Mitch started fooling around. It was obvious something was going on. He started exercising for the first time in his life, lost weight, bought new clothes, and spent more time grooming and more time away from home.

Joyce thought it was a phase, a midlife crisis, something he would get out of his system. But there were others. How many she didn't know. The final straw was when she found out Mitch was paying for an apartment for Sherri, a girl in his office. That was it, she moved out, filed for divorce, walked with half their assets, $350,000, her freedom, and, maybe best of all, she didn't have to hear about dental procedures any more.

Joyce moved to Palm Beach and bought a fifth-floor, two-bedroom condo at the Winthrop House, with views of the ocean and the orange tile rooftops of the trendy shopping district. She applied for a job at Sunset Realty, and got it, but put off her start date for a week so she could take her niece, Jenni, to Munich. Joyce hadn't been back since the war.

They were having a wonderful girls' day, shopping all morning, walking along Leopoldstrasse when she saw him coming out of a restaurant. Recognized him, mind racing, trying to remember when, and pictured him wearing a gray SS uniform, holding a riding crop in gloved hands. Joyce approached him and said, "I know you."

He glanced at her and smiled, thinking she was an old friend.

"You're the Nazi from Dachau, the murderer."

He frowned now, moving away from her, signaled a taxi. She dropped her shopping bags and went after him. "Stop him, he's a murderer." People on the sidewalk were looking at her like she was crazy, keeping their distance.

Jenni picked up the bags and followed her, surprised, embarrassed, Joyce could tell, by her outburst.

"Aunt Joyce, what's going on?" Jenni looking at her like she'd flipped.

"It's the Nazi murderer from Dachau."

"That was thirty years ago," Jenni said. "How can you be sure?"

Jenni called her friend Adele, who worked at the Anti-Defamation League in New York, explained what had happened. Adele suggested they contact the ZOB in Munich. Joyce called and talked to a woman named Lisa Martz, and arranged to stop by their office the next morning, to look through archival photographs of Dachau Nazis.

Joyce was calmer, more relaxed after that. She and Jenni went back to their hotel, napped and went out to dinner. When they returned to the room there was a swastika painted on the wall, their clothes were all over the floor. Joyce freaked. She wasn't going to go through that again, called the airline and they flew out that night.

Three weeks later Mitch, her ex, and Sherri, his fiancée, were murdered. A Washington DC detective named Taggart had flown down to question her. He was a nice-looking dark-haired guy, although she couldn't say much for his taste in clothes. He wore a green dress shirt and a brown plaid sport coat.

"Nice view," he said, looking out the window at the ocean, Virginia twang in his voice.

"That's why I bought it."

"What's a place like this run, you don't mind my asking?"

She told him and he whistled hearing the amount.

"You want to sit down, Detective?" She was in one of the blue Baker Regency chairs. He crossed the living room and sat on the couch.

"Get back to DC very often?"

"I flew up for the funeral." She had paid her respects to Pitsy and Jarvis, Mitch's parents, and joined them for shiva.

"How about before that?" Taggart said.

"The day I moved."

"How'd you feel when you found out your husband was having an affair?"

"Which time?"

"How many were there?"

"I don't know for sure. Three or four, at least."

"How do you know?"

Joyce said, "You married, Detective?"

"Uh-huh."

"Ever have an affair?"

"We're not talking about me," Taggart said, getting defensive.

"When a guy has an affair things about him change. I knew what Mitch was doing."

"Did you know Ms. Shore?"

"She worked in Mitch's office," Joyce said. "I saw her occasionally. We weren't friends if that's what you mean."

"How'd you find out about it?"

"He rented her an apartment. The bill came to the house. Dumb, huh?"

"Were you angry?"

"No, I was relieved. I'd had enough. I said, you want her go right ahead. I'm leaving. You know when your marriage isn't working, don't you?"

"Do you own a gun?"

"I don't believe in guns."

"Did you kill your husband?"

She looked him in the eye and said, "No."

"You know who did?"

Joyce shook her head.

She escorted him to the door, sure he was going to ask another question like Columbo always did, Peter Falk looking scruffy and disheveled. But Taggart wasn't Columbo. He walked out. She closed the door and stood on the balcony, watched him come out of the building and get in a car and drive north on South Ocean Boulevard.

241

Chapter 36

Hess was wearing the new yellow golf shirt, khakis, sunglasses and the Breakers cap. He had parked on the side of the road and stood at the gate, studying the house and grounds of the estate. According to the description in the brochure it was Mission-style, 12,150 square feet, eight bedrooms, movie theater, bowling alley, private beach and beach house across South Ocean Boulevard, circular drive made out of stone to match the color of the tile roof.

A white Cadillac approached, the gate opened. The driver waved. The Cadillac drove in, parking on the circular drive. Hess pulled in behind her.

She stepped out and came toward him, a blonde Jew, fifties, Dachau thin, heavy make-up, an excessive amount of jewelry.

"Mr. Landau, I'm Lenore Deutsch."

She had a New York accent and offered a cold bejeweled hand. Hess shook it.

"I understand you're from Atlanta. What part? Wait. Don't tell me. Let me guess. Sandy Springs. Am I right?" She smiled.

"How did you know?" Hess said. He could see the dark roots of her hair under the dyed blonde, and evidence of plastic surgery, skin tight across her face, and lips that curled up like a duck's.

"I assumed you were from Fulton County. I sold an oceanfront property to the Watt family not too long ago. Do you by any chance know Mr. Josh Watt? He's a major developer."

Hess was already tired of listening to her.

"You're without question an astute and savvy buyer, Mr. Landau. There is only so much ocean frontage. And

Palm Beach, as a one-of-a-kind enclave, will never lose its luster." She paused. "Now would you like to tour the estate?"

Her onslaught of words was exhausting. "What happened to Mrs. Cantor?"

"Ms.," the blonde Jew said. "She's divorced, went back to her maiden name. Mitch, her ex, was murdered. In Georgetown for God's sake, our nation's capital. Can you believe it? Horrible, a real tragedy. What's happening to the world?"

Hess waited for an opening but she kept talking.

"Joyce, God bless her, has taken a leave of absence. Needs some time off to get her head on straight. Who wouldn't? Poor thing."

"I would like to say hello. If that is possible."

"No one knows where she is."

"Joyce came highly recommended."

"Who referred her, if you don't mind my asking?"

"A friend in New York."

"You're not going to tell me, are you? I'm sure you have your reasons." She smiled. "I can assure you, Mr. Landau, you're in good hands. I was realtor of the year in 1970. I've been selling property in Palm Beach since the early fifties. I know the island better than anyone."

Modesty wasn't one of her attributes.

Hess endured her for another hour while they walked through the house empty of furniture, the woman explaining architectural details: beamed fourteen-foot ceilings, leaded glass, marble bathrooms, teakwood paneling, her voice sounding distant to him at times as he withdrew and thought about killing her. Throwing her over the upstairs railing onto the French limestone foyer thirty feet below. See if that would silence her.

When the tour was complete Hess told the woman he was impressed, however he wanted to see some other estates for comparison before he made his final decision. He was sure he would make a purchase within a few days, a week at the most.

They got off the Turnpike, Harry paid the toll and took Southern Boulevard all the way to Palm Beach, going over the bridge and going left on South Ocean Boulevard, Cordell wide-eyed looking at the oceanfront mansions set back behind sculpted hedges and sea grape. Scattered palm trees giving a lazy relaxed feel.

"Harry, you see that?" Cordell pointing at a ten-thousand-square-foot faux Tuscan villa with a circular brick driveway behind an iron gate that made Harry's Huntington Woods house look like a shack.

"Like it?" Harry said.

"No, why would I want to live in a place like that?" Cordell grinned at the thought. "Where all these people get their money at?"

"Maybe they sell heroin," Harry said. "I understand you can do pretty well."

"Oh, I see you got your sense of humor back."

They came up on Worth Avenue, went left to South County Road, passing shoppers, passing Mercedes-Benzes, Rolls-Royces, passing glitzy storefronts.

"Where's Joyce at?"

"An estate. I think it's right up here."

They passed Royal Palm Way, Cordell looking down the row of evenly spaced palm trees with their long straight trunks and high plumes.

"What's the plan?"

"I don't know."

"Come again?"

Harry passed the Breakers, pulled over and turned around. "I'm going the wrong way." They went back along the water, south on the beach road to 1960, the address Joyce had given him. The island was narrower along this stretch, the estate property extending from the beach road to the intercoastal. There was a decorative iron gate closed across the driveway. He went right on a narrow lane just past the house, and drove along a white seven-foot-high wall bordering the property. Another paved lane behind the estate led to a four-car garage.

He went back out to the front gate and rang the bell. A woman with an accent—Spanish or Italian—answered the intercom.

"Yes, who is this, please?"

"Harry Levin."

The gate opened. He drove in and parked on the circular drive. A plump dark-haired woman, mid-thirties, wearing a light-brown uniform, came out the front door and approached the car. Harry got out.

"Welcome Señor Levin. You must be tired from your journey. Please come in. My name is Josefina."

"Nice to meet you. Where's Joyce?"

"I am sorry, the Señora is not at home."

"Where is she?"

A Nazi might be coming to kill her but she wasn't going to skip her maintenances. She could see her auburn hair starting to turn gray at her temples. Joyce had been getting her hair colored for about ten years, freaking out when she saw the first signs of gray when she was thirty-eight.

She would have Josefina drive her to the salon on Peruvian, and pick her up. If Harry Levin called, tell him where she was. She would wear a sun hat with a wide brim, hide her face, slip in and out of the salon without being recognized.

No one except Lenore knew about her situation, or where she was staying. Joyce had to confide in someone and trusted Lenore. They were good friends. They had talked a couple of times since she went into hiding. Lenore was showing an oceanfront estate to one of her customers, a referral, Southern gentleman from Atlanta. "Sounds like Clark Gable doing Rhett Butler," Lenore had said. "Heard you're wonderful."

"That part's true," Joyce said. "What's his name?"

"Emile Landau. Nice guy, very friendly."

The name didn't ring a bell. "Who referred him?"

"A friend from New York was all he said."

Joyce had sold a property for a man from Manhattan, Bob Meisner, but he hadn't called and recommended anyone. "What's he look like?"

"Fifty, six feet tall, hair slightly gray, wears a golf cap," Lenore said.

"You just described half the men in Palm Beach. The other half is older. He have a goatee by chance?"

"Not that I noticed."

Hess followed her for the remainder of the afternoon. She met buyers at houses on Seabreeze and Brazilian, each showing lasting forty-five minutes to an hour. He was getting impatient, imagined the woman talking in her annoying, never-ending stream of consciousness.

At 4:30 p.m. he saw her white Cadillac sedan appear coming out of the driveway on Brazilian. He followed her back to the real-estate office, parked on Worth Avenue and waited.

At 5:10 he saw her come out of the office and walk east to a restaurant called Ta-boo. She made her way to the far end of the crowded bar, joining a group of friends. The noise level seemed to rise with her arrival. He sat at a table near the entrance and could hear her voice over the din.

Hess ordered a Macallan's neat and two appetizers: shrimp cocktail and smoked Norwegian salmon with capers and onions. He was hungry. He had not eaten since breakfast, eight and a half hours earlier. He wolfed down the appetizers, finished the single malt and ordered another. At 6:15 he saw Lenore moving along the bar, coming his way. She noticed him and stopped.

"Are you following me?" Lenore smiled, seemed looser than she was earlier, face animated. "Just kidding. What you don't know about me, Mr. Landau, I'm a natural-born kidder." She took a breath. "This is my favorite restaurant. Great food. The owner, Jim Peterson, is a good friend. Would you like another drink? I've had enough myself but I'm happy to buy one for you."

"I am good," Hess said.

"Well, I'll see you tomorrow. Is ten a.m. OK? We can meet at the office. I'll take us around."

And with that she was out the door. Hess left fifty dollars on the table and walked out after her, keeping his distance, followed the woman to her white Cadillac parked across the street from the Town Car. Not as concerned about being seen—it was dark. People strolling on the sidewalk. Lights from the storefronts aglow.

Lenore Deutsch lived in a modest house on Queens Lane, situated at the north end of the island. No lights on. Hess had noticed a wedding ring, but could not believe she was married. Who could listen to her? She parked in the driveway and went inside and turned on the lights. He parked on the street, opened the glove box and took out the Walther. He waited a couple of minutes, then stepped out of the automobile, crossed the street and knocked on the door.

The maid, Josefina, had given Harry directions to the beauty parlor. He went there and waited in the lounge till a petite woman, five two, with reddish-brown hair walked through the beaded curtains. He had never seen Joyce Cantor in his life but he knew it was her. "Joyce!"

She turned and looked at him. "Harry?" Moved toward him, put her arms around him. "I can't believe you're here."

Now two hours later they were at the estate owned by a rich guy from New York named Frankel. Harry was checking on Cordell in the pool-house living room. He brought him a turkey sandwich, cottage cheese, chips and a Coke. Cordell was stretched out on a couch, watching TV, a nineteen-inch console.

Harry said, "You don't have to stay out here like the hired help."

"Think this is slummin', Harry, never been to a slum. Check it out."

He already had, asking himself how many two-bedroom pool houses with a cathedral ceiling and a big living room he'd seen? Appointed like the main house. Sixty-foot Italian marble pool right outside.

"Don't worry 'bout me. I'm watchin' *Soul Train*."

"You hear anything, see any Nazis, give me a call." Harry handed him a piece of paper that had the phone number to the main house on it.

Joyce was standing at the island counter in the kitchen, opening a bottle of Morgon, two stemmed glasses on the black granite top.

Harry said, "I remember seeing someone running into the woods as I climbed out of the pit."

Peter Leonard

"That was me. I don't remember you though." Joyce cleared her throat. "But I knew your mother. She was on the last truck, forty-seven of us from the women's camp. It was late afternoon. They told us we were being transferred to a sub-camp at Halfing. I believed them because I wanted to."

"We all did," Harry said. "Thinking anything was better than where we were."

"When we got to the woods I could see SS guards standing at the edge of a clearing, talking and smoking cigarettes. I didn't know what was happening until I saw the mound of dirt behind them. We were marched to the edge of the pit and I saw the bodies. Words can't describe... I have never in my life seen anything like that." She caught her breath. "Harry, where were you?"

"I had jumped off the back of the truck," Harry said. "I was hiding behind a tree and saw everything."

"I can still see Hess with the pistol in his hand. He told us to jump in the pit. No one moved, so he shot a woman in the face. There was a little hole in her forehead, blood coming out of it. She fell to the ground, and all at once we jumped onto the stacks of bodies. Many were still alive, the pile was moving, and then the guards started shooting at us like it was a game. I crawled between two bodies and the next thing I remember it was dark. The pit had been covered over with dirt. I couldn't breathe. I started pushing my way through corpses until I felt the cool air. It was night. I ran to a farm and hid in the barn. The farmer found me the next morning. He and his wife kept me till the war ended." She took a breath. "Harry, I can't believe you're here. How can I ever repay you?"

"Help me take down Hess."

"Of course." She poured two glasses of wine and handed one to him. "To us, Harry. Mazel tov."

He clinked her glass and tasted the wine. It was dry and slightly bitter.

"Josefina, the housekeeper, got it for me. The man at the wine store said it was good. I usually don't drink red wine, it gives me a headache."

248

"Hungry?" Harry said. "I can make us omelets if that's okay."

"Good-looking and you cook too."

Harry went to the refrigerator, took out six eggs and a wedge of English cheddar.

"Tell me where you lived in Munich," Joyce said, handing him a bowl.

"Sendlinger Strasse." He cracked the eggs, found a whisk and mixed them.

"We were near Gartnerplatz on Klenzestrasse. Remember Isaac Jacob's store?"

"The milk dealer, right? I used to go there with my mother."

"We were right down the street." She sipped her wine. "What butcher did you go to?"

"Joseph Bamberger. He was a friend of my father's."

"I can picture the storefront." She looked across the kitchen. "My family preferred Julius Lindauer."

Harry said, "Where did you go to school?"

"Jewish Elementary and then the gymnasium."

"I did too. I'm surprised we never met."

"Harry, why did we survive?" She paused. "I've been asking myself that for thirty years. Why not my brother? He was better than me, smart as a whip."

"You sound like you're apologizing, like you did something wrong."

"I didn't deserve it."

"You deserved it as much as anyone."

"I was the rebel of the family."

"That's why you're here. You're tough."

"I don't feel tough," Joyce said. "I feel guilty."

"It's not your fault," Harry said. "Stop blaming yourself. Think about what they did to you. Doesn't it make you mad?"

"I've never thought about it that way."

"Do it, you'll feel better."

"Is that what you did, Harry?"

"You're damn right." He drank some wine. "Remember Dachau? All we thought about was surviving."

249

"Get through the day," Joyce said. "And don't think about tomorrow."

"Well, here we are."

Lenore opened the door and saw Mr. Landau from Atlanta, hesitated, feeling the effects of the two drinks she'd had at Ta-boo. He had followed her, but why? He was smiling, a big Southern teddy bear. "All right, you. What's going on?" He looked different without the cap, pale skin that could use some color, dark hair flecked with gray.

"I hate to dine alone. You are the only person I know in Palm Beach. Will you join me?"

She invited him in, wondering if it was a mistake, then thinking about the commission she'd make on an oceanfront estate. She escorted him into the kitchen, opened cabinet doors showing where she kept her glasses and liquor. "Help yourself. I'll be right back."

"I have to ask you something."

He reached behind his back and brought out a gun with a long black barrel, pointing it at her. She could feel her heart race, scared to death, knowing now he was the Nazi.

"Where is Joyce?" he said, German accent, not pretending any more.

"I don't know."

He came toward her, aiming the gun. Lenore wanted to run but couldn't move. She was frozen. He put the barrel against her cheek, pressing it into her face.

"Let's try again. Where is she?"

Chapter 37

At the commercial, Harry went out to check on Cordell. It was a beautiful night, clear sky, sixty degrees. He looked up at the stars for a couple minutes, spotted the Big and Little Dipper and the North Star. Then he crossed the yard and went to the pool house. Cordell was asleep in a double bed in one of the bedrooms. Harry turned off the lamp on the bedside table. Walked through the living room, turned off all the lights, locked the door and went out.

At 10:00 when *McCloud* was over he escorted Joyce up the stairs that wound through a turret to the second floor, dark oak planks with a Persian runner. Josefina had gone home. According to Joyce, the security company came by every few hours, checked the doors and windows, and patrolled the grounds.

Harry lifted his shirt, showed her the Colt stuck in his belt. "Hess comes—"

"Harry, you have a gun? What kind of a Jew are you?" She smiled, put her arms around him. "A tough one. What can I say? You're a mensch. I should be so lucky."

The master bedroom was at the end of the hall. Joyce opened the door and went in. Harry followed her, impressed by the room that had to be sixty by forty feet, with a sitting area in front of the fireplace, four-post antique bed with a canopy, two TVs. He looked out the windows at the front yard and circular drive, the view extending all the way to the ocean, flat and dark, blending with the sky.

On the other side of the room, French doors led to a balcony off the back of the house, view of the pool and

251

pool house. "If you're afraid I'll stay with you, sleep on the couch."

She smiled. "I'll be fine. There's an alarm system. Anyone tries to get in, the security people will be here."

"'If you want me,'" Harry said, "'just whistle.'"

"Who said that? No, don't tell me." She glanced across the room looking for the answer. "Lauren Bacall. She said it to Humphrey Bogart. What was the movie?"

"*To Have and Have Not*."

"Know what Lauren's real name is?"

Harry shook his head.

"Betty Joan Perske."

"You know your movie stars, don't you?" Harry held her in his gaze. "Unless he has a ladder there's only one way in. So keep your door locked."

"Thanks for everything, Harry."

"I haven't done anything."

"You're here, aren't you?"

Harry went to his room. It was half the size of the master but still twice as big as the bedrooms in his house. The windows looked out on the back yard, and French doors opened onto the balcony. He pulled the spread down, propped pillows up against the headboard. Slipped out of his shoes, turned off the light, and got on the bed, holding the Colt next to his right leg. His eyes adjusted and he could see the dark shapes of furniture in the room and the soft glow of lights from the back yard. He started to doze off.

Next thing he heard was the deafening high-pitched shriek of the alarm—re-er, re-er, re-er.

It was 3:27 a.m. He grabbed the Colt, got up and went to the window, saw a flashlight beam sweep across the front of the pool house. He went in the hall, looked left, the door to the master suite still closed. He ran to the staircase, looked out the front window, saw a white sedan, lights flashing in the circular drive. Ran back, knocked on Joyce's door. "It's Harry. You okay?"

"What happened?" she said, voice muffled by the alarm.

"I don't know."

The alarm stopped. The door opened, Joyce was standing in the shadow, pulling her robe closed. "The security guys are downstairs. Stay here. I'll talk to them."

"I want to go with you."

Hess sat 1970 realtor of the year Lenore Deutsch at the kitchen table, aiming the Walther at her, tears staining her cheeks blue with eye shadow.

"Okay, I'll tell you, but you'll never get in. There is a state-of-the-art security system."

A gun pointed at her, and still she smirked, giving him her insolent tone again. He knew how alarms worked. He had a system at his estate in Schleissheim. "Who is in the house with her?"

"Maybe the housekeeper, I don't know."

It didn't matter. "Do you have rope?"

"Why?"

"So I can tie you."

Lenore Deutsch said, "You don't bring your own rope?"

The arrogance of this woman. It was beyond belief.

"It's in the garage."

They walked through the kitchen. She opened the door, turned on the light. It was space for a single automobile cluttered with pool supplies and gardening equipment. She handed him a spool of heavy string.

"This is all I have."

He picked up a shovel with a long handle.

"What are you going to do, bury me?"

It was a good idea, but he had something else in mind. Hess escorted her back through the house to her tidy bedroom and through that into the bathroom, pink tile and towels, large tub in the corner and next to it a glass shower.

"I have to wash my face," Lenore said.

He could see her in the mirror, wiping off the blue smudges under her eyes and off her cheeks with a wet cloth, and patting herself dry with a towel.

"Get on your knees," Hess said.

She did, putting her hands behind her back. He walked across the room, closed the window and tossed

253

the spool of string on the floor. He wasn't going to need it after all. Hess moved toward her, aiming the Walther at the back of her head, firing, spraying the walls with spatter.

Hess drove along the southern perimeter of the estate, parked off the road behind a green wall of foliage on the neighbor's property. He took the shovel and walked back toward the house, feeling a strong breeze coming off the ocean, palm trees swaying, moon waning behind heavy clouds that had moved in. The estate was sealed off, surrounded by walls on three sides and a gate in front. There was a narrow lane behind the western perimeter, and a wall with a gate in the center extending to the four-car garage.

He held the end of the handle, reached up and swung the shovelhead at the phone line until it broke free from the main line, glanced at his watch. 3:17. He waited behind the wall of foliage on the neighbor's property south of the estate. Two white security sedans arrived at 3:25. One in front, the other drove along the southern perimeter to the rear of the estate. The alarm sounded at 3:27, delayed ten minutes so the security team could be deployed.

"No sign of forced entry," the security man said to Harry.

He looked about forty, gut bunching the shirt at his beltline, brown hair over his ears, wispy Charles Bronson mustache. He wore a dark-blue uniform shirt with red epaulets, Harry thinking except for the gun on his right hip he could've been an exterminator. He'd introduced himself as Tony Cloutier, a French name he pronounced in down-home English.

Now they were in the kitchen.

Cloutier said, "Did you see or hear anything?"

"Not till the alarm went off," Harry said.

Joyce said, "I was sound asleep. It scared the hell out of me."

"Scare an intruder too, there was one," Cloutier said.

A second security man came in the back door now, guiding Cordell, hands cuffed behind his back. He was younger, bigger than Cloutier and wore a blue jacket over his uniform.

"Harry, will you tell this—"

"What're you doing?" Harry said, cutting Cordell off. "He's a guest."

"Sir, I didn't know."

"Cracker see a black man, middle of the night, got to be a criminal."

The security man unlocked the handcuffs. Cordell rubbed his wrists.

"I'm sorry."

"I'm sorry too motherfucker, I can't pop your dumb ass."

"Take it easy," Harry said.

"This is Ms. Cantor and Mr. Levin," Cloutier said. "Meet my over-zealous partner, Ted Tambke."

He nodded at Joyce, shook hands with Harry.

"Windy out there," Tambke said. "Phone line's down. I have to believe that's your problem."

Joyce said, "What does that have to do with it?"

Tambke said, "Severed line triggered the alarm."

"Can you fix it?" Joyce said.

"Not till morning, I'm afraid," Cloutier said.

Joyce said, "Are you saying the system won't be on?"

"I'll hang around till daylight," Tambke said. "Keep an eye on things."

"Just stay out the pool house," Cordell said, giving him a look.

The security men left.

"I see you're feeling better," Harry said. "Got some energy back."

"Have some cracker rent-a-cop cuff you down, try to break your wrists see how you do." Cordell still charged up, angry.

"Why do you think he's a racist?"

Cordell grinned. "Don't think, Harry, I know. Been dealin' with motherfuckers like him my whole life."

"Stay here?" Joyce said. "God knows we've got room."

"I'm cool where I'm at. See you in the morning."

Cordell went out the door. Harry locked it and walked Joyce back up to her room. It was 4:18.

The lights from the security vehicle were still flashing red and blue off the estate wall when Ted Tambke moved through the gate to his car, pissed off and embarrassed by the way the scene had played out in front of his boss. Fact was, you saw a black guy in the middle of the night he usually was involved in a crime.

Tambke saw something out of the corner of his eye, someone coming around the side of the house, aimed the flashlight, unsnapped his holster and put a hand on his .38. It was an older man wearing a cap and a yellow golf shirt, moving toward him.

"Excuse me," the man said. "Is there a problem? I live right there." He pointed to the property directly south.

Tambke glanced over the hood at him. "Sir, you scared the bejesus out of me. What are you doing out here in the middle of the night?"

"I heard the alarm," the guy said.

"It's all over. You can go home now." He didn't say it mean but just about. "Everything's under control."

"What happened?"

"Wind severed the phone line and that triggered the alarm."

"I am interested in a security system for my own home," the neighbor said. "Do you have a card?"

"Yes sir," Tambke said, trying to shift gears, be friendly now. Employees got ten per cent of the net for any new business they brought in. One of these Palm Beach mansions, it could be ten grand. Cloutier made fifteen thousand dollars one time.

Tambke opened the door, sat behind the wheel, reaching in the console between the seats, grabbed a couple business cards. When he turned back the neighbor was standing next to the car. "Here you go." He reached out, handed the cards to him.

"So nobody broke in?"

"No sir."

"The neighborhood is safe?" the man said, smiling.

"Yes sir. I'll be here till morning just to make sure."

"Let me ask you something," the neighbor said. "What size is your jacket?"

Tambke, puzzled, said, "Extra large. What do you want to know that for?"

Earlier, Cordell had been standing at the window looking out, listening to the alarm, thinking there was a fire but dint see no flames. The door opened, dude looked like a cop shined a light in his eyes, aiming a gun at him.

"Freeze," the cop said. "Put your hands up."

"Be cool. It's okay. I'm stayin' here."

"Sure you are. Get on your knees, put your hands behind your back."

He did. Cordell, fugitive from justice, wondering how they found him. Thinking it had to do with his trouble in Detroit. Dude cuffed him but soon as they were outside Cordell could see he was a rent-a-cop, and relaxed.

Now he was back in the pool house wide awake, 4:30—nothing on TV, wonderin' what to do when he saw something move by the window. Got up for a better look, saw the cracker rent-a-cop heading toward the house. There was something different about him, but Cordell couldn't quite put his finger on it.

Chapter 38

Hess shot him once in the chest at close range with the silenced Walther PPK, the round bouncing around inside him, tearing up vital organs. He removed his cap and jacket, took the house keys, flashlight and sidearm, turned off the flashing lights, pulled the security man out of the automobile, and dragged him by his feet across a narrow strip of grass, hiding the body in the dense foliage on the south side of the house.

Hess unlocked the gate and entered the property, walked by the pool and pool house, across the lawn to the door that led to the kitchen. He tried several keys until he found one that fit the lock, opened the door and stepped in, listening—not a sound. He gripped the Walther, starting through the house, enough light to see where he was walking. Made his way through large rooms with high ceilings to the foyer, looking at the winding stairs, and started up.

Joyce was almost asleep when she heard the door open and saw the security guard come in. Now what? She sat up. "You've got to be kidding."

He closed the door and came toward her, took off the cap and now she recognized him.

"You were expecting me," Hess said. "Were you not?"

Joyce was so afraid she couldn't talk, couldn't get a word out.

Hess smiled at her. "You were on the last truck that day in the woods, a teenager with fair skin and red hair. How old were you?"

"Eighteen."

"That is a good age. I remember when I was eighteen," Hess said, smiling, sounding sentimental. "Were you in school?"

"I had just graduated from the gymnasium."

"Were you planning to attend the university?"

"Jews weren't allowed." Who was this lunatic? Came to kill her and he was making small talk. But she tried to keep the conversation going.

"That's right," the Nazi said. "I enrolled in the Technische Hochschule."

"You must be very smart."

He brought his hands up in slight embarrassment, the right holding the gun. "You know, I didn't do too bad." He paused. "Do you miss Munich, Bavaria?"

Harry heard voices, picked up the Colt, went out to the hall, moving toward Joyce's room. Stood next to her door and listened, tried the handle, it was locked. He went back to his room, moved out to the balcony, crouched low, going toward the master suite. Looking in the windows but couldn't see anything, the shades were pulled. Harry squatted in front of the French doors. The drapes were closed but not all the way. He could see a narrow slice of the room: the rug, part of the bed and armoire. Now he saw a khaki leg, yellow shirt, the edge of a face in profile.

Hess moved out of view and came back, arm extended. Harry couldn't see what he was holding, but knew what it was, imagined Joyce in bed, scared to death. Hess was about thirty feet away, the same distance as the paper targets he practiced on at the shooting range. But the paper targets were lit up and straight on and nobody's life was at stake if he missed.

Cordell followed the rent-a-cop, saw him open the door, go in the house. What was up? They got more trouble with the alarm? Then it occurred to him, something wasn't right about him 'cause it wasn't him. This dude was wearin' khakis. Other one had on blue uniform pants.

He stepped in the kitchen, pulled a serrated knife with a long blade out of the holder on the counter, slid it in his belt and went up to where the bedrooms were at, movin' slow with his bad leg. Walked down the hall. Didn't see the Nazi but had to believe he was up here. Pulled the blade, went into a room, door to the balcony open. Saw Harry squattin', lookin' in the next room like a peepin' Tom. "Yo, Harry—" he whispered.

Harry squeezed the trigger twice, glass exploding, pushed the French doors open, and went in the room, aiming the Colt. Hess was gone, Joyce was sitting with her back against the headboard, afraid, but alive. "You all right?"

She was staring at the gun in his hand. "I think so, Harry. But don't do anything, please! Let him go. We'll call the police."

No way. He was going to end it right now. He ran down the hall to the stairs, saw Hess at the bottom and went after him. Raced through the living room and dining room, caught him in the kitchen, Hess moving past the island counter halfway to the door. "Take another step you're dead." Harry aimed down the gun sight, arms extended, two hands on the Colt. "Put it down, and do it slow."

Hess stopped, glanced over his shoulder. "You think I am a fool? I put the gun down you will kill me."

Harry had been thinking about this moment, but didn't see it happening this way. He wanted Hess looking at him when he pulled the trigger. "All right," Harry said. "We'll both do it. Put them down at the same time. But I'm telling you, make a move it's all over." He lowered the Colt, resting it on the countertop. Hess reached back and laid his semiautomatic on the black granite, turned, facing him.

"I have been wondering, who is this Harry Levin? And finally it occurred to me. You must have been the boy hiding in the woods. How did you get off the truck? The prisoners were counted as they got on, and then again when they arrived. But somehow they missed you."

"I've been thinking about you, too," Harry said. "I remember you shooting my father, showing your men how to kill Jews."

"I should have paid more attention to you."

"Then passing out bottles of schnapps to celebrate," Harry said.

"It was not to celebrate but to relax the men. I underestimated how they would react. To my surprise many of them broke down. Some were deeply shaken. They needed relief."

"You killed six hundred people," Harry said, "you were worried about relaxing your men?"

"I was following orders," Hess said.

"Whose orders were you following after the war?"

He didn't answer.

"I saw your souvenir collection. You're still at it, huh? Can't stop yourself."

"You think the world is going to miss a few more Jews?" Hess said. "Killing your daughter was a bonus, Harry. What can I say? I was just lucky."

"I am, too," Harry said, picking up the Colt.

Hess went for his gun, and Harry fired. Hit him in the upper chest, just left of center, the velocity blowing the Nazi backward off his feet, gun flying. Harry walked across the kitchen, stood over him, Hess looking up, eyes open. "Help me."

"You're not going to make it," Harry said.

Chapter 39

"We have to call the police," Joyce said, staring at Hess on the kitchen floor, blood pooling under him.

"You want to be involved in the killing of a Nazi war criminal?" Harry said. "Bring all that attention to yourself? Have the nuts come out of the woodwork, looking for you?"

Joyce said, "We don't have a choice. We are involved."

Cordell at the kitchen table said, "Harry, what you sayin'?"

"Get rid of the body. Bury him."

Joyce frowned. "You're not serious?"

"You have a better idea?"

"Harry, somebody has to have heard the gunshots and called the police," Joyce said.

"If the police were coming, they'd be here by now."

"What about the door upstairs?" Joyce said. "And the bullet hole in the armoire? How're we going to explain that?"

"You picked up one of those terracotta planters on the balcony," Cordell said, "broke the glass by accident."

Harry glanced at him. "That's not bad." He paused. "I wouldn't worry about the bullet hole. Who's going to notice it?"

"Got another one, Harry," Cordell said. "What about the security dude?"

Harry'd found him dead in the bushes behind the south wall. "Somebody shot him. We didn't hear it. We don't know what happened. We don't have to explain anything."

"And Hess' rental car," Joyce said.

Harry'd found it parked on the neighbor's property to the south. "We don't know anything about that, either. Name on the rental agreement is Gerd Klaus." It was also the name on his passport and international driver's license. "You know someone named Gerd Klaus? I don't. Nobody knows he's really Hess except us. All the police have is a rental car. Without a body there's nothing to connect us." Harry had searched him and found a ring of keys and a room key to the Breakers Hotel.

Joyce said, "What if he told somebody what he was going to do, and they come after us?"

"Why would he?" Harry said. "If you were going to kill someone, would you talk about it? For Hess it was personal. He was taking care of the last connections to his past." He looked at his watch. It was 4:53. "We don't have a lot of time. Somebody is going to come looking for the security guard, and then the police are going to be involved." He glanced at Cordell. "What do you say?"

"Otherwise you be lookin' over your shoulder," Cordell said, eyes on Joyce.

"I don't like it, Harry," Joyce said. "I feel like a criminal. But I agree with you. I wouldn't bury him, though. The ground's too soft. He could wash out during a heavy rain. I'd dump him in the ocean, let the tide take him out to the sharks."

"What about this?" Cordell said, picking Hess' gun up off the floor.

"I'll get rid of it," Harry said, taking the gun and sliding it in his pants pocket. He went outside, crossed the yard and went through the gate, walked to the far side of the property, took the gun out and threw it as far as he could into the Intercoastal.

Harry went to the garage looking for a tarp, and found a roll of Visqueen. He took it back to the house, wrapped Hess in plastic. He and Joyce dragged him outside and lowered him from the steps into a wheelbarrow. Harry'd take care of the Nazi. Joyce and Cordell would clean the kitchen floor.

Harry wheeled Hess down the narrow lane to the beach road, slight breeze blowing his hair back. Light

was breaking on the horizon. He crossed the road and
went down a slope of soft heavy sand, put the wheelbarrow down, kicked off his shoes and rolled up his pants.
The tide was on its way out.

He wheeled Hess across twenty yards of hard wet
sand that had been underwater a few minutes earlier,
and dumped him in the shallows. Harry glanced over his
shoulder making sure no one was following them. When
he looked back he saw Hess' leg move, foot jerking under
the plastic. What the hell was that? Harry'd checked him
in the kitchen. Hess was dead, wasn't breathing, didn't
have a pulse. But now Harry wondered, had his doubts.
He bent down and pulled the Visqueen coffin into deeper
water, up to his waist, gave it a push and watched the
current take Hess out to sea, watched till the Nazi disappeared and he felt better.

Harry thought about what Hess did to his parents.
It had been hanging there in the back of his mind for
almost thirty years. Now finally, they'd been avenged.
He thought about Sara, felt some relief knowing she, too
could be put to rest.

He got back to the house a little after six. Joyce and
Cordell had cleaned up the blood. The floor was spotless.
Harry locked the kitchen door, went up, showered and
got in bed.

At 6:30, Cloutier returned, patrolled the grounds,
found his partner, and called the police. Harry was ques-
tioned by a cocky Palm Beach detective named Conlin.
Harry told him he hadn't heard a gunshot, hadn't seen
an intruder, and had never heard of a businessman from
Stuttgart, Germany named Gerd Klaus. Joyce said pretty
much the same thing, and although Harry was convinced
Conlin didn't believe them, they were released.

Cordell, on the other hand, had an outstanding warrant in Detroit. He was arrested and taken to county lock-
up in West Palm for twenty-four hours, till Stark was able
to appeal to a black judge sympathetic with Cordell's situation. Young man in the army, serving his country, being
discriminated against, and all charges were dropped.

Voices of the Dead

"Appreciate the legal assistance," Cordell said when he walked out of jail and got in Harry's car. "Thank Counselor Stark for me. You were right, man knows his shit."

Harry said, "What're you going to do now, go back to Detroit?"

"Reinvent myself," Cordell said. "Going to stay down here. Going to see what looks interesting, what I can get into, figure out how to make money at it."

"Ever want to get in the scrap business, give me a call."

Cordell shook his head and grinned. "That's a tempting offer, Harry, but I think I'll pass."

265

Chapter 40

While Cordell was being held, Harry'd driven to the Breakers, knowing it would take the police a little time to figure out where Hess had been staying. He had to make sure Hess didn't have anything the police might find that would connect them.

The room had an ocean view, bed made, everything neat and clean like the maid had just been there. First he checked the closet. Two sport jackets on hangers, half a dozen long-sleeved dress shirts, two pairs of pants, two pairs of dress shoes, one black, the other brown, red Breakers golf shirt. Hess' suitcase was on the floor in the corner. He went through the pockets of all the clothes and the compartments in the suitcase, didn't find anything. He moved back in the bedroom, checked the dresser, opened the drawers, saw socks in one, underwear and undershirts in another. Three drawers were empty.

Harry sat at the desk in front of the window that looked out at the ocean. Saw a freighter creeping along the horizon. He glanced around, noticed a briefcase tucked under the desk on his right. Reached for the handle and pulled it up and put it flat on the desktop. Tried to open it, but it was locked. Harry took out the key ring he'd taken off Hess. There was a small key with a black plastic cap on the end and a hole through it. He slid it in the lock and the briefcase opened.

There was a stack of business cards tucked in a leather sleeve, identifying Gerd Klaus as Midwest sales manager of an international auto parts company. Harry took out a pile of receipts: Statler Hotel in Detroit, an Eastern Airlines flight, Detroit–West Palm, Hertz car rental, all in the name Gerd Klaus, all paid in cash. Under the receipts were surveillance photographs, close-ups of Harry at several Munich locations, and a couple shots of Harry and Cordell. Under the photos were half a dozen auto parts brochures. Hess had gone to a lot of trouble to look authentic.

On the bottom of the briefcase was another business card, Dana Kovarik, assistant manager, SunTrust Bank, with an address on Royal Poinciana Way, Palm Beach. He put the card, keys and photographs in his pockets, walked out of the room and closed the door.

Chapter 41

Harry watched Colette come through the gate. He'd been thinking about her, but seeing her had an effect on him. She was looking around, saw him and ran over, kissed him and they put their arms around each other, standing there, the exiting passengers moving around them.

They drove down the coast, checked in a motel on the ocean called the Ebb Tide. It had twelve efficiency apartments, a pool, private beach, and it was right near the inlet where the fishing boats came in.

When they got to the room, Colette showed him her article, six pages in *Der Spiegel*, featuring current photos of Hess and his bodyguard, Hess at the Blackshirt rally, and sepia-tone photos of Hess in his Nazi uniform, posing in front of the mass grave. The article read like a suspense thriller. He finished it and looked at her. "This is amazing," Harry said. "Shooting Hess' bodyguard with your father's military sidearm. You couldn't make that up."

"It was self-defense and I still feel bad about it."

"Of course you do," Harry said. "You're a good person. How's your mother?"

"She was in shock."

"I can imagine. Must've scared the hell out of her."

"But she's fine now, hiking in the mountains again."

"I was surprised you didn't mention Hess' souvenirs."

"We know he was a serial killer, but we can't prove it. My editor wouldn't allow it."

"My favorite part, of course, is the daring escape by an eye-witness survivor who is prepared to come forward to help prosecute Hess."

268

"I thought you'd like that." Colette sat on the bed. "Here's the strange thing, Harry. The article appeared a few days ago and Hess has disappeared. Reporters converged on his estate in Schleissheim and his Munich apartment. His wife and daughter claim they have no idea where he is."

"You believe them?"

"I do. I think he's left the country. Gone into hiding."

"You're probably right." Harry didn't tell her what really happened. That Hess was dead. At least Harry hoped he was.

About the Author

Peter Leonard is the author of nine novels. He lives in Birmingham, Michigan.